To

Day

Happy Reading

AHpurse

-x-

Dead Bodies

Do

Tell Tales

A Jack the Ripper Novel

BY AMANDA HARVEY PURSE

Published in 2013 by FeedARead.com Publishing – Arts Council funded

A CIP catalogue record for this title is available from the British Library.

Front Cover Design

By

Artist and writer

Coral De Anne

Other written works by Coral De Anne are:

Be with Me

And

Requel

Other Works by the Same Author

Jack the Ripper's Many Faces

A set of four linking short stories in which the reader travels through the centuries with the aim of finding out who wore Jack the Ripper's Face while meeting a few famous people such as Dr Crippen, Inspector Walter Dew and Sir Arthur Conan Doyle as Dr Watson.

Victorian Lives behind Victorian Crimes e-book series:

Vol:1 The women who made Jack the Ripper famous is where the victims of Jack the Ripper talk about their lives as if they were in the same room as the reader, with photographs of the murder sites as they are now.

Vol:2 The Poisoning Men has the famous Poisoners of the Victorian era such as William Palmer, H.H Holmes and Dr Cream explaining their deadly deeds with the medical and literature history of the poisons used.

Vol:3 It's a Hanging Job Now has the famous criminals such as Charles Peace, Mary Ann Cotton, James Bloomfield Rush and Amelia Dryer tell the reader their life stories to the point in which they were hanged. It also has the life stories of the hangmen, such as John Billington and William Calcraft.

The Tails of Binky the Tabby Cat e-book series:

1: The Detective Tails of Binklock Holmes, Purrirot and Miss Meowples this is the first in the funny series where Binky the tabby cat becomes her favourite detectives and gets involved in similar but cat like versions of their favourite stories such as The Speckled Collar, Murder of the Feline Express and Pocket Full of Cat Nip.

Praise for Victorian Lives behind Victorian Crimes

Vol:1 The women who made Jack the Ripper Famous

'Amanda Harvey Purse has had the neat idea of having the Ripper's victims tell their own stories in their own words and she has executed it entertainingly.'

Described by Paul Begg (author of Jack the Ripper: The Facts and co-author of Jack the Ripper A-Z) in the Ripperologist Magazine, issue 130.

For my husband who is a constant source of encouragement and support.

For my family and for the cats that are no longer with me whom I all love and cherish.

For my darling pussy cats who are always a source of entertainment,

Mischief and Binky.

Prologue

Jack the Ripper had killed again. Is there anything he can't do? As I walk around the streets of Whitechapel it is hard for me to imagine being anywhere else. The dilapidated houses decorated the streets; the overall slime that covered every cobbled stone is our friend. The odour of the local docks and sewers are everywhere I go, I can't get away from the smell of rotting flesh and decaying animals that lined the snot trodden mush sides of the great Thames River that flowed from our great British Capital to people like me.

Without people like me, there would be nothing to compare too, no way of showing how prosperous and wealthy the City of London is and to who can live there. We have meaning; why else would these Top hat and tails come here in the murky and freezing hours of the night?

It is our pubs, our secret clubs and our ladies that bring the gentlemen folk here. It is the atmosphere you cannot get anywhere else; it understands that if you were to throw a sovereign on a table all your secrets and darkest thoughts will be delivered and undisclosed to anyone who may ask. Everyone is equal, no one is looked down upon, and you are with friends.

We are the height of fashion when it comes to social endeavours; we were the first to use the new crop from China that allows you to travel to new worlds and entice senses you never knew you had. We were the first to realise the wonders of the purple poppy and brought it to the masses, teaching them how to cook the Opium until it turns into a dense and concentrated black liquid that you inhale through a wooden pipe. We are teachers, people learn from us.

That is why I am here, I would not be anywhere else, I have accepted my fate for I belong to the lower class of people and where else would the lower class people be, but Whitechapel?

I have known of the dangers that haunt the alleys, the threats of the brawny gangs as you pass from one area to another, the men that think they own the women of the night. The bruises and cuts you have to hide, the pain inside yourself from every nights work. The emptiness of not eating, the peril of the public house and vice it holds within. All this I know and yet twenty five years on I am still here, I have survived for I am strong. I have never truly been frightened of my home, for this is the place I feel a part of myself blending into, much more that my place of birth.

But now with this mad man that hunts within the smog and poorly lighted alleyways to kill for no real reason is within my City, and that there is no way of understanding why he can take someone's soul with the sweeping of his knife, a part from believing a gateway must have opened and allowed this devil to walk through, I am now fearful and terrified for my life.

Chapter One

Ten Years on

'Help me! Help me Thomas!' She screamed at me. I reached out to her, I could almost touch her. Then I woke up...

No! Not again! Why can I never get to her?

I suppose I better start at the beginning, my name is Thomas Dunn, and I *was* a famous writer of my time. I was the writer that made the Silver Publishing Company survive through the bad financial season a few years back, my book *The Coffin Bell Rings* was a hit.

'One of Mr. Dunn's best works, its fills the reader with a morbid sense of pleasure that seems to be the in thing at the moment... Mr Dunn is a credit to his generation'.

But with every generation there is another, following shortly behind and now I am out of date; my books are not selling, just gathering dust of someone's shelf. *These days I can walk around London without being noticed*, my funds are running low and if I don't do something soon, my debts and the Billing Club will come to hunt me down.

Add to this with my terrible dreams and I am in disarray. I used to have these same dreams when I was younger, a new person around town, ready to try the new sights and experience how seedy the underbelly of London can truly go. Now these dreams are back and I can't get rid of them. I have come to the conclusion, that instead of fighting these dreams I must go with them, for I must reach her.

The woman in my dreams is young; her hair is long and wet. In fact her whole body is damp; the clothes are of the lightest blue but are so sodden, that the material clings to her body shape tightly. She is standing in the middle of a lake; there is nothing but water all around her feet and the darkness seems to cover her like a shawl but I know I am standing on land. She turns around and looks at me, she tries to move towards me, but something I cannot see, pulls her back, she screams. She calls my name but I can never get to her.

'Thomas!' A man's voice I hear call to break me from my trance; I turned around on the spot.

'Charles!' I said happily but in truth although this man was my dearest friend I never did like his manner sometimes, but he had connections *and I truly couldn't imagine my life without him.*

'Thomas, may I walk with you?' Charles asked as he caught up with me.

'Well yes,' I said thinking on the spot for now I must change where I am going.

'Capital! It is good I saw you Thomas, are you writing anything new at the moment?'

'Yes, I have a few things in the post,' I lied.

'Oh I am sorry to hear that, what a shame!'

'Oh? Why is that my dear friend?' I asked.

'Oh it's nothing really. I heard a story while I was at the Club and it just sounded like one of your types of stories, I thought you could use.'

'Well I am open to new opportunities,' I said. This might be something I hoped.

'Really? I mean are you sure?' Charles asked looking quizzical at me. 'Well that is just Capital my dear boy!' I his man uses the word, capital far too much. 'Let's get to the club and I will tell all!'

When we reached our destination, the doors opened for us, for we were regular clientele. The familiar smell of cigar smoke hit us when we walked through the second door, and found our seats by the window.

'So what is this story?' I asked.

'Well, there's this Mortuary Keeper in the East End, he has been sacked!'

'Story not sounding too good at the moment, Charles,' I said as I was passed my favourite port, even though it was lacking my much-loved ingredient.

As Charles, took a slip from his whiskey glass, he said 'wait one minute, Thomas. I haven't told why he was sacked.'

'Did he steal some tools?' I asked.

'No he was sacked because of losing bodies!'

'Losing bodies you say? How can you lose a body? Let alone a dead body?' I asked.

'Bodies I said, plural, my dear Thomas.'

'Come on Charles, he was probably caught out selling the bodies and that's why he got sacked, there's a lot of that going around.' I said, as I leaned back in my chair.

'Believe what you will, this man swears he never touched the bodies, windows were smashed, and door broken into.'

'Well that settles that, someone broke into the shop and stole the bodies,' I said.

'Or the bodies broke out,' Charles said.

'Come on now!' I proclaimed disbelievingly almost spitting out my drink, causing me to lean forward in my chair.

'Look my dear fellow, believe it or not, but I have managed to get us some firsthand research.'

'How did you do that?'

'You have known me long enough not to ask those questions,' Charles said with a wink.

'Fine, I will play along with you,' I said. 'But do you honestly believe the bodies just walked out?'

'Well when you read stories like the one of yours, it is very hard not to believe.'

'But that's exactly what they are Charles, they are stories.'

'They must have come from somewhere, my dear fellow.'

'You are meaning, what exactly?' I asked.

'Every writer does his research, so what research did you find?'

'I don't know what you mean Charles; the story just came to me.'

'So you are able to think up a story involving dead bodies moving around London replacing their empty coffins with live people? Why can't you imagine it happening in real life?' Charles said.

'What one can think up, another one can believe, I suppose,' I said.

'That's the ticket, so do you fancy a little trip down the East End Thomas? It will remind us of our youth.'

'Yes, the less said about that the better, Charles,' I said, suddenly feeling the room was crowded.

'Oh yes I forgot Little Tommy has never done naughty things, has he?' Charles laughed.

'Stop joking around Charles, what time do we meet?'

'Let's say in three days from now, that will give you enough time to go wherever it was that you were going before I disturbed you and for you to spend enough time there,' he said with another wink, I didn't reply. I didn't need to justify myself.

I got up and started to move away from the oversized brown leather chairs that our club was famous for when I felt no body behind me so I turned 'You are not leaving?' I asked my friend as he seemed to have not moved a muscle.

'I don't have to my dear boy, I get everything I need from here,' he said as he looked out the window. Other people would have thought that was a slight poke at people like me, and my habit but I knew he was speaking the truth. I knew what he was starring at through the window.

Across the street from the club was a little known theatre called The Willow and The Owl. It wasn't an upper class place, but you wouldn't feel self-conscious of being there. It had a lovely atmosphere with pleasant enough seating and you could really get to see some fine acting. But that wasn't why Charles was starring at it.

Ellen was a fine actress, she was lovely and sweet. Charles fell for her straight away and not many people could blame him. But in the end she turned him down, so he never had a chance to hold her on his arm. He had said to me once, 'she has turned me down Thomas!' he boomed as he burst into my study.

'What?'

'Ellen, she has turned me down, can you believe it!'

'Did she say why?'

'Only that *her heart was with another man* can you believe it?' Sadly I could believe that she told him the truth. A girl like Ellen was never short of men following her every footstep, a girl like Ellen could pick and chose who she wanted to be with and my friend Charles although seemed wealthy enough for most girls, most girls aren't Ellen.

'Come on Charles, pull yourself together, there will be other women,' I said as I patted his shoulder.

'Not for me Thomas, not for me,' Charles replied and despondently he was very much correct in his statement because years on, Charles has never been with another woman, his heart was firmly on Ellen and even though Ellen had moved on and does not act in that theatre anymore, Charles can't help himself but stare at the place that once held his love.

I left the club and turned sharply eastwards, it amazed me how walking just a few yards further along the town could change. The place grew darker, the smell had the hint of the River Thames and rotting flesh, the places were grubber and dirtier to match the people that were walking or in most cases lumping the streets around it. The gas lamps were of poor quality and never did give out much light, it didn't matter as I knew my way.

After walking down a few alleyways I reached the Kingsmen Opium Den. I tapped the top of my walking stick on the lightly painted green door. The door opened, I could smell the sweet, delightful smell of my favourite drug flowing out into the night time air, the Chinaman that answered, looked at me for only a short moment and then moved to one side, allowing me to walk in.

As I walked in and allowed the smell to heighten my senses, I saw the den was quite full with mummified bodies, all slowing dying and wilting as they lie around the filth filled floor. There was one girl with a mixture of soot and sweat showing on her face at the far back of the room who was laughing. But what a laugh, was certainly slow and haunting, giving me goose bumps as I walked passed her. You had to be careful when following the tiny Chinaman as there were other exotic living animals, set in wooden cages that hung from the ceiling, these you would sometimes have to dodge to one side or even have to bend low down to walk past.

'Upstairs,' the Chinaman simply said to me in his broken sounding English.

I moved up the creaking wooden stairway that hardly had any space for me to move comfortably and contentedly. As I reached to top I moved towards one of the rooms, the Chinaman that was now behind me, reached in front of me and pulled back the wooden beads that they used for doors, and I walked into my room, the Chinaman followed bending over to light the candle on the side table and laying a wooden pillow on the bed. But in truth I didn't care, for I had noticed the drug on the side table waiting for me to try it, it almost felt as if that little black liquid was teasing me.

When the Chinaman left, I untied my shoes and placed them to one side of the bed, I also made sure my hat and cane were left where I would remember them and sat down gracelessly on the hard bed. I moved towards the pipe and let the smoke enter my body and excite my veins.

'Help me Thomas, help,' I reached out for her, I seemed to be getting nearer to her. I still didn't know this woman but there was something about her, I felt like I should know her. She looked so frightened, but frightened of what? I can't see what holding her back...

Back to the year of 1888

Jack the Ripper, as the newspapers are now calling him, had already killed two women a few streets away from my dwelling but they were so much more than just any two women, they were my friends. They helped me move from the criminal Radcliff Highway to the lodging houses of

Dorset Street which I really thought was a step up in the world; I had my own place to live and did not have to share with anyone else, a part from my Joseph.

I loved them as if I was their birth sisters; they made up for the hole that my own family left in my heart. But at the present the hole is re-opening again as I am now in mourning for them, I wear a black, dying rose in my hat for each of them, now I must find two more.

For this night on the 30th September 1888, Jack the Ripper had killed again. But this time he had upped his game and butchered two in one night. The thought of this made me feel ill, I feel lightheaded and woozily. I can taste a poisonous, lumpy fluid entering my mouth, I cannot hold it in, for I am going to be sick.

'Oi! I wouldn't do that too often Mary, clients may think you are fallen!' shouted a fellow worker of the night as she laughed with her friend. They did not wait for me to answer them but pushed passed me and pulled open the wooden door to the Ten Bells Pub.

What did they know? They knew nothing for the world besides their own lives, they know nothing of the love between a group of friends, living and working together within one area of London. All looking out for each other, we were friends; we were sisters, a band that cannot be broken even in death. Their lives will live on I can see it, I can feel it, call me silly if you like, for I just know it.

Poor Lizzie, there were moments in her life where she could have really been one of those high class ladies, sipping tea with other ladies and eating fish paste sandwiches and what not. She owned a coffee shop in the Square Mile of the City with her husband and things were going grand. But her husband had a vice, and it was a vast financial one, the vice of gambling. He gambled in the highest of clubs and lost a huge deal, including the coffee shop. Lizzie and her husband parted company and she was left to fend for herself and that led her slowly and ever so surely to Whitechapel and to working the streets at night. She had another chance of love with a man from the government but something went wrong and he was no more.

I am unsure how she had met Michael Kidney, but he hanged around with her for many years. He was a vile and despicable man. He would not have any guilt feelings against beating her with his belt whenever he felt like she had needed one and then he would blame her if she could not get any business that night because of the visible bruising he caused. But I understood why she would stay with him.

'Mary, I know he hurts me but I don't want to be alone no more, I am not young and pretty like you, my time has come and gone. Michael is all I have.'

'But how are you meant to get the Coattails if he keeps beating you?' I had asked while placing a hot, wet cloth over her eyes.

'We have discussed this, he was meant to just beat me on my back this time, but his temper got the better of him,' she paused 'I know you are shaking your head, even if I can't see you,' as she lifted up the cloth, tried to wink and then placed the cloth back over her eyes.

'I am sorry Lizzie; don't think I don't understand because I do. It's just hard when there are so many pains in our lives that we have to deal with, coming home to other one is hard for me to bare.'

'Doesn't Joseph?'

'Doesn't Joseph what?'

'Beat you.'

'He tries, we have arguments but I always tell him where to go.'

'And he goes?'

'Yes, for a few days, then he comes back with money, so I don't have to work the streets for a bit of time.'

'You don't know how lucky you are Mary.'

'Oh I know, I truly know,' I said as I took the cloth away and stared at Lizzie's bruises. As Lizzie looked back at me there was a moment of silence, which Lizzie broke when she said.

'You are the strong one of us Mary; you will live us all out.'

'Stop that dark talk; you will be around for many a year still!'

'Nice of you to say so Mary, but I hope not, I really do hope not.'

Well Lizzie at least when you met Jack the Ripper in Berner Street tonight, he stopped the beatings and the iciness of emotion you got from Michael, what will Mr. Kidney do now without you Lizzie? I hope, for your sake he falls on his arse!

The ghastly little man deservers nothing more, whereas you on the other hand didn't deserve to have your throat cut and have your body left, lying on the cold and damp ground as the your blood left your neck and ran into the drain disappearing into the sewers. It is almost insulting, that Jack the Ripper wasted your life, he got no satisfaction in killing you as he was nearly caught and had to run away. You did not deserve to be wasted. But at least you did not meet his true anger that sadly lay in store with my poor Kate Eddowes.

1898...

I awoke with shapes of colours in my eyes, when the shapes faded away I sat up. I had no idea how long I had been there. Time has no meaning, significance or value when compared to a higher, stronger being such as the drug I had just consumed. This isn't working; I had hoped that embracing my habit, my wanting you could say, I would be able to see more of my dream, understanding it a little more, but it wasn't happening. I have a headache and feel unwell. The poppy has a dark side to it, you don't notice it at first because it is clever and fools you but it slowly creeps up and takes over and the euphoric feeling you first experience *dies away* leaving the bad taste of depressingly wretched and dismal desolation and its black magic is casting its spell on my whole soul. I must take my leave of this voodoo place and make my way to the comfort of my home. I was in my study, when the maid dropped a letter by my side.

Thomas, please come to Blissful Hill to start our adventure...

The message was short and sweet, just like Charles himself. I guessed tonight was the night I would see the firsthand research, maybe see the mortuary, the place of death. It's funny; I guess I should feel like I'm going *home.*

With all the stories I have written about death, why do I unsettled about this whole adventure? In all my research, I have travelled to some deep and dark places, in which strangely I have felt more at ease and more relaxed to be around death, than life. I never seem to have many friends; I do prefer my own company. That way I can do what I like, when I like and don't have to pretend to be charming to anyone, I do detest acting and playing the role of a noble and prosperous young gentleman, somehow it doesn't feel quite right, it feels as if something is wrong, all I know is *it's not me*.

Death in the East End seems common place these days, and perplexingly it was the death of four women in the East End a few years back that made me feel more *alive* than I have ever been, my life seemed to *start again*. I don't really seem to remember my life before the Whitechapel Murders, my imagination juices were flowing at that time and I was able to write more clearly and more morbidly. I could feel the murders happening as if I was truly *there.*

Now ten years on, if Jack the Ripper decided to return he would have to do a better job to hold one's attention. It almost feels common place to read or hear of a murder that has happen in the eerie hours of the night, Jack the Ripper would have plenty of competition these days. The East End would seem to be very hectic and full of murderous activity at the time Jack would normally get to work, he would have to change his habits.

It is amazing how life can change in just a few years; in 1888 Jack the Ripper shocked and jolt the public into disbelief, would he be able to do that now? Would I be so fascinated and engrossed in Jack the Ripper now as I was then?

I used to read as much as I could about the murders, they interested me; I began to travel to the East End and specially to the Whitechapel area at night, as the place had more sinister, mysterious and almost threatening atmosphere, to get my darkest imagination to emerge. I talked to the locals, and to the ladies of night. I become one of their people. I started to feel close to the victims, almost connect with them. I could feel their pain.

The first victim was Mary Nichols, I never got to meet her *personally*, but I heard a few things about her, she wasn't just anybody, she was someone's daughter, someone's wife. None of the newspapers, made me feel about her in the same way as when the locals spoke about her.

I actually got to speak to her father, Edward Walker once. He was a proper gentleman, living in the west end. When I got to see him, he was full of remorse and was actually blaming himself for her murder!

'If only I had let her back into the family home when she needed me to!' He cried.

'It isn't your fault, you weren't to know,' I ended up saying to him.

'I know she was drunk sometimes, but she was still my little girl!' I could feel his pain and I absorbed it. 'I should have been there!' But the problem was quite simply he wasn't.

What surprised me was that some people was less forgiving, her ex husband, William Nichols was one of them. He had an almost loathing and revulsion against even the slightest mention of her name, he claimed it was her drinking that torn them apart and broke their marriage, their children seemed to believe this too and although they didn't have the same amount of disgust for their own mother they certainly was no fondness for her. Her ex-husband undoubtedly worked his powers of persuasion on his family, close friends and primary on me when I initially interviewed him.

But there was this sensation I could feel from him, it was almost as if he was hiding something rather menacing behind the angry ex-husband mask he was wearing. It took me a while to see what this important piece of information that Mr Nichols was concealing was but the locals helped to enlighten me on one crucial factor, I was told that Mary and William needed help with the five young children so they hired a nurse, a rather attractive nurse or so William thought and he and the nurse started an affair, it had been carrying on for weeks but then they were caught, so Mary left the family home and her children giving William the means and the opportunity to change the view of his marriage setting himself up to be the saint, a role he was still playing up to and after her death. Maybe he had taken the chance to become a saint because now Mary could never have the chance to give him the forgiveness he needed so, in a sense he could forgive himself.

I could see what interesting lives these people live in the dark undertone of City life, but what are more interesting to me and to many other people was their deaths and at the time I didn't care how evil that made me sound as I was safe in the knowledge that is what most people were thinking, so it was normal to be interested in the way they died.

Mary was found in Buck's Row, just a few hundred yards from the London Hospital. I went there; I couldn't help it I needed to see the place where Mary Nichols saw what we all wish we could see, where she seen her killer. It was a gloomy, small back street, not much light and a very quiet place to be. I could pin point the place she died as the blood still stained the cobbled stones. I bend down by the stain and said a few words, a pray perhaps. It did seem fitting to the scene. I stayed there for a few minutes but then I had to leave as, silly as this sounds *I felt death was following me*, waiting silently around the corner, plus it was raining and I had a very far way to walk. I had caught a fever that night.

I spent many days and nights confined to my bed chambers, never seeing many people, which pleased me. The maid was my only source of amusement, as I watched her fuss over me. The doctor she said had given her a nice, brown liquid called 'Collis' to give to me daily and I was becoming very fond of it. The rest of my time was spent remembering and researching my time in Whitechapel. Within a few weeks, I was back on my feet and back in the East End, but carrying one extra item, my trusty 'Collis Brown Liquid'.

The second victim was Annie Chapman; she was a little rougher around the edges as I heard she had got into a fight, just days before her death over a bar of soap! The way the papers described her death, was horrifyingly sensational. The murderer had slashed at her insides and her head was almost cut fully off! I was writing all this down.

The police seemed to be after a man nicknamed 'Leather Apron'. Not a great name for a killer, a taker of lives, I would have to change that, his real name was John Pizer, not a great name either. John Pizer was a local shoe maker, who had been known to get a little heavier with the street walkers than he should and they only went with him when it was necessary. The police were after him, but everyone knew, so in turn his people were hiding him. He was found not guilty and sued the newspapers that said he was the killer.

But the newspapers are not all bad; they gave the world a better name to the killer, Jack the Ripper. That was much more superior, it was a better quality of name, why didn't I think of it?

Victim three and four happened on the same night, that night I will forget as one of the victims I had seen and spoke to only days before, She was the fourth but she was so much more.

Liz Stride was killed first, in a dirty, old back yard of the Working Mens Educational Club, in truth I didn't care too much for her as not many people seemed bothered that she died, and her death didn't thrill me at all, just had her throat cut and she laid there bleeding to death. Not much for a writer to go on. But the fourth victim that was a different matter. Oh how shocking it truly was. Jack did seem to go to town on her, poor Kate Eddowes. She was a charming old girl, always had a smile on her face and a story to tell. Once when I was drinking in a local pub, adding my new favourite ingredient to my port, *when as if I was in a dream* she came up to me.

'I've seen you a lot around here.'

'Yes?'

'You are not a journalist, but you write.'

'How could you tell?' I asked.

'A woman knows these things,' she said as she sat down beside me. 'If you buy me a drink, I will tell you something else this woman knows.'

She said it in such cheeky way; I had to buy her a drink. She took it gladly. After she took a mouthful, I asked 'So what do you know?'

'Well my lovely, I know who Jack the Ripper is!' She said with a wink, I was unsure whether to take her to the mad house or not.

'Have you been to the police?'

'No, don't need to.' She said deprecatingly.

'How come you don't have to?'

'What would happen if I went to the police?' she asked. I looked at her puzzled. 'Well, what's in it for me?'

'They will pay you a reward.'

'That's only if they believe me, what happens if they don't? What happens if they think I'm just another mad person trying to get some money? And what happens if the higher ups know what I know and know I know it?'

'Yes I can see you point, as you are starting to sound a little loopy now,' I said, as she laughed.

‘I guess I am. It’s the drink. Anyway, how do I make sure I get some money?’

‘I don’t know.’

‘Ah, see what a clever little person I am,’ she answered proudly. ‘I go and see the only person who knows I’m right and that I’m telling is the truth.’

‘Who is that then?’ I asked.

‘The man, himself.’

‘Who?’

‘Jack the Ripper,’ she said as she finished off her drink. I was shocked.

‘That’s a dangerous game to play.’

‘But that’s life isn’t it?’ She said has she walked off. But that’s also death, I thought.

Chapter Two

1888

Jack the Ripper cut you to pieces didn't him Kate? He was so angry at being almost caught he took it out on you.

Catherine Eddowes was a motherly sort of woman. She was very plump and podgy as she did like her food and drink when she could get it. She was the first one to take me under her wing and introduce me to the other women in the group, she made going out on the streets seem a lot less frightening for a new beginner. She explained everything that was going to happen when I met a client, she went into detail about the pain and the bleeding it may cause, but we were all in the same boat and coped. She even went with me the first few nights, to hold my hand if you like and promised everything was going to be fine by the morning, when I would be sleeping it all off. She wouldn't even take any money for helping me, like the older ladies were doing with young starters.

'Your money is your money dearie,' she said as she had hold of my hand and led me down some dark alleyways. 'Don't let anyone tell you anything different; you are not doing this for the fun of it, are you?'

'Certainly not,' I replied.

'Good, well then. You need all the money you can get, don't you?'

'I guess so.'

'That way you might not get to be here at my age, things are a lot harder to get when you get older, your eyesight fails you, you have to buy more material to fit around you and you can feel your bones creak and ache with every move you make,' she said. That statement made me stop in my tracks and look back at her.

'Oh Catherine, how can you talk like that?' I proclaimed.

'How many times do I have to tell you? It's Kate to my friends and you are my friend. Don't start feeling sorry for me love, we are all in the same boat in one way or another and it's not all bad.'

'No?'

'No love, look I still have my teeth!' She said showing me her pearly whites, which ironically were stained yellow.

All this love in your warm heart and now you are lying on a cold slab in Golden Lane, surrounded metal tools and liquid filled jars. You are being washed down and sewed back together by two lonely and creepy attendants, who couldn't care less who you are and what you have done for other people. They are hanging you on their wall by a rusty hook as a last humiliation to you so the police can take their new fangled photographs, capturing the way you died for all time; can't they just let your soul go to god without people knowing what the devil did to you?

That last thought I made me taste that vile fluid in my mouth again, I spit it out, I need a drink! I walked a few more yards towards the wooden door of the Ten Bells Pub, I knew if I opened it I would be sucked in to the atmosphere of the cheering and the talking, just the environment of being with people and to pretend for just a few hours that these people in the public house are your family and they love you, that's why you are all in the same room is very temping. Silly as it sounds, it is what we cling to, to get through the day. You could spend all day clinging on to that thought, all the while not realising you're slowly wasting your life away in there. Of course the mischievous sprite that is served within helps as well, all this I knew and yet I still opened the door...

1898...

'There you are!' a familiar voice shouted to me.

'Here I am, Charles,' I answered the voice, turning around to face my friend.

'I thought you were going to threw one of your famous fevers.' He replied as he walked to me and tapped me on my shoulder.

'I didn't know they were famous.' I said feeling a little sheepish and that statement.

Charles just winked at me, perhaps sensing my embarrassment. ‘Well you are here now, let us get on and meet our Mann.’

‘Who is he?’

‘The sacked Mortuary Keeper I had mentioned before.’

‘And what are we doing?’

‘We are to ask questions.’

‘Why?’

‘That’s the ticket, come on,’ he said as he waved him to follow him, this I did down dark alleys and side roads, getting deeper and deeper east, we went past the streets and dens that I knew and I was feeling lost.

‘Do you know where you are going Charles?’ I asked with hopes that he might relax my thoughts.

‘Yes and no,’ was his simple and uncomforting reply.

‘Charles!’ I shouted, surely he was *playing games* with me and I was in no mood for silly answers.

‘Oh come on my boy, what life without a little mystery?’ He asked without turning around to face and I watched as his shadow disappeared for a second in the smog. I felt as lonely as ever so quickly followed his footsteps into the gloom.

We went deeper into the dark pit of London, the smell of The Thames was the strongest I have ever smelt it and when we turned a corner I could understand why. We were standing on a long stretch of a wooden, rotting pier, looking out across the Thames.

'What are we doing here?' I asked, looking at the planks of wood that was dark and wet, wondering if at all it would hold my weight.

'We are waiting.' Charles simply said.

'Waiting for what?'

'We are waiting for a Mann.'

'A man, you say?' I asked as I looked towards the outline of my friend because although he was only a few feet in front of me, the dense smog that filled the air allowed me to not see my friend in detail.

'Yes,' said the shadowy creature.

'Come on Charles, you are not being fair with me!'

'Have I not been?'

'No Charles, you have not!'

'But I have answered all your questions.'

'Not correctly.'

'Maybe you haven't asked the correct questions,' he said as he turned sharply at me and then sharply back at the river. It was through the mist I swear his eyes were glowing red, what is wrong with him? Is this environment that we are standing in changing him somehow?

'What do you mean by that?' I asked starting to feel a little confused at my friend's strange behaviour.

'Always ask the correct questions, Thomas,' he said as he looked from the Thames towards me and seeing me facial expressions this time, he said, 'fine, you asked who he is? He is the Mortuary Keeper. You then asked why? Not what is his name? So I answered, to ask questions. You asked do I know where I am going. I answered yes and no. As I know that I wanted to get to here, but from here I don't know where we are going, so yes and no. Then you asked what are we doing here? I replied, waiting as we are waiting for our guest here.'

'But then I asked you, what are we waiting for? And you replied, a man.'

'Okay maybe that was being unfair.'

'Thank you.'

'But only a little bit, we are waiting for a man, a Mr Mann, Robert Mann.'

'Not many people say my name,' said a voice. We both looked towards the Thames, to see a small wooden rowing boat coming into view. 'Hop on.'

'What have you got us into, Charles?' I said.

'The correct answer is... I haven't got the foggiest my dear boy!' he laughed as he jumped aboard. What choice did I have? Jump aboard a strange boat with a strange driver and even stranger friend or be left on the dock side of the East End alone, at this time of night and not knowing my way back home. I did the only thing I could do; I jumped aboard dreading my choice the instant that I did so.

'So what do two gentleman wants with Robert?' asked our driver as he started to row away from the dock. My thoughts were firmly on the safety of the dock that we were now leaving so Charles answered.

'Why were you sacked?'

'Robert was not sacked, Robert still works.'

'But I heard about the missing bodies.'

'Ah, missing bodies, yes Robert knows about the missing bodies.'

This was getting useless. 'So what happened at the mortuary?' I asked.

'Robert does work at the mortuary.'

'When did the first body go missing?' asked Charles.

'Wednesday last.'

'Do you know where it went?'

'It got up and walked off.'

'Oh come on! This is getting hilarious!' I shouted.

'Robert doesn't like shouting men!'

'Okay, okay, what makes you think it got up and walked off?' Charles asked.

'Robert goes into to work, he finds doors swinging open and an empty hook on a wall where there was a body hanging when Robert left, the night before.'

'What was the body's name?'

'Marie' That name, it must have been the way he said the moniker but it made me shiver and cold to the touch, I was *dead cold.*

'French?' Charles asked.

'Didn't look french to Robert, they all look the same. Everyone looks the same, dead. They all come to Robert dead; they all need Robert dead or not. Robert cleans them, cleans their souls, ready for the maker. They all have to go through Robert first; you will have to go through Robert, when you *will meet your maker.* '

I have had enough of this, 'Look Charles, you may enjoy this odd conversation in this odd surroundings, but I don't and I want out!' I shouted.

'And where do you inspect to go Thomas? To the bottom of the Thames by chance, because that is the only place you can go *now,*' Charles said without looking at me.

There was darkness to the tone of Charles's voice, a threatening quality that I had never heard from uttered from his lips before. Being around this strange mortuary keeper was unquestionably rubbing off on my friend; I did not like this one bit.

'I want off this boat!'

'Will you calm down Thomas; we are in the middle of the Thames having a little chat with our new friend here that is all. Answer me this Thomas, why are you getting so angry?'

'Why? Well don't you think this is all a little odd?'

'Not at all, now Robert was there anything special about her?'

'Special you ask? Robert doesn't understand your special when you say it; Robert's special is special, real special Robert thinks.'

'You know what I mean, was there any tattoos, marks on the skin, a crooked nose perhaps?'

'She was special; she was perfect in every way. She was Robert's kind of special. I told her so, so I did. I told her she was special and I told her I would look after her and Robert did. I looked after her real good, I did.' he answered. I didn't like this guy, there was something disturbing and baleful about him. I took a drink from my flask and let the warm, delightful liquid fills me needs and calm my nerves as I looked to the murky depths of the Thames.

‘How did she die?’

‘Drowned, she was so wet. Puddles, puddles here, puddles there, and puddles everywhere!’ he laughed childishly as he waved his damp wooden oars in the air, splashing Charles and I with a splatter of the river’s putrid smelling liquid. As I wiped my cheek I looked over the side the boat, for one horrifying moment I swear I saw a face looking back up at me.

A face where the flesh was peeling away leaving fragments of the skull for everyone to see and yet it felt like I was the only one seeing it, the eye sockets were empty as the eyes themselves had rotted away and there was no skin left on the nose bone making the face look sickeningly unnatural, all the while the face was looking at me it was smiling, one last deathly smile. I watched with revulsion as the face floated downwards out of my sight to lay on the shadowy gloom of the waters bed. I couldn’t quite get over the scene I had just witness, why are these demons haunting me! What do they want from me?

‘I want off!’ I suddenly shouted, but as I stood up I lost my balance and fell back, I hit my head on the back of the boat and there was a splash.

‘*Thomas, help me. I need your help’* She shouted at me. *She was struggling, ‘Let me go!’ She shouted.* ‘Thomas, Thomas can you hear me?’ I opened my eyes to see my ceiling; as my eyes then looked down to see my maid looking at me for I was back in familiar surroundings and in my own bed...

1888

'You better behave missy or I'll Whitechapel you!' said 'Old George' to one of the same girls that had shouted at me outside. This was the scene that greeted me as I walked through the public house's doors. It has almost becoming the normal thing for the chaps around here to threaten that towards girls like us, ever since Jack the Ripper has turned up in our district. Whitechapel is now famous, famous because of a murderer; oh how depressing can lives truly get I wonder?

'Oh come on George! Everyone knows you are good for a pint! Get your coins out, there's a good boy!' said one of the girls.

'And what's in it for me?'

'Well if like, I could take to the alleyway out back'

'Oh George, you can't turn that down!' Said another man as a group of men laughed behind him, all drinking from their glasses and it seems to me that they had been drinking for a while. On a normal night, my eyes would have been shining bright at the thought of all those intoxicated guys with all those pence's weighing their pockets down, but tonight is not a normal night and I am not the normal Mary.

'You are not my type,' said George sternly.

'No? I have never known you to be picky dear old George' she said as she wrapped her arms around his neck. George looked to so uncomfortable and embarrassed, I was starting to feel sorry for him when I noticed a strange thing. I don't know how he is managing to do it but his skin around his eyes was turning a devilish black. How can that be so?

'Again I must say, you are *not my type!'* George shouted at her as he pulled at her arms and pushed her away quite severely that she hit her back against the bar. This time she took the hint, maybe she saw the dark rings around his eyes too. While she was rubbing her back she replied back to him.

'Okay then, are you going to tell us all who is your type? Because we are all *dying* to hear, aren't we?' She asked an uninterested crowd.

'Well,' George began as he glanced passed the girl towards me as I was still standing by the door. The girl followed his glaze.

'What her? What makes her different from me?'

'She has class,' was his reply.

'Don't make me laugh! She's carrying.'

'Carrying?' he asked.

'Come on George you know what I mean, she is with child. That is how classy she is!'

'I don't believe you,' he said angrily.

'Suit yourself, no skin off my nose!' she said as she moved on to the next unwilling client.

'Mary!' George shouted over to me as he nodded me to move nearer.

'Not tonight George, I'm not in the mood,' I said as I got a drink from the bar and moved to the back of the pub. George looked hurt but then carried on talking to the group of men.

'Alright dearie? You are looking a little pasty tonight, anything wrong?' said the ugliest woman I had ever met, her hair was fragile and easily broke at the ends as well as turning a horrible shade of grey, she had gigantic, dark and hairy boils across the bridge of her nose making it look as if she had one, rather large eyebrow. She had missing her two front teeth which made her mouth shape revoltingly repulsive and every time she opened it, you could see the other teeth were black as the night and smelling an obnoxious stench.

My god please don't let me turn into a hideous monster like her, I'll take anything, anything but not that! Let me stay young; let me stay as I am for all time.

'I am fine,' I said as I took a sip from my glass and looked straight ahead of me.

'You not expecting me to believe that are you? Since when have any of us been fine?' She replied as she sat down beside me.

'Let's try it another way then, I don't want to talk.'

'At least you are now being honest.'

'Since when have any of us been honest?'

'Very true, my love,' she heartily laughed as she threw her glass down on the table that was in front of us, almost knocking the entire contents over. As I watched the browning liquid swirl in the glass she carried on talking. 'So what gets you down tonight?'

'What's it to you?'

'Come on love, I'm only being friendly.'

'I'm not friendly.'

'I can certainly see that; let's try it another way then. I am trying to help.'

'Help? Help is such a powerful word, why would someone like you want to help me.'

'Because I can sense you need it, probably more than anyone else in here tonight.'

'Why is that?'

'Haven't you realised yet?'

'What am I meant to have noticed?'

'How special you are?'

'Special? Are you some kind of joker or idiot?'

'Most people seem to believe that I'm a bit or both.'

'I can see why,' I said butted into her sentence.

'You really can't see it can you? I had always thought that when I finally meet you, you would know how unique you are, you are the maiden after all.'

'The maiden you say?' I asked I seemed to always attract the screwy ones.

'The maiden is the supreme being that can wander through the forest of worlds,' she said straightforwardly.

'That settles that then.'

'Settles what? My lovely.'

'You are an idiot, don't get me wrong I'm not frightened of you although I guess I should be, but there are a lot of you guys around here. Just waiting to be dragged into an asylum where you can carry out your craziness behind closed doors and padded walls and it is only because I have heard that you would not be treated right in there that I don't call the wardens in now. Just go, leave me be and a few more drinks down the line I promise I will forget this whole conversation.'

'You don't want to forget this conversation.'

'I think you will find I do,' I said as I finished off the contents of my glass 'One down another two the go I think.'

'They said the maiden will need to be shown the way through the first forest by the shepherd, I now understand what they are on about.'

'I'm glad somebody around here does.'

'I am the shepherd, why didn't I see it before?'

'I was wrong.'

'Oh?'

'I think I am going to need three, no best round it off to four drinks to forget this and to forget you.'

'Why would you want to forget me?'

'Because in case you have not realised yet, you are loopy. You are not normal, you are a crazy person. You are nice and kind but still crazy.'

'But I am the shepherd.'

'Yeah you said,' I said hopelessly.

'But the shepherd is here to help you.'

'I don't want your help or anyone else's in fact.'

'No?'

'No, I'm fine on my own.'

'But that exactly what you are,' she said as she grabbed her drink and left the table.

'What exactly am I?' I said towards her back.

'You are on your own, you are the only one left now' was her reply...

Chapter Three

1898

'What happened?' I asked my maid, as I said those words to her an out of the ordinary thought crossed my mind, it is quite quaint of me to think this and at this moment in my life but it feels like I had known my maid for years, I have a warm, cosy feeling when I see her, as one has when they look deep in the eyes of one's own mother, but as I look at her ageing face I don't ever remember not seeing those lines on her face, I don't remember seeing her dissimilar to how I see her now.

'Charles said, you wanted to play some midnight Cricket, in which Charles thought was odd but as he is such a good friend, he went with you and because it was so dark, he hit you on the head with the ball and you went down. Why did you want to play at that time of night Thomas? It will not do your fevers any good.'

'I don't remember any of that.'

'He did say he hit you quite hard, as he is such a fine sportsman.'

'That's sounds like Charles,' I said.

'The doctor has been and wants to you to start taking Brown again, there you go, down the hatch.'

'Wait!' I shouted but it was too late, the cool liquid had entered my mouth and as natural impulse started, I began to swallow and drink it. I had learned a few months back that Collis Brown had Opium in it and was probably the reason of my constant trips to the aberrant East End dens and now I have just had a double dose that thought stayed with me as I shifted into medicated slumber.

Thomas, help me! Thomas, help me! Thomas I can see you, why are you not helping me! Why did you not help me? She reaches out, but something stops her. I feel within myself the emotion of trepidation and concern for this anonymous lady. I know I want to help her as a brother would want to help his sister but I don't understand why, this lady is not known to me as yet I am being made aware of the familiar identify this lady holds. I can feel myself moving to be of assistance to the woman that haunts me but I feel the walls closing in around me, I feel trapped and spellbound. What were once wide open spaces now are not. I reached out; my fingers are bleeding as push hard against the walls that surround my very being. There is blood running down the brick walls. I look back at the woman and with a desperate plea I shout I can't help! I can't get to you! The woman looks at me with terror in her eyes as her body falls...

I awoke sweating; I had sweated so much that my bed sheets were soaked through and sticking to me. My head was still lightly spinning but I would see the outlined shapes of the bedroom objects that were known to me. I forced my body to sit up higher on my silk pillows as I tried to force my senses to reline with each other.

These dreams are disturbingly alarming, and I can make no suggestion to the purpose of these eerie notions that seem to have latched on to my soul. But why are they happening to me? What is so special about me?

I gathered my bed sheets together and after tripping over them a few times with my slippers, I managed to get to the hallway while the door to my study opened and the maid was standing in the doorway staring at me.

'Sir? What are you doing sir?' asked the maid.

'I,' I garbled. 'I want new sheets so I thought I could get rid of these first.'

'Let me take them Sir.'

'No, no it's fine.'

'No Sir it isn't fine,' she said as she tugged at them as they lay in my arms, she won the tug of war. This maid has some strength and is quite surprisingly forceful in her approach today. As she stepped back with the force of me letting go, she started looking at the sheets at which point I was fighting with myself whether saying the word sorry to a maid was right or not when she asked 'Are you hurt or in pain Sir?'

'What a silly question, no I am not hurt and no I am not in pain, what's the matter with you girl?'

'I only ask Sir, because your bed sheets are covered in blood.'

‘Blood you say? No surely it is sweat you see before you.’

‘Unless you sweat the red stuff then I’m sure this is blood.’

‘Red?’

‘Look Sir’ as I looked at the sheets she was holding, they were indeed stained with blood. Why did I not see that before?

‘I don’t understand,’ I was all I managed to say. The maid still had a puzzled look upon her face as she gazed at the discolouration on the bed sheets; she seemed to take a deep breath and then said.

‘Don’t worry sir, I will get rid of them,’ with a questionable look and me and then back at the bed linen she then started to walk away, talking to herself. I was too far away to hear what she was actually saying but I don’t have to be Inspector Dupin to guess what the subject was about, for the subject would have been about how crazy she thinks her master is.

As I was left alone, standing in my own hallway now empty handed my thoughts ran over the confusing incident I was just involved in and which I don’t understand, I wasn’t cut or hurt in any way. What was going on? I straighten myself and decided I needed some fresh autumn air so I walked out the front door and got my stride in full swing.

The day was shining bright and the streets were busy, I liked it this way, the busier the streets the more I could think. I tried to forget the peculiar occurrence between my maid and I and of course I needed to forget my spine-chilling imaginings for I needed to write a story, more to the point I needed some money. What story could I write? Should it be Charles's story of missing bodies? What would the title be, 'The strange case of Robert Mann'? I would hate to admit it but how ever odd that Robert Mann seemed to me, from a writer's point of view his character is interesting, should I find out more?

It was then, when I had that thought that I felt something rather unusual on the heel of my foot, it was distressingly cold and damp so I looked down and saw a wet amber coloured leaf had landed and wrapped itself around my heel. As I took a moment to bend down and release the leaf's grip of me, I was startled to realise I had left my lodgings in my slippers! I had become a gentleman's disgrace.

'Do I know you?' questioned a pair of old, tatty men's boots. I looked upwards and was surprised to see a young lady looking down at me, I stood up. I was a little taller than her.

'No I'm afraid to say I have never met you,' I said. She was quite pretty and although what I had just said, there was something about her I felt I knew.

'Are you sure?' She said.

'I'm sorry madam, I do not know you.'

'But it is strange is it not, for I know you.'

'How do you know madam, have you read any of my stories by chance?'

'Stories Sir, are in your own head, you do not need someone else to write them for you. I have stories Sir, I have many stories to tell but alas I cannot write or even read Sir, but what interests me is that you have story to tell.'

'Why does that interest you, what is special about my stories?' I asked, this lady although I could easily was of the lower class and possibly quite ill, she was fascinating and appealing to me.

'Is there something wrong with your ears Sir?'

'I should hope not.'

'Well maybe it is the fact you do not how to use them Sir.'

'I beg your pardon!' I exclaimed.

'What do you beg at my pardon Sir? I do not understand, you are rich Sir are you not?'

'I come across that way, yes.'

'Then why are you begging at me Sir?'

'I think we do not understand each other.'

'You have only just thought that Sir? Then you are very slow as well as deaf.'

'Why do you think I am deaf Madam? We are having this conservation are we not?'

'But you are not listening Sir, you are talking but not listening' She said as she itched her nose with the top part of a rather dirty hand.

'Am I not?'

'No Sir, I said what interests me is that you think you have a *story* to tell, just one.'

'I can tell you Madam, I have written many a story.'

'I don't care for the stories you have written, I care for the story you have inside of you.'

'I do not understand.'

'I can sense you have a story inside, as I know you have a story inside because I know you.'

'How come you claim to know me?'

'Because I have said I do.'

'Oh, where do you know me from?'

'I know you in a past life.'

'Look lady, I don't know what you are on about.'

'Why are you here?'

'What do you mean why am I here?' I looked around to find myself standing outside the women's help in need building. 'I stopped here to remove a wet leaf from my heel' I said as I turned back to her, I heard a voice.

'That's very nice Thomas, thank you for sharing.'

1888.

As I ran outside the Ten Bells public house and halfway along the road, I could hardly see a thing as the autumn showers had started while I had been inside and was now in full swing. I was getting soaked just standing there but in truth I had no idea which way the rather strange lady had gone, she had just disappeared.

'Mary!' I heard someone one shout, as I turned I could see the outline of a man half in and half out of the pub 'Mary!' he shouted again.

'George, is that you?' I asked, as I saw the shape of the man running up to me.

'Yes, I need to know.'

'You need to what George?'

'Was she right?'

'Was who right George? Look I don't know if you have realised but I getting sodden here, and these are my best clothes.'

'Yes they are,' he said creepily.

'Yes well, I must get home.'

'Back to Joseph I presume?'

'No, Joseph and I have parted ways again.'

'Is that so? You are on your own again; you shouldn't be on your own Mary, what with this murderer around.'

'I won't be on my own for very long, Joseph always comes back.'

'I care for you Mary, I truly do. If you just let me show you, I can protect you, I would never leave you side not for one moment.'

'Thank you George, but I don't need protecting but I do need to get out of this rain.'

'But don't you see how special you are.'

'Will people stop saying that to me, I am not special. There is nothing unique about me, I live in the dirty streets of Whitechapel earning a living doing things that are nasty and unspeakable like everyone else around here, people will not remember me.'

'I will make people remember you, if that is what you want. I will give you everything you want.'

'Please George,' I desperately pleaded.

'This murderer is killing in your home town, he is killing your friends, and no one is safe.'

'Don't you think I know this, don't you think I have fear every time I leave the house, but I do leave my house because I have to work the streets, handing out sexual favours.'

'Don't talk like that Mary! I won't hear of it, you are different. We are different together I saw it in your eyes, your lovely eyes that you felt it too.'

'You have got to be kidding me, you think there was something special between us, even when you paid me afterwards!'

'I paid you money because I can look after you and wanted to show it, I thought you knew this.'

'You paid me George because I am a prostitute, nothing more.'

'No Mary, please don't talk like that, you don't understand that is all, you are young you don't know a good thing when you see it. I will protect you Mary I will always protect you, no one knows who this killer is, so I will always be there,' he said as he ran back inside the pub.

A very bad and horrifying thought entered my mind then and there; maybe just maybe good Old George could be the killer, George the ripper?

'He could be but I don't *that* answer' said a voice from behind me. I turned to see the perplexingly idiosyncratic woman that I had been talking to inside the pub, leaning on the only gas lamp in the street as if it wasn't raining down hard.

'Where did you go?' I asked.

'A more important question is why were you following me?'

'I don't understand.'

'Well you are the one that said you didn't want my help, that you were fine on your own so I begs the question what was the sudden need to follow me out of the pub and into this rather showery weather?' she said as rocked one of her legs to and fro without looking at me.

'I need to know.'

'Need to know what?'

'What you know.'

'I know a lot of things.'

'I need to know what you know about me,' I said as I moved closer to the ridiculous woman.

'I know a lot about you,' she said still looking at her one moving leg.

'You know I am the only one left.'

'Yes, you are,' she whispered as the leg stopped.

'How do you know that?'

'It has already been written.'

'It is my destiny you mean.'

'In a way.'

'You can see what will happen to me, you mean?'

'I know what will happen to you.' she said quietly.

'I need to know.'

'You need to know what?'

'What it is that makes me so special.'

'Ah there it is, you have accepted your role from your shepherd, the shepherd can show you the way now but are you ready to know?' she asked as for the first time she glanced a foreboding look at me. Was I ready to know what was going to happen to me?

1898

'Charles!' I almost shouted at him in astonishment of seeing him suddenly appear in the same spot the strange woman had only a moment ago stood.

'That is what people call me, yes,' Charles laughed, whether he was laughing at me calling his name or the way I called it, I never asked.

'Did you see that girl?'

'I see many girls, what are you doing here?'

'What is it, with people asking me that?'

'I don't quite follow you my dear boy, anyway why in heaven's name are you publicly showing your sleepwear to the world, don't you realise it's a gentleman's disgrace?'

'Yes Charles, I fully understand what I am wearing and where I am showing it off too.'

'Yes, well I am glad you *fully* understand the situation you have put yourself in.'

'Yes, well I ran out the house you see, to get some fresh air and I bumped into this woman.'

'Was she endearing?'

'What? Yes, no. I mean did you see her?' I asked as I felt like I had taken a wrong turn somewhere and found myself going crazy.

'Look Thomas, there has been another missing body,' he said while showing me a newspaper. As I looked towards the paper and started reading the thoughts of the bizarre lady faded away from the depths of my mind.

'Charles, why has this story got such a hold on you?' I asked.

'Seven out of ten, for that.'

'What?'

'I marked your question, seven out of ten, getting better. But please, read about the body that's missing,' Charles said, it was only then I noticed the red rings around his eyes, Charles had been crying. I took the paper from Charles's hand to read it more closely, while holding back the pages that the slight autumn wind was trying to take from my cold stiff fingers, I finally saw what was making my friend so upset.

Once again in the evil East End of our great London town there has been another ghostly happening. If it wasn't enough that this poor women was murdered in the back alley of the Willow and Owl theatre but now the dead can't even rest, as her body disappeared from the Mortuary last night.

'It's Ellen, coming back to haunt me,' Charles said

'Charles, please, you need to let her go.'

'Thomas, I feel you are the only one that will understand, please try to go with me on this, I don't want to do this on my own. And if you don't come with me I'm afraid no one will, and they will cast me off to the mad house and then whatever message she is trying to give me will be lost.'

'Charles, I don't know how to deal with all this.'

'I'm not mad Thomas, please help me, help me Thomas,' my friend pleaded to me but with the echoing of my dreams rushed upon me, I felt weak and lost my balance. I felt into the road.

'Thomas!' I heard with the noise of a horse shying, women screaming, children laughing. I hit my head and my ear drums burst, giving me a bubbled sound of everything that was going on. I couldn't find the courage to open my eyes.

'Thomas, my friend, can you hear me? Oh Thomas forgive me, you are not well and your friend does this to you, Thomas!'

'Take me home,' I managed to say.

While I was laid up in bed I had noticed the sheets were different. 'I am so sorry Thomas, I should never have asked you,' Charles said after the maid had pumped up my duck feathered pillows and had left. I looked at Charles, he needed my help, in my dreams I can't help the woman, maybe it's because I am meant to help here.

'Charles, what makes you think I can help?' I asked.

'Because you write about this stuff, the afterlife I mean. I had hoped you believed in it too. Plus you are also quite mad yourself,' he said with a wink.

I laughed. 'How can I refuse?' I said.

'Really? But your health my boy,' Charles said leaning forward.

'Charles, it was a shock to hear you plead in the way in which you did that is all. I am here to help. I am unsure where you are going with this but I will be at your side, health or not health.'

'Where will I be without my Doctor Watson?'

'So now I am your sidekick, where do you want to start?'

'Robert Mann.'

'Again? I was getting quite sick of that man. He was very intensely creepy.'

'It was at his mortuary, he may tell us more than the local rag.'

'Robert Mann, okay. So are we having a row in a boat?'

'No, we can meet him at his workplace, after hours of course.'

'Of course Charles, I don't expect to meet a man like him in the bright hours of the day, now do I?' It was Charles's turn to laugh at my statement.

'How do you feel about tomorrow night?' He asked.

'Fine, meet me at the club,' I said.

'I will leave for you need to rest.'

And that is what he did. I looked towards my window, it was funny for a split second, weird as it sounds but I was sure a panel of glass had been smashed but as I shook my head the window was back to normal. I heard the birds singing and fell under their spell, I drifted off to sleep, a natural sleep.

Thomas, Thomas, help me! Why didn't you help me? I pushed at the walls until I can't push anymore. I can see blood dripping from hands. My hands are covered in blood, my eyes move from the girl back to my hands, I see blood running from my hands and hitting the floor, it was like I was watching a fountain of my own blood, there was blood around my feet. My feet were splashing around in my own blood; it was not a lake of normal water at all.

‘Thomas! For god’s sake, wake up!’ My maid screamed at me. I awoke, sweating. At least I hoped it was sweat. ‘Thomas, wake up! Stop doing that!’ I at once noticed I was on my side and stretched out. I looked over to my maid, ‘No wonder there was blood on your sheets, look at what you are doing,’ I followed her line of eyesight to my hands that were lying on the top of my pillow covered in blood, my blood. I had been scratching the wall behind my bed.

My hands started to shake; I have never felt so terrified of my own self before. ‘I, I don’t understand, I was having a bad dream.’

‘I think I should let the *doctor* know about this,’ said my maid.

‘No, no I’m fine; it’s just a reaction to the medicine. It’s very common for someone to have bad dreams.’

‘Is it Sir?’

‘Yes, of course if this gets worse, I will have to see the doctor.’

‘Very good, sir,’ she said as she took my blood stained pillow case away. When she closed my door, I checked my sheets, there was no more blood. I washed again. I walked out, taking my trusted liquid friend with me.

All the way to the club I was debating whether to carry on walking to Kingsmen, its felt such long time since I had been there, I still didn't know the answer when I reached the door of the club which was opened for me, I wavered on the door line, 'Does sir want to come in?' the guard on the door said. I turned to face him, his face slowly turn towards me. He had no eyelids and there were cuts of his cheeks, freshly cut as the blood was still pouring out of them. He looked as if someone had tried to take the skin completely off his face. I was horrified, my mouth was open and I tried to moved away but the guard was moving slowly towards me! 'Is sir okay?' the frightening and most appalling face said.

'Keep away! Keep away from me!' I shouted. I fell on the stairs and had to crawl backwards towards the railing, where I hugged my knees to my chest. I was crying.

'What is wrong sir?' said the face again.

'Please, please! Why are you doing this to me?' I cried.

'What am I doing to you, Sir?' said the same voice but I dare not look at him. I closed my eyes. After a few moments, when all was quiet I opened them again to see a familiar face looking back at me. It was the woman, she was sitting on the stairs with me and the guard was gone.

'Where did the guard go?' I asked her.

'I saw no guard, but you *did*.'

'What does that mean?'

'What did the guard look like to you?'

'Ghastly.'

'Why?' She asked.

'Because he had no eyelids and had these awful cuts on his face.'

'No, I mean why did he look that way for you?'

'For me you say? I don't understand.'

'You must understand it's the only way,' she said as she rolled two sovereigns towards me. I watched them hit my hand and I picked them up, as I looked at them I noticed they were not sovereigns at all but polished farthings.

'A way for what exactly?' I asked as I looked back towards her, but she was gone.

'Thomas! My dear boy! What in heaven's name are you doing down there?' Charles said as he looked down at me from the doorway of the club. 'I thought you weren't coming.'

'Charles,' I breathed, seeing my distress Charles brought me to my feet and carried me inside and placed me in my chair.

'You look like you need a drink,' Charles said, I just nodded. After I took a few sips of port Charles asked 'feeling any better?'

'Much.' I lied.

'What's going on with you Thomas? Are you very ill?'

'I don't know. Can I be honest with you?'

'Yes, please. It might help talking about it.'

'And you won't send me to the mad house?'

'If I do, I'll meet you in there,' Charles laughed. I smiled, but my smile dropped as I tried to think of the best way I could put it all, of what has been happening to me.

'I have been seeing things, things that I know are not really there, but they feel real. My dreams seemed to be filtering into my real life, it takes me a while to realise what is real and what is not. I used to be able to control my dreams, I have lately lost control and I don't know why. I used to think my dreams were trying to tell me something and that if I followed them, followed all the clues, I would find out what I need to know and would stop having those dreams, but now I just think I'm having a meltdown.'

'Maybe you need a break from London, you always liked Paris.'

'I have?'

'Yes, don't you remember? You had been there once and you had said you wanted to leave this unpleasant town and go back there.'

'I did?'

'This isn't helping you, your dreams can you talk about them?'

'There is this woman.'

'Isn't there always, carry on.'

'She has long hair and she is wet. At first I thought she standing in a lake, now. Well now I not so sure, she is calling out for my help, she knows my name. I try my hardest to get to her but I can't.'

'So you have put yourself in the role of a knight in shining armour, hey?'

'I guess, I never thought of it that way before.'

'*I'm not doctor* but maybe you are meant to help me on my quest, with my Ellen. She is a woman is distress,' Charles suggested.

'But we don't truly know this is Ellen do we?'

'I believe it is, and just for a short while can you believe it too?'

'For a friend, yes I will.'

'Thank you, now are you ready? We are already running quite late.'

'Yes, I'm up for a midnight adventure,' I said in the cheeriest voice I could muster.

'Well come on Watson, the game is a...toe?' Charles said looking at me for correction.

'Foot Charles, the game is a foot.'

'Elementary my dear Watson' with that we were on our way to the Mortuary on Old Montague Street.

Chapter Four

1888

The strange woman and I were walking along past the turning I would have taken to get home to Miller's Court. I took the time to notice how saturated my clothes were becoming from the cold and heavy downpour we had just experience which had turned to a light spiting, when she seemed to pick up her pace, splashing in every puddle that was in her way. I was struggling to keep up the pace she had set, so I shouted for her to slow down to which she didn't hear or at least pretended not to. I picked up my skirts and started to run; jumping over the murky puddles rather than going through them, when I finally reached her I asked 'What is the sudden rush?'

'We need to get away from the busy sights.'

'It is almost the early hours of the morning, the streets are quiet.'

'Quiet you say? What with the bells of Spitalfields church ringing every hour?'

'The bells you say? Oh yes, I forgot about the bells, living so close by, you do get used to them but surely the bells can't disturb us, can they?'

'No, but the fact that the market porters will be soon on their way to Spitalfields market, across from the pub just well might.'

'So where are we heading to in such a rush?'

'Somewhere quiet and out the way, somewhere a little more comfortable and out of this rain.'

After a few turns to the left and a few turns to the right, plus taking a short alleyway between a tobacconist and a candle stick makers, the strange woman abruptly turned down a *dead* end road, Old Montague Street. The name rang a memory bell in my mind, I know I had never been this way before, but I knew the name. It took me a few seconds of searching the *depths of my mind* to realise I have heard the name being read to me by Joseph from the newspaper articles of the murders of my dear friends.

'Doesn't this street have the mortuary on it?' I asked.

'Yes, it is the small shed at the bottom of this road, the one with the blue door.'

'You live here, on the same road?'

'I work on the same road, yes.'

'Doesn't that scare you?'

'Why would that scare me?'

'Being around the place of death,' as I said that statement she stopped walking and turned to me.

'Are you scared of death Mary?'

'Aren't you?'

'Everybody dies at one time or another; it is a progress we all have to go through, like being born.'

'I guess.'

'Never guess, you cannot fear death, you must embrace it,' she said as she turned and started walking off again but slower this time.

There was something sinister about this road; it was off the beaten track making it a lonely and secluded, the only sound I could hear was the sound of our own soggy boots hitting the pavement. On one side of the street were a few small dirt encrusted houses that casted an infected shadow across the stretch of cobbles and reached to the long grubby brick wall that was situated on the other side of this conventional side street of the East End.

'What is on the other side?' I asked, as I felt a little lost.

'A completeness of your whole being,' was the obscure reply.

'I'm sorry? I was asking what is on the other side of that wall.'

'Oh I thought. Never mind, are you feeling a little disoriented Mary?'

'To be honest I am feeling a little adrift with everything that has happened tonight.'

'Is that so? Well I hope you have the stomach for what is coming next,' she said. In truth I didn't like the sense of meaning behind that statement so I stopped walking and watched bewilderedly at this impenetrable woman who was walking off ahead. It took a few moments for this mystifying lady to realise I w as no longer walking along with her 'What is wrong?' she asked me as she turned to face me.

'I was just thinking I don't even know your name.'

'Names are not important.'

'Oh? Don't they define us, and make us who we are?'

'Not in the larger scheme of things, no. What defines us is our lives and what we do with it.'

'What have you done in your life to define you?'

'I am walking along this road with the maiden; this is my most defining moment and you? Well your defining moment is what you will do when you leave my home.'

'Isn't it already written out there, somewhere what I will do?'

'Yes it is, but I am giving you the choice, it is for you to choose what you have already chosen.'

‘As simple as that then,’ I said, everything about this night is completely bewildering, why did I think I was going to get a sensible answer?

‘You are right; it is as simple as that.’

‘Why are you bothering then? For I have already chosen my future, it is something I cannot change until my *dying day.’*

‘What then?’

‘What then what?’ I answered, puzzled with my own question.

‘What will you do after that day?’

‘Nothing, for I would be *dead.*’

‘That is interesting, *disappointing* but still quite interesting.’

‘Do you ever talk right?’ I almost shouted at her, I was starting to get to my wits end with the conversations I keep having with this woman.

‘Depends what you think of as right, in my eyes I am talking right in yours I presume I am not.’

‘No you certainly are not.’

‘You don’t trust me do you?’ she asked as she slowly walked back to me.

‘Do you blame me? A woman that I never met before and who won’t give her name starts talking to me about how special I am, about maidens, forests and shepherds and how she can show me my future, wouldn't you feel a little distrusting?' I asked.

'Put it like that and I can see it might seem a touch odd.'

'Thank you for seeing my point.'

'But I didn't drag you out of the nice, warm and dry pub, did I? I didn't make ran out and get yourself chilled to bone because you followed me, did I? I didn't make you walk with me here did I? No, I didn't because you chose to do those things; don't you think you have behaved somewhat odd tonight too?' she was now so close to me that when she finished her sentence I could feel her breath on my face.

'I guess.' I managed to say.

She decided to stand a little further back, sensing my awkward feeling of her being too close when she said, 'You have been guessing a lot tonight Mary, would you like to know something a little less of a speculation?'

'You mean about my life?' I asked as I carried on walking with her in the direction we had already headed for.

'In a way, yes you are right. You know, I do not lie Mary. I may not always speak in the right way but I never lie, you are special and you deserve to know why.'

'Should I know why? I mean won't that change history?'

'There is only one way to find out,' she said as she stopped to push open a shed like door and walked inside. She turned around to face me, waiting for me to follow her into the gloom of her own home. I stared up at the house that I was standing in front of; it was as eccentric as its owner. It was still as filthy as the other houses it was attached to on this street but there was something different about it, it had a splash of colour. The first colour came from a plant that had grown with the house and had fastened itself to the border of the residence reaching high over the second floor windows. The plant looked healthy, looked after and very green, the peculiar woman had also painted the brickwork of the accommodation in a dark red colour, how she had managed to paint it such a dark colour I have no idea but with the green plant it looked almost delightful and singular.

My eyes spread to the roof where I could just make out from the broken chimney smoke rising high up into the air. At that moment I felt like an invisible spirit circling around my whole being pulling me in, whether it is the promise of being warmed by the fireplace I am unsure but I *chose* to let the apparition guide me in as I walked across the threshold.

1898

'You seem to know your way around here,' Charles said to me as we walked down a series of alleyways and streets.

'Well I must admit I do feel at home here. I don't know what it is about this place but Whitechapel seems to have a hold over me. Yes I can see the dirt, the down and outs and the danger in the air with every corner we take, but I feel more safe here than anywhere else.'

'Even compared to Paris, Thomas?'

I stopped in my tracks, 'Charles, I don't remember Paris, I don't remember saying I liked Paris.'

'Strange isn't it?' He said with a wink as he carried on walking past me.

'What's going on with me?' I asked to myself as I had to break into a jog to catch up with Charles.

'Charles, how comes *you* know your way around here?' I asked as I walked along beside him. He stopped which made me have to turn head to look back at him.

'What?'

'Well we all know why I know this area, but how do you?' I asked.

'Why are you asking me this? What is the meaning behind what you say to me?' he asked quite angrily at me. The expression on his face was horrendous; I could see the thunder of hatred rolling around his face, it was quite dreadful to look at so I turned away.

'I don't know, it just hit me, maybe it's being here and things are..'

'Things are what Thomas?' He said as he walked up to me and placed his arm on my shoulder.

'I don't know, Charles,' I said still not having the courage to look Charles in the face, so I glanced at the cold pavement instead hoping for something to catch my eye and change what I was thinking about when I glimpsed Charles's shoes, standing heels together in front of me. It was quite an odd sight to see really; amongst all the dirt, grime and rubbish that were lying around on the old East End walk way, was a pair of heavily polished black shoes, without a peck of muck on them, well apart from the slightly dark patch of the right shoe anyway. It wouldn't have been very easy to notice if it wasn't for how shiny the rest of his shoes were and that fact was why I was still staring keenly at them.

'What were you going to say? Think Thomas' Charles said as he shook me to look up at him. The darkness in his face had subsided somewhat, I could still feel tension in the atmosphere around us but at least the unknown irritation had released its hold of him.

'I was going to say, things are coming back to me. But what those things are I don't understand myself, Charles. Am I going mad?'

'I hope so my dear boy, the best people I know are mad. Look, *I'm no doctor*. But maybe you haven't quite got over your fever, or maybe you're lacking your medicine.'

'Lacking my medicine?' Could that be true? Could I be missing my beloved dens? I felt for my flask in my inside pocket of my jacket and took a drink of it, I let the warming liquid fill my needs. I looked at Charles to see him smiling at me. 'Shall we crack on?' He asked.

'Yes, yes,' we only had to walk a few more yards before we were at the start of the famous Buck's Row. In just a few years the little common, cobbled street had changed its name to Durward Street because now it had become the most notorious and recognized road in the world, which came as a dislike to many of the people living here, so they change the name. But I don't think people will ever forget this street, the street that started it all for Jack the Ripper. To my surprise Charles, walked on, passed Buck's Row and was headed towards the London Hospital.

'Charles, surely it would be quicker if we walked down Buck's Row.'

'Yes, you are right Thomas,' he said as he turned back on himself and walked down the well-known street.

As we walked down Old Montague Street, I was wondering where exactly this Mortuary was as there wasn't much in this little side street, a few uninhabited houses and a brick wall on the other side but that was all. As we walked past the houses, I wondered to myself of all the families that had lived in those houses, all the different trades and professions they must have had, were a wonder to think of. I stopped outside one of them, it looked slightly different somehow.

'Why are you stopping here Thomas?' asked Charles as he walked back towards me.

'I have no idea really, it just struck me.'

'What struck you?'

'How beautiful this house must have been for its owner.'

'Oh?'

'Don't you see it?'

'I can be honest when I say, no I cannot see the beauty of this house, it looks the same as all the other deserted homes in this street.'

'Think of it five or even ten years ago when the paint was not flaking away and dull, when those dead branches held a strong and vigorous green plant rising high up the side of the house, think of it then. Think how different it must have looked then and how different it was for its owner. The owner must have been someone quite *special.*'

'You say special, I say quite mad. I mean who would paint the outside of their house a rather. What is it, a dark red? It's all quite, quite mad.'

'All the best people are Charles, you have just said that yourself.'

'Yes well, we should be on our way,' he said as he carried on walking down the road.

'But are we in the right street?' I asked as I caught up with him.

'I do believe so,' he said as he turned towards me, 'Why Thomas, you didn't expect to find a nice building for the mortuary did you? This is Whitechapel you know, there is not much love for the people that are living here, and so can you imagine what they do to the people that are dead?'

'Yes, I understand that, but I had thought what with newspapers highlighting the problems of this area with thanks to...'

'The Ripper' Charles whispered, then laughed.

'Yes him. I thought certain things might have changed, especially when dealing with death.'

'But alas! Nothing has changed, even a serial killer on the loose, changes nothing. What hope is there? So you can understand I can't leave this matter to the police, they are *fools.* And they will probably laugh at me anyway, but all that doesn't matter. For I have my Watson after all,' he said as he smiled to me. 'Oh, that is capital! Here we are my dear boy,' he said as he stopped outside a wooden shed.

'This? This is the Mortuary? I can't believe the dead are put in here!' I said.

'Ah yes, I forget you would not have known what this place looked like,' Charles said as he tapped on the door. 'We are here, Robert,' he said as he pushed open the peeling blue painted door with the top of his walking cane and walked inside.

'No wonder, bodies are missing. He leaves the door open!' I exclaimed.

'Capital Thomas! You are letting your brain work! But alas I do not think the door is meant to be left open.'

'What makes you think that?' I asked.

'Did you see the lock? It has been changed, probably when the first break out occurred. But the new lock has been smashed in and of course this,' he said as he pointed to the work table over in the corner.

There in the light of the candle that was sitting on the work bench, was Robert Mann surrounded by jars of all different acids protecting all manner of human parts. My first thought would have been that he had fallen asleep while busy working, but the long knife that was shining ever to brightly in the candle light and was sticking out of his back, told me that was not the case!

'My god!' I screamed.

'Well he won't have to be moved far will he?' Charles said in a huff.

'Charles, please! The man is dead!'

‘And we are left here, no further in our quest.’

‘WE MUST get the police!’

‘For the good that will do, that will probably hang around outside for a few hours, while they wait for a higher up to come, the higher up will take his time, and the long and short of it will be the ‘murder by person or persons unknown’ I have just done all the that in a few seconds, let us move on.’

‘And leave him here?’

‘He is not about to get up and walk away is he?’ He said as he walked out, then he stopped and turned back to me ‘Or is he? Did you want to wait and see, Thomas?’

‘No I do not!’ I said as I raced out of there.

‘I thought not.’

‘What do we do now? There was certainly a struggle before Robert Mann met his death, the murderer might still be close by, watching us and we could be in danger,’ I whispered. I was starting to feel panic rising within me.

‘Struggle you say?’ Charles asked as he calmly started to light his pipe.

‘Well yes, I mean there was a smashed jar on the floor and the acid had stained the floor by his desk.’

'Well done Watson, credit when credit is due. I don't suppose the police will notice that at all! What a brilliant mind you have.'

'What do we do?'

'Let me think about it, Thomas, well its getting light now and there is a nip in the air, which will not do your health any good and we must keep that brilliant mind in tip top shape to help with our quest, let's go home. I will pop into a police station on the way.'

My head was already starting to spin, and with the sight of seeing the strange Robert Mann killed in his place of work was overwhelming, the thought of going home seemed almost delightful for I needed to lie upon my own pillow as I was feeling sleepy.

Thomas! Thomas, help me! Why aren't you helping me! Let me go! I can't reach her! I'm screaming. There is blood on my hands, dripping from my fingers. She is wet with blood, there is blood everywhere...She falls, she lies in the blood. Help me! Help me Thomas! I can see you...Why didn't you help me? You need to let me go! You need to help me! Help me! You are the only one that can! You are the only one who knows! Who knows me!

'WHO KNOWS HER?' I screamed out aloud as I awoke from my dream, I was out of breath and glad I was at home and in the safety of my warm and quite moist bed sheets. It was also the maid's day off, meaning I was alone and no one was able to hear me as I was unsure how loud I was. I looked down at my hands, it had become almost an accepted part of my usual routine to see whether I was bleeding, anomalous as that sounds.

This time I was sure there was no blood to be observed from any angle of my vision, so I decided to turn my attention to my side table, which had a crystal vase holding one single rose, to this day I cannot remember when I brought that vase or why the maid is replacing it with another living one when this one dies, *for it must die mustn't it?* As the sunlight hit the crystal it sent beautiful colourful sunbeams across my ceiling, they seemed to be dancing together as if they were at a private ball and I was being an onlooker too lame to join in.

Sitting close to the vase was a whisky glass filled half way with a thick cream, although it had no label I was sure that was my medicine, waiting there inducing me to drink it. I reached over to the glass almost out of habit but just as my forefinger felt the solid glass, I snatched my hand back as if the glass had just bitten me. No, not today I will cope without the sickly drug inside of me, for who knows I might feel better for it.

I pulled back the burdensome covers and swung myself around, placed both feet in my checked slippers, left my divan and headed for my wash stand. I let the cold water splash against my skin and awaken my sanity a little more, as I tried to make sense of everything that has happened in the last few days. I had met a mysterious and a quite slow-witted man who seemed to have a rather unhealthy not counting his disgusting devotion to the dead bodies that are in his care, the thought of what he must have done to them when he was alone with them was too horrendous and ghastly to think of.

But now I have seen this sickening creature dead in his workplace surrounded by his own tools at his own worktable, he certainly was odd and a little sick in the head but did he deserve to die in such a gruesome manner? *Does anyone, no matter what they have done deserve to die by someone else's hand?*

Who would have wanted this man dead? What could Robert Mann have done to someone living in this world to make them want to kill him? It makes no sense, but then does anything make sense anymore the way things are going I was seriously doubting it. There are of course my dreams that I have no understanding towards although *I can feel they are very important to the narrative of my life* and there must be an earth shuttering reason why I am having them.

Now I am having visions in my real day today life as well, these petrifying hallucinations of dead people with flesh stripping of their bones and bloodied cut across their faces are terrorizing deep down in my very soul and giving me a mental picture of a mad person. But the most shocking of all is the girl that I have seen twice now, was she following me and if so why? What is so special about me? The moment that thought entered my brain I felt a strange sensation around the word 'special'. This girl seemed to turn up magically and speak in tones of the all seeing prophecy. Does she know the future? And what does that mean for me? I am meant to know something important and is there a connection between her and my dreams? Is she the woman I mean to save?

I dressed and left the house, somehow I felt a little unsafe being outside in the busy streets on London on my own, but I shook that feeling off and walked east wards towards the club but more importantly to the theatre of the Willow and the Owl.

1888

As I entered the colourful house I saw in the gloom ahead of me was the shadow of a flight of stairs that had four steps missing halfway up. 'How do you get upstairs?'

'I don't.'

'Oh, I just thought there may be another family living up there.'

'There was, but died or left early in the year. Nice family really, the Turner's were. The mother, May was a good old woman, looked after me pretty well when I first moved here. I was young you see, alone too and May was the mothering type, well she had five of her own and she was worried for me, bless her. I was sad to see her leave in that old coffin.'

'What about the other members?'

'Well after May died, James the father carried on for a bit. He even painted the front of the house for me, he said he didn't mind as red was May's favourite colour and it would be in memory of her. The oldest child left home, I think his name was Jimmy went to be a bar tender in some little theatre in the West End somewhere I believe, anyway the youngest Victoria died in the arms of Martha her sister. In truth I never thought James recovered from the death of his youngest, sweet little girl she was, everybody liked her. James died shortly afterwards from a broken heart I would say and Martha was left to bring up the other two children, Maria and Lewis. Lewis sadly went to prison for stealing a neckerchief, I haven't heard anything of him since. Martha and Maria went to work in the workhouse in Lambeth, I saw Maria a few months ago so she must have left the workhouse. I hate to say it but she looked awful and tatty and I am sure she is working the streets.'

'I wouldn't wish that on anyone.'

'I can understand that.'

'What happened to Martha?'

'Martha? Didn't you hear? In the dead of night, a few months ago Martha Turner was murdered.'

'Murdered!' I exclaimed. For I hadn't heard anything of this, why! I feel like death is following me everywhere I go. I cannot get away from it no matter how much I try! Why is everyone dying around me? Why do I feel a presence of the devil looking over me as I was a prawn in his sickening and twisted game? The devil called Jack the Ripper.

'Yes, quite a sad story there as always, Martha had left the workhouse and started to work the streets too, she was with another girl and two soldiers. They left The White Hart pub, you know the one in Whitechapel High Street?'

'Yes I know the one.'

'Of course you do, well anyway Martha left with one of the soldiers and went down Angel Alley to service him while the others waited for them, but they were taking their time so the other two left. Martha was found a few yards away from Angel Alley and had forty nine stab wounds made by two different knifes.'

'No! Poor Martha!'

'I believe it might have been the start of Jack the Ripper spree.'

'Do you?' I asked, there I hear his name again, Jack the Ripper, Jack the Ripper. It seemed as if his name was being whispered hauntingly down every alley, on every street corner and I will always hear it. Will I be forever disturbed by this mad man? Will my name, Mary Kelly be forever linked to Jack the Ripper? Something was telling that this might be spine-chilling so.

'Yes but who would listen to the ravening's of a mad woman' she said pointing to herself. So she knows she is mad? That doesn't bear me in good stead for tonight. But wouldn't a mad person really not know that they are mad? So knowing that she is mad makes her almost sane. Or quite possibly I am turning mad thinking of all this madness.

'Quite,' I whispered more to myself than to her.

'So you can understand that I have no need to go up there, as there is a bad spirit that haunts over the top floor, I can feel it every day reminding me of things to come.'

'Spirits? You mean ghosts, there are ghosts up there?' I said pointing to the stairway.

'Do you believe in them, by chance?'

'I guess I should,' I alleged as my head turned back towards the spooky stairway as if I was going to see a ghostly figure staring back at me, waving.

'You would guessing correctly my dear girl; never shut your mind to anything that may be possible otherwise the maiden's soul will not come and you will end as you stand now. That is not how your destiny has been paved for you.'

'When you said 'reminding you for things to come' you meant to say things that have come to pass, didn't you?'

'Did I mean that? Of course that would make more sense to you wouldn't it?'

'Yes it would seem most sensible.'

'You need to let you go of all sensibilities and probabilities before you enter my door missy.'

'What do you mean?'

'Tonight there will be things that sound odd to you.'

'Things already seem a little odd.'

'Not this kind of odd missy, there will be things you will not understand, could not dream to comprehend, it will change everything you could possibly imagine.'

'My destiny you mean?' I asked.

'You cannot be the maiden; you cannot enter a new forest unless you embrace the end of this forest.'

'How will I know it is the end of this forest?' I said trying my best to talk to this strange lady in the same words she was using.

'The spirit of your own self will be shown to you, through a looking glass.'

'Sounds simple,' I joked

'I am glad you say so, most people don't get this far.'

'I take it, you don't bring many people back here,' I said as I managed to laugh a slight bit.

'On the contrary, my work brings many a person here. Tall, short, rich or poor, they all find their way to me, although it is different for you, in many ways.'

'Different ways you say?'

'Why yes, normally the curious seek me out. But I had to seek you, something told me to wait in that pub tonight and I was going to leave just when you walked in.

With your bright red hair, just standing by the door looking abandoned and lost, I knew you were the one I was waiting for. You see, I have dreamed about you.'

'Dreamed about me?'

'Oh yes, for quite some time too. I knew I was looking for a Mary and there you were.'

'That is nothing special, Mary is a common name around here and if I remember correctly I did not give you my name.'

'And yet when I called you Mary, you have always answered.'

'Well yes it was natural too.'

'Exactly, what could be more natural than answering your own name? But there is more.'

'More?'

'Oh yes, so much more and I know that is main reason that you have followed me home tonight, as the little sheep you are. For tonight is the exceptional night, you will understand why you will be always remembered in the hearts of people *in this life and the next.'*

Chapter Five

1898

I was standing outside the entrance to the Willow and the Owl theatre pondering whether I should make the final step inside when 'Mind out the way fella, I got to get to work' said a voice from behind me.

It was Jimmy the bar tender, he was young in looks but what gave away his real age was his greying hair and probably the main reason why he always was seen wearing his flat cap that his father gave to him before he passed away.

'Sorry Jimmy, is it just you on tonight?'

'Almost but I can't complain, it brings in the dosh and I need all the money I can get for me and Maria.'

'How is little Maria?'

'Not so little now Sir, she has managed come off the streets, with a little help and decided to change her last name too, a sort of fresh start. Named herself after the family pet, 'Harvey' so she has.'

'Oh that is good.'

'I think so, she is working here as a char woman most nights and she is living with me now.'

‘Oh?’

‘Well you know we have got to look after each other, we have been the only ones left for nearly ten years now after Martha was.’

‘Yes I remember someone telling me about the death of Martha.’

‘Yes that was an awful way to go, but let’s not talk anymore on the past Sir, it is not wise.’

‘I guess you are right in what you say, Jimmy.’

‘Are you coming in tonight? We have some fine acts tonight, all magic tricks.’

‘*I am not a fan of being tricked* Jimmy, I came here to ask a few questions.’

‘Are you being the new Dr Watson now?’

‘I’m sorry?’

‘Well Dr Watson worked with police, asking questions and I only ask Sir because he and you are an author.’

‘Oh I see now, no I am not working with the police. I am doing research for a new novel.’

‘A new novel did you say Sir? Oh I am ever so glad; I did like your other one Sir.’

‘You might be able to help me with this new one.’

‘It would be an honour if I can Sir.’

‘What do you know of an actress that worked here a good eleven, maybe twelve years ago by the name of Ellen?’

‘Yes the name does ring bell, it was when I first came here. She was the singing nightingale wasn’t she? Sweet to hear and even sweeter to look at.’

‘That is the one.’

‘You are writing a story on missing persons then?’

‘She is a missing person then?’

‘That is what I believed at the time Sir, and her mother did too but not at first might I add.’

‘Oh?’

‘I remember it quite clearly. For you see Sir, Ellen’s mother was a recluse. She spent most of the day inside her home on Courts Row, only coming out at night. So it was a shock to see her. Most people thought that she belonged in Bedlam and that night, when Ellen first disappeared I mean Sir. Well her mother came rushing in, when we were at our busiest I might add and she screaming and carrying on, much more unnerving than when women normally carry on, I will tell you Sir. I could understand why most people thought the madhouse was the best place for her; she crazy that night, maybe she always was I don’t know Sir. All I know is she looked terrifying, her dress was torn and falling apart and her scars Sir were shocking. But the noise

Sir, the noise coming out of her mouth was like the devil coming alive as I never heard a woman scream with tears so loudly since. It brought a chill to my spine Sir. She was like a mad woman, shouting that her beloved daughter had been murdered.'

'Murdered you say?

'That is what she shouted Sir.'

'Did she shout anything else?'

'She did seem to say something, I can't remember what Sir. But I remember her face Sir; it was horrid I can tell you.'

'What was wrong with her face, Jimmy?' I asked as I looked up at him. Jimmy wasn't looking at my face but up to the skies behind me, he looked terrified as if the thought of the Ellen's mother face was still harrowingly crossing his mind. 'Jimmy? Jimmy, are you all right?'

'What? Oh Sir, I just had a fright that's all. Look Sir I hope you don't mind at all but can we talk about this inside, I am running late as it is.'

'Oh yes Jimmy that would be fine for a few minutes, but only a few minutes.'

'Yes, yes Sir. Let's get inside now,' he said rather hurryingly as he patted my back, pushing me forward.

Once inside the theatre Jimmy seemed more himself and a little more relaxed, 'Right Sir you sit over there in that booth and I will follow once set up here, and can I get you a drink? On the house so to speak.'

'Why yes Jimmy that would be most appealing, my usual if you please.'

'Righty oh Sir, be with you in a jiffy,' he said as he pushed the door marked 'staff' at the same time another member of staff came walking through it.

'Hey Jimmy there will be a delivery at the back door soon, when he knocks answer it for me will ya?' the member of staff asked him.

'Yeah, yeah,' was Jimmy's reply as he walked through the door, disappearing out of sight. I moved towards the booth that was pointed out to me and sat down in the comfortable seating and looked around.

It was rather odd to see the theatre unmanned and empty, it seemed the same from the outset. The same wooden stage was there with the gas lamps lighting the edge, the same dark red curtains with gold trimming were pulled together as if a show was about to start. The same seating and the same smell was all there but one thing was missing, the people, the public, and the common old customers that come here every night for the best entertainment was absent leaving the theatre alarmingly sinister. But what was more sinister was the spine-chillingly high pitched sudden scream that came from behind the door marked 'Staff'. As I ran over to the door, a woman was slowly walking backwards out of it with a hand over her mouth; she had been crying a whole heap.

'What has happened?' I asked as I grabbed the woman by the shoulders.

'It's horrid! It is sick!'

'Tell me, what has happened?' I repeated as I shook her a little to make her notice that I was in front of her. Her eyes moved towards me very slowly.

'There is so much blood!' she screamed at me.

'Oh my dear God!' I shouted as I ran passed her and through the 'Staff' door. I don't know what I thought I could do about the situation for I knew what I was about to see, but I kept running down the stairs as something was telling to see what I already knew was true.

When I got to the bottom of the stairs there was a group of three people standing this side of a set of double doors. The two men, young in stature were standing like a pair of waxworks, frozen with shock and the other girl of about the same age was sitting on the floor, rocking herself gradually to and fro while crying uncontrollably. I moved passed them to the double doors and put my hand up against it, about to push it open when I felt a cold hand on my shoulder that stopped me and made me instantly drop my hand to my side.

'I would do that if I was you Sir, the sight will turn your stomach,' the hand seemed to say; as I turned to see what the cold hand was attached to it repeated itself 'turn your stomach it will,' I could now see the hand was connected to one of the men that must have melted the wax away for him to be able to move along and touch me.

'It is Jimmy isn't it?' I asked even though I knew the answer, at the sound of his name the woman screamed out an deafening noise which made the other man run over to her stating that it would all be fine.

'Yes Sir it is he.'

'What has happened?'

'He has been murdered Sir.'

'Has anyone called for a doctor or the police?'

'We are all in a state of shock Sir, but yes you are right the police need to be called as I know a doctor doesn't,' he said as he turned to walk up the stairs.

'Maybe you should take this lady with you, she could do with some air don't you think?'

'Yes Sir that is a fine idea indeed,' he said as he grabbed hold of the sobbing woman and held her all the way up the stairs, when I heard the door on the higher level swing open and then shut I turned to the remaining man, who had decided to stand beside me.

'You want to look in Sir don't ya?'

'Yes I need to know what has happened to Jimmy.'

'But why Sir? It is sick and horrid.'

'So I hear.'

'And you still want to go in.'

'I need to know for reasons of my own.'

'Then you are sick Sir!'

'Excuse me?'

'Well tell me why you would want to go in there and not take my advice? I mean for heaven's sake it is like Jack the Ripper has come back to life!' he screamed at me as he ran upstairs, not giving me much chance to reply and leaving me alone, with a door between me and hell. I must see hell in the face.

1888

The hauntingly look on the strange woman face froze my soul; I tried to speak but felt unable to. The hallway I was standing in suddenly felt cold and bitter to match the pungent taste in my mouth, I became aware of everything turning rapidly to solid ice and I would imagine I would have been freezing to the touch. I tried to breathe but every time I opened my mouth, what felt like piercingly sharp cold air came rushing in, suffocating me. The last three things I remember was that my arms started waving around hastily and then the strange woman asked,

'Are you all right?' and then there was nothing.

I push open a cold, unyielding door and I peer in. The room was empty of objects and feeling, no love here. I stand in the doorway feeling unable to move forward, some unknown being is telling me to look down but I don't want

to for I already know the scene that lays before me. A revolting and vile scene, a scene I will never forget. 'Horrid' they will say, 'ghastly' they will call, 'dreadful' they will shout. And here I am standing within the scenery of frightening set, for I am a part of it, I have always been a part of it.

This place feels detached from anything I have seen before and yet I feel strangely attached to it. The table I see before me I recognize as if it was mine own, the used fireplace stands strong while holding the worn out kettle is bubbling away within its belly. Someone should take it off the heat; the spout is going to melt.

Then the moment happens when my eyes wonder naturally towards the horrendous picture that lies before me. The colour hits me first, so bright a colour I had never seen previously or had I? Something about it rang a bell with me; I had seen it I am sure but from where? As I looked down and my eyes stayed on the pile of bloodied meat that was still bleeding, I felt a number of different emotions. The first one being such a frightening horror I could actually sense my eyeballs shaking inside their sockets, then came fear as I feared for the soul that had been recently taken from this world and lastly came sadness. I undergone a sense of sadness for what had happen here, someone had died as I believed that once this pile of flesh and bone had once been a person but they had been butchered like a pig. They were not human anymore; the killer had taken the very essence of someone being alive.

The body laid on its back, its head was fleshless, the colourless eyeball were laying loosely in their sockets, the neck was cut open and the past pulsating red liquid had congealed around making a horrid red neckerchief. The insides of the human form was laid outside on the table, leaving a huge bloodied hole below the head up to the start of the legs which was still there, missing their skin.

This person is dead and I am the first to see it, this poor man is dead for the body is a male.

I awoke from my nightmare tired and confused, my eyesight had not fully returned to me as what I was seeing was hazy and unclear, I felt like I was lying on a cold, hard slab. Had I died? Was I now lying in the mortuary which was not far away?

No, as my sight slowly became a little more normal I could see that I was face to face with some kind of papers that were lying on the floor with me for I had fallen and was now lying in the strange woman's hallway; she hadn't bothered to catch me or pick me up. How long had I been lying here? I would never know. I rolled on to my back and looked up at the mouldy ceiling, why was I here? Why did I follow her? What had I done? What had I changed? Maybe nothing, maybe this would just be a night I would never forget and that would be the end to it. My eyes wandered to the left of me and to the stairs leading up to the death and lonely rooms of the Turner's, was there really a ghost up there in the shadowy gloom? Maybe it is the ghost of Mrs Turner, the kind motherly type of person, still looking out for her neighbour who lived downstairs. Was she looking at me right now I wondered as I look towards her? Was she looking after me when I was knocked out and the strange woman had just left me here?

The door standing beside my feet opened and the light from the room within hit my face, I covered my eyes with my arms and noticed that my arms ached.

'You are awake then?' said the strange woman as she walking a little further into the hallway and shut the door, leaving us again in the gloom.

'No thanks to you.' I replied.

'No need to be like that, what was I meant to do? I tried to move you but you were a *dead* weight, there was no blood so I thought you would wake up in your own time.'

'I could have died!'

'Oh no, I knew you wouldn't have died here,' she said as she reached out her hand to help me up, as I grabbed it I asked.

'So how long have you lived here?'

'Depends how you think about time.'

'What do you mean?'

'Well if you think of time as one continuous line, then I have lived here for quite some stretch but if you think of time as floating line with many different time lines being able to come of it then I have not lived here very long at all.'

'I don't understand.'

'In truth not many people do, but you should for you are the maiden.'

In truth at the this point I wanted to turn around and run away from this strange woman, all this talk of me being a form of maiden in a world full of forests was somewhat disturbingly worrying but there was something remarkable and attention-grabbing about the woman that was standing before me. I can't quite think what it was, was it because she was different and refreshing? Or was it quite simply that I did not want to be alone and she offered company, a strange and peculiar company but company all the same so I closed the shed like front door and was left momentarily in the dark.

The odd woman then opened her side door again and the light from one candle that was standing tall on a wooden pole beside a multi-paned window flooded the hallway I was standing in and that is when I noticed the flooring was covered in not just paper but newspapers, all different kinds of newspapers too. I couldn't read but there were titles I know the look of, there was The Strand and The Evening Times but there were newspapers titles I had never seen before and some had colour that I have certainly not set eyes on in previous times.

'Why do you keep so much different newspapers?' I asked.

'Do they interest you?'

'Well the different ones do.'

'What do you mean when you say 'different'?'

'Well the ones printed in colour and with different letters.'

'The ones in colour, you say? You can see the ones in the same colour as my house?' she asked in a fascinated way.

'Yes, what of it?'

'It is interesting that you can see them, it tells me something.'

'Oh? And what might that be?' I asked. I felt like I was in a tug of war of questioning and I wasn't about to lose this time.

'It tells me I was right about you.'

'I am glad for you,' I replied, for I didn't know what else to say and had lost the tug of war.

She nodded a 'thank you' at my response before she asked 'So would you like to read The Sun newspaper?'

'Is that what the newspaper is called then, The Sun?'

'Yes, can't you read it?'

'Joseph reads to me, well what I mean to say is Joseph read to me, about the murders only mainly. I hope you don't find that perverse of me, but I wanted to know how they died for they were all my friends and I do miss them so, well hearing about them, even their deaths keeps them alive, in a mixed up kind of way. '

The woman turned around to face me before she said 'So am I to take it that Joseph has already left you?'

'Well yes, but I don't see how that is any concern of yours.'

'I guess you couldn't, but it does mean something though.'

'Oh? And what is that?' I asked or I was starting to get engrossed.

'It means time is running out and I need to work fast.'

Chapter Six

1898

As I faced the door to the devil's playground I braced myself for the worse possible sight, I relaxed my shoulders as I found that I had been tensing them tight since I had ran down those stairs, there was a part of me wishing to run back up them without peering into the room before me but there was a greater demon pulling me forward for I must see the horrid, I must see the sick.

I placed my shaking hand against the icy door again and was willing my leg to move when I heard a clanging of metal. Is there still somebody in there? Another witness maybe or could it be the murderer? With the words of my friend Charles running around in my mind 'So you have put yourself in the role of a knight in shining armour, hey?'I suddenly in a fit of heroism I burst open the door.

The room was small and I guess would have been quite dark if it wasn't for the second door leading to the outside being open and flapping to and fro on its hinges. That is why it was so cold in here, or was it the devil's touch? Although the second door was making a slight creaking noise it was not the same metal clanging I first heard, that was coming from the lid of the kettle that had been left boiling in the diminutive square fireplace, it had been boiling for some time as the spout had melted a little at the top. For some reason, maybe it was natural instinct or some divine higher spirit telling me to do so, but I removed the kettle from the heat using a piece of white silk that was lying on the floor for protection, the noise stopped and there was silence, a *deathly silence.*

At last I took the courage to look at the bloodied mess that lay on its back in the middle of the room. Jimmy was no more, no more a human but miming perfectly a butchered pig. His throat had been slit from side to side, so much so that his head was lying in a very unnatural manner, his eyes were staring blankly at the moving door as if his last sight followed the murderer leaving the scene of the crime. The was one long and jagged cut running from the neckline to where I would imagine Jimmy's belly button would have been as it had now dissolved into the red liquid of his blood, there were organs outside of his body, some thrown on his shoulder others laying just by the side still attached to the insides. It looked as if the killer had tried to peel of the rest of Jimmy's skin but had run out of time to finish the job; it was a sad and sorry state of affairs for a murder like this to still happen in my life time and to happen so quickly. I was about to close my eyes to say a pray for the parting soul when a shadow of a person casted over the remains of Jimmy, I turned to look and saw a small boy standing in the entrance of the open doorway.

'Delivery for the Willow and the Owl,' he stated to me just as his little eyes fell on the cadaver that laid before me, I watched as his tiny eyes grew wide and turned a ghostly white. 'Oh my god! Are my eyes playing tricks on me Sir or am I actually seeing a corpse?'

'Sadly so my dear boy,' I said as I looked back at what was Jimmy the bartender.

'Are you a policeman investigating the crime? Or are you?' the boy stopped in his tracks.

'Am I the murderer by chance?' I finished the sentence of for the young boy, still looking at the dead body, when the boy didn't answer me I looked back at him to see him staring in horror at me.

'Are you Jack the Ripper?' his teeny voice managed to ask.

'Do you remember those murders then my lad?' I asked.

'Remember them Sir? No Sir, I am but fifteen years old now Sir. But other people have mentioned him and my mother fears he is still alive.'

'Your mother is a sensible lady.'

'So you are Jack the Ripper?'

'If I was Jack the Ripper would I still be standing here having a nice conversation with you?'

'I guess not Sir,' he said as he eyes fell back to Jimmy.

'Now my boy, take your eyes away from this sight and finish with your deliveries.'

'Yes, yes Sir' he said as he looked back towards me, nodded and turned to leave.

'Oh and boy!' I shouted.

'Yes Sir,' he answered without turning back.

'Try to forget the sight you have seen, it will do you no good to remember this.'

'The same can be said to you Sir,' he replied as he carried on running and by the speed he was moving that young lad was running for his life.

Just then the door that I had used to enter the room flew open and a tall, lean man with sleek black hair ran in, almost landing head first on top of Jimmy. The man, in a waxed suit stood back a few paces and dusted himself down. 'So what do we have here? A murder and the murderer by chance? I can see what part you play in this act young lad' he said to the remains of Jimmy 'You are the murder, so that would make you the murderer,' he said as he turned to me.

'No I am not the murderer.'

'Oh? So what is your role then?'

'I am. I am Jimmy's friend.'

'Who is Jimmy?'

'The guy lying before you and as you are throwing names around, would you kindly tell me who you are.'

'I am Inspector Foresight.'

'You must have seen this coming.'

'Ha ha ha, I see you are a joker Sir, well I am here to tell you that this is no joke, this is murder Sir.'

'I know Inspector, I know.'

'Well then what are you doing here?'

'I was trying to pay my last respects.'

'Oh? He was a dear friend then?'

'No not really, he was a bartender here.'

'Oh I see? So you spilled out your life story to him, did you? Then you realise what you had done so you came here and murdered him.'

'And then I just waited around longer enough for you to arrive to arrest me did I Inspector? No I think you will find Inspector it does not wash, you have the wrong man.'

'It is amazing what can wash with a little twisting in the right direction.'

1888

The room I was hushed into was a lovely quaint little space; I had never been in such as picturesque and curious dwelling. The wooden floor creaked as I walked in and there was at least a month's worth of grey dust on it causing me to leave footprints of my damp boots everywhere I went. There was a rather large fireplace that took up most of one side of the room, with a black cauldron which was chipped around the edge sitting inside of it. There were two arm chairs that were heavily worn and at the sides the red fabric had been torn apart and sagging down to reach the floor. There was a rather strange looking table in the middle of the two chairs with something written on it but as there was only one candle lit within the room which was by the window, it was casting a shadow over the table and I could not see what was displayed on it. There was a sense of love in this room, it had been well lived in and was very homely to me, I guess anything is homely compared to the streets.

'You leave a candle lit when you go out?' I asked.

'It is cheaper than a lock.'

'I guess.'

'Now that should be the last time you do that' she said as she hurried around the room lighting the other candles in the room. As the warm glow of the candle light flame filled to room I could see a large number of other objects that lived here. There was a book case at the far end and although I could see that there was a lifetime's worth of cobwebs spread across the books that have resided there, certain titles seemed to be alive and the words were dancing around in the light, drawing me closer to them. I didn't walk over to the book case, I floated over to them, I didn't feel my legs move once, but all of a sudden I had my nose so close to them I could see the woodworm and smell the oldness and knowledge in the volumes. ‘You like the classics then?’ I was asked.

‘Classics? How can these be classics?’ I answered as I carried on looking at them.

‘What do you mean?’

‘I don’t read much, I mean big words are not easily looked at for me, but I do recognize some words, Sherlock Holmes being one of them and Dickens being another.’

‘So?’

‘Well these are new stories are they not? So why can these be classics already and why is there a layer a dust that shows they have been here for years, but that can’t be so.’

‘Why is that then?’

‘Well they must be new, but how you could afford new books I would hate to imagine but then to allow them to get into this state I don’t understand.’

‘I brought them in that state.’

‘But they look old.’

‘That because they are,’ was the spine-chilling reply.

‘I’m sorry?’ I said as I turned around to see that the strange woman had lit a fire underneath the cauldron and was slowly stirring the contents inside.

'Come, have a seat. I am cooking soup, you must be as hungry as I am,' she said still with her back to me. I moved slowly over to the chair that was opposite her and answered

'Yes I am hungry,' as I sat down.

'I don't where Mischief is?'

'Who is Mischief?' I asked.

'She usually here at this time.'

'Who is Mischief?' I asked again although a little louder.

'Oh yes, you have not met my Mischief yet, she is the cutest thing, a little too proud to be living with me but she keeps me company and stops me from going insane.'

'Stops you from going *insane*?' I questioned to myself.

'She will be missing out of some dinner,' the weird woman whispered, I think to her own self but I cannot be sure. Why was I so surprised to know that this queer woman not only talks to herself but sees and speaks about things that are not there, this poor woman should be in an asylum not living here on her own talking about imaginary friends. Who or what this Mischief is, she is clearly not real.

'Well then, I will give that another five minutes to boil' she said as she sat down to face me. My face must have given away my thoughts as she then said ‘You think of me as strange don’t you?’

‘Well things seem to be not normal.’

‘We live in an age of un-normal. We live in the same city as the rich folk, in fact we are inches away from them and their wealthy homes and yet we live like this, eating things like this’ she said pointing to the cast iron pot. ‘You have to do what you have to do to survive these terrible times and harsh winters, and I, well let’s not talk about me but do you think that is normal? My only faith I have is that one day things will change but even still we now have a killer in our mists, killing our women.’

‘Killing our friends,’ I interrupted.

‘Killing our friends,’ she said with a nod, ‘this just isn’t normal, and I know that in one sad day people will have talked about him to death making him seem normal but the truth is the things he does to these women is un-normal, he is un-normal and we are the ones that have to live through this and see this and feel this not the future generations. They will read about him in books, they will read about us in books and they know what we are not meant to know.’

‘What is that?’

‘The ending of the book, will he be caught or will he not be caught that is the question.’ she said in a dream like state.

'He might, one day,' I said with optimism. God I do hope so! There are opposites in every life; the devil made Jack the Ripper so God must have made a man to catch him. I just wonder where this man is now I would look him right in the eye and ask him whether *he can save us.* As I thought this, a piece of glass I had been carrying fell out of my pocket and landed on the floor, it didn't break but only smashed a little, as I picked it up and did the most natural thing to do, look into it, I could see my hair was a mess but it was my eyes that shocked me the most. I mean for a split second even though I knew they had to be my eyes *they looked different and new somehow*. I placed the piece of glass back in my pocket before the strange woman said.

'Yes, well you cling on to that hope,' she said as she turned towards her cooking pot.

'You still haven't answered me.'

'Have I not.'

'About those books.'

'Why do they bother you so?'

'Well how can they be new and old at the same time?'

'They are not; they are new in your eyes in your own time, but old in another person's eyes and in another person's time. Can you see how special you are? You can see what the books look like new and what they look like old, not everyone can do that. In fact only a selected few, you are a maiden.'

'I don't understand.'

The strange lady filled two bowls full of boiling hot liquid and handed one to me, 'You soon will Mary, you soon will.'

Chapter Seven

1898

The building standing before me was a powerful place, a place I had passed many times on my way to the dens of the East. It stood tall and commanding, it allowed people outside to know that there was something formidable and mighty and sometimes if you get on the wrong side of it there will be something quite crushing inside. Today, I seem to have placed myself on that wrong side as I have arrived here in a police cart, under guard and in chains.

'Welcome to Commercial Street Station, funny boy,' said Inspector Foresight.

'What a lovely place, with a little housekeeping it would be quite delightful.'

'Glad you like it, for it is my own. But I warn you now, don't get too used to it because if I have my way I will be taking back into the City.'

'Thank you Inspector, I could do with being taken home, this journey was very tiresome and I have had quite an unusual and remarkable day.'

'You get me all wrong Sir, I would willingly take you back into the City but not to your home, I will be taking you to Newgate!'

'Oh that is a disappointment.'

'It is, isn't it? Bobbie, take Mr Joker here to a cell, I will deal with him when I'm good and ready,' the Inspector said to my guard.

'Righty oh, Sir, one prisoner taken to a cell Sir,' was his reply, the Inspector nodded at him and walked up the stairs to the police station. The guard started tugging at my chains, forcing me to move forward and follow the same route the Inspector took.

'So, do you love the Inspector Foresight as much as I do?' I asked the guard.

'I am not allowed to talk to prisoners.'

'Oh? Well you have just broken that rule.'

'Broken it Sir, but how?'

'You have just broken it again.'

'Oh I see.'

'And again.'

'Come along Sir, I am in no mood for jokes.'

'I don't think you have quite got the hang of the 'non-speaking to prisoners rule' have you?'

'Quite Sir, I don't think I have,' he said with a smile as he pushed open the police station's door.

After being introduced to yet another peeler I was told to sign my name 'if I could sign my name,' in the rather used book that they kept behind the front desk, I found it highly amusing to try to sign my name in hand chains, but I guess the peeler didn't find my situation very funny as he snatched the feather out of my hand before I had finished and stating that 'there is no need for me to be an artist now,', he then gave orders for me to send downstairs into the cells to wait for Inspector Foresight.

As the same policeman who took me through the front door was also now taking me down to the cells I felt as if I had stuck a rapport with him, this thought was clarified by when we were alone he spoke to me again. 'If you don't mind me asking Sir, but you seem to be taking this all very lightly.'

'I guess I am.'

'You are being charged with murder Sir.'

'How hilarious it is!'

'Hilarious you say Sir? I don't quite understand.'

'In truth I don't either,' I said with a laugh. I don't know what it was today, but I felt carefree and untroubled I don't quite understand why, I mean I had just witnessed another murder, a murder most horrid but yet I am joking. I have been arrested for the murder of good old Jimmy Turner and am now being lead to a cell where the likelihood of going two places, either to Newgate or to the hangman is a high possibility but yet I am laughing.

‘If I was in your position Sir.’

‘You would have legged it when you had the chance?’ I butted in.

‘Well it sure seems strange for you to wait there.’

‘Don’t you think that alone proves my innocence?’

‘Not really Sir, you could have killed the guy and not run away because that is what a murderer should do so you wait there until the police turn up, to do the thing we didn’t expect you to do, so that in the end you could walk away.’

I looked at him blankly, trying to figure out what this policeman meant, when I thought I had, I answered ‘Well if all that is true, it didn’t work for me did it?’ shaking my chains at him.

‘Well no it didn’t, but then you didn’t expect to meet a guy like Inspector Foresight did you?’

‘I don’t think anyone ever does.’

‘He is quite a character.’

‘One worthy to be wrote about in a book.’

‘I quite agree Sir. There you go, don’t tell anyone but I have put you in the best cell so to speak.’

‘Best cell?’

'Oh yes Sir, it's a real beauty. It's just been cleaned out and it is the only one that has the grate in the ceiling, so you will be able to see the shoes of the Londoners walking above you,' he said pointing into the cell. I followed his quite grubby finger to inside my new abode.

The three walls were the colour of a murky grey with some creepy looking green and yellow slime running either up or down the thick set corners. In between the cracks of the brick work was some kind of plant growing, taking in to account the damp held in the cell because of the open grate in the ceiling and cold I could feel approaching from the cell that I was to now going to live in I would guess the plant was a form of moss. There was a wooden table to one side that I was to take as my bed because of the dirty thin blanket placed on top of it.

'Oh, how perfectly charming, and how thoughtful of you,' I lied.

'But don't tell anyone, I am meant to have stuck you in with Stinky Pete, he likes ears,' he said pointing to a cell next door, I moved closer to it. The cell was very dark and smelt badly of manure, I thought there was no one in there until I heard.

'Pete needs to hear, Pete needs to hear, PETE NEEDS TO HEAR!' he shouted as he suddenly appeared in front of me behind the metal bars, his face was gruesome. He was wearing a dirty eye patch and had red, pus filled boils covering his whole face, and he started licking his lips. 'Pete needs to hear with your ears!' he said as he tried to grab out at my ears but missed.

'Such a nice gentleman,' I said.

'Yeah, well he has been here too long,' said the policeman, 'I wouldn't get to close, not if you like your ears attached to your head.'

'Ah well I have become fond of my ears.'

'Here is your cell, I wouldn't lean against the slime, it causes ugly rashes and if you need to go to the toilet, pick a point and use the same point every time. My advice is to pick a point furthest from where your head will lay. '

'Thank you my kind Sir and I must say again what a lovely abode.'

'It is the best Sir.'

'Tell me, why you are giving me 'the best'.'

'I don't know why, I mean after all you could be a murderer.'

'I just could very well be,' I butted in.

'But I like you.'

'What is your name?'

'Robert, Robert Abberline'

'Abberline you say? Are you related to Fredrick Abberline, the policeman who almost caught Jack the Ripper?'

'Yes, Fred is my father. I joined the force to make him proud.'

'I bet he is.'

'Thank you Sir,' he said as he moved to one side to let me in the cell and closed the metal barred door behind me, 'One more thing Sir.'

'Yes?' I replied as I turned to face him as he pulled the bars across the doorway, locking me in.

'It probably doesn't mean much to you, but I don't think you are a murderer. I don't think you could kill anyone.'

'You are wrong.'

'Sir?' the policeman said shockingly.

'That does mean a lot to me, coming from an Abberline.' I said with a wink, he winked back and replied,

'Very good Sir, very good.'

1888

'Waltzing Matilda! Waltzing Matilda! Da, da da, da, da, da,' sung a young girl as she burst through the strange woman's living room door. As I glance around from my seat to look at this new stranger I noticed that she was very young indeed, her face looked fresh and bright which still held the babyish fatting. Her eyes were of the most vivid blue and showed that she was still filled with wonder and delight. Her hair was of the warmest brown that I had only ever seen on the coldest of autumn days, when the strapping wind takes hold and blows a perfectly formed dying leaf from a elderly tree in one of London's distinguished parks all the way East to be walked on by the likes of me. She was wearing a dress that was two sizes too big for her, which meant it was three sizes too big for a street worker as tightest is always best and was of the colour of dirty green. She was not too young to be drunk though as I recognised the certain leaning on the wall, that was trying to look normal and casual but failing dreadfully.

'Ah Maria, there you are. You are drunk again I see,' said the strange woman without looking up.

'You say drunk Miss; I say just an teeny bit tipsy. Merry shall I say, yes that's it, merry I am Miss.'

'I see.'

'Waltzing Matilda, waltz...'

'Yes Maria we can all hear you have a lovely singing voice.'

'Why thank you misses, I always thought I had, everyone tells me so; they say I'm even better than that old Singing Nightingale from the West End theatre.'

'And we all know what happened to her,' was the mysterious reply from the mysterious woman.

'Well there is a lot of that going around here, too many people I'll say. That's the cause of it, too many people not liking too many other people.'

'To true Maria dear, I feel sorry for her mother.'

'I wouldn't.'

'Maria! Don't talk bad my love, for it isn't nice.'

'Don't get me wrong, I heard she was sad, crying all the time and such like. She went mad at one time, 'the crazy woman at the end of the street' they called her, don't you remember?'

'Ah so they did, it was nice not to feel like the only one that people thought was crazy,' she said smiling at me. 'But she went through something a mother should never go through, if she decided to go a little fanatical then we can't blame her Maria.'

I don't quite understand why I felt compelled to enter this unfamiliar conversation but enter I did as I asked 'Who is this 'Singing Nightingale' you are mentioning?'

'Never been to the West End have you love?' asked the drunken girl as she moved slowly around the room to face me, she stood by the side of the quite baffling woman I had come to known. At that moment the strange woman looked up at me too, having four eyes suddenly stare at me, made me almost jump with fright but there was something else, something I was seeing but to the life of me I couldn't quite figure out what it was. But sensing what I was feeling with the two of them staring at me, the strange woman coughed and turned away from the drunken girl; in the back of mind I thanked her for that. I turned to the girl known as Maria and said,

‘I have actually, once. Not for very long mind, I went to Paris after that.’

‘Oh a frenchie are we? Why come back here?’

‘I have often asked myself the same thing, but I never heard of this ‘Singing Nightingale’ you speak of.’

‘No? well I am surprised about that, she was quite famous you know, yes she acted a little but it was her voice that made her stand out, she was said to be aiming for the wonders of America.’

‘And that is what made her mother mad?’ I asked and it was then that the strange woman took up the story.

‘Oh no, it was nothing like that. The ‘Singing Nightingale’, Ellen I think she was called anyway. She was due to leave for America, but she was stopped.’

‘Yeah, I’ll say!’ Maria laughed.

‘Maria don’t you laugh at the dead!’ replied the strange lady.

‘She is dead!’ I shouted in shock.

‘Yes I would say so, quite dead.’ Maria joked.

‘Maria, please behave yourself.’

‘Yes, well, sorry. But I find it hard to feel sorry about the whole affair considering the money the mother got.’

'God forbid if you were to die Maria, it would be acceptable for people not to care if, I don't know say Jimmy got some money would it my dear?' said the strange woman.

'Well I, I didn't see it like that I did I?' she said like a child and then slumped herself down on the floor.

'Sorry about that,' the bizarre lady said to me 'Yes Ellen is dead; her body was taken to the Mortuary at the bottom of this road rather quickly by orders of that gentleman.'

'A gentleman you say?'

'Yes, Ellen had a gentleman friend that often visited her at the theatre, there were rumours of course about them being an item but somehow they didn't quite seem right together.'

'No?'

'No, she seemed a little too forward thinking for him, anyway he had money and paid for the funeral, but somehow her mother wasn't very happy with him and a few days later she was screaming the theatre down saying that her daughter had been murdered.'

'Murdered?'

'Yes, saying she could feel it in her bones that her daughter had been murdered.'

'A crack pot,' Maria butted in.

‘Yes well, that as it may be. The gentleman was very nice and instead of putting her in the asylum, he gave her money to leave the East End, so she left for a short while.’

‘Maybe not such a crack pot in the end then, I guess.’

‘Quite Maria, quite right.’

‘A sad, sad story,’ I replied.

‘Isn’t it just,’ Maria said proudly, ‘So is this another important person?’ she asked, changing the subject and pointing to me. It was at this moment that the strange lady looked down towards the drunken young girl.

‘This is Mary and she is my friend, she could be yours too if you were to be nice and not drunk.’

‘How do you do Mary?’ she said as she mockingly waved her hand at me.

‘That’s enough now Maria, do you want some soup before you go home?’

‘Nowadays it feels more like home here than it ever does on the streets.’

‘Why don’t you find Jimmy, he will look after you.’

‘Yeah well I think about it.’

'So just soup and maybe if we are lucky a little friendship is all we get tonight,' replied the strange lady not really to anyone as she turned to the melting pot.

1898

I had no idea what the time was as the kind policemen had taken my pocket watch but judging by the lack of daylight coming from the ceiling gate I would say it was getting quite late and I had missed my supper, and I surely wasn't meant to be fed here by orders of Inspector Foresight no doubt.

Suddenly pieces of broken bread started to rain heavily inside my cell, I sat up and walked over to the ceiling grate and looked up to see the same working man's boots I had seen before. 'Excuse me, lady?' I shouted up, the bread stopped.

'No one has called me a lady before,' was the eerily reply.

'What would you like to be called?'

'I wouldn't like to be called anything.'

'What is with the bread?'

'I thought you might be hungry.'

'Thank you but how did you know I was here?'

'Full of questions aren't you?'

‘And you have the ability in not answering them,’ I said, there was silence and then I noticed the working man’s boots were tapping the pavement, she was thinking of an answer.

‘Why are you here?’ she asked.

‘Why are you?’ I answered, the boot started tapping again.

‘I asked first.’

‘I have been arrested for murder.’

‘That you didn’t commit?’

‘Yes.’

‘Did you see him?’

‘Jimmy? Yes he was in a horrid state, the sight was truly unpleasant and yet.’

‘Yet what?’

‘Now you come to mention it, the sight seemed familiar somehow. I was standing there with Jimmy’s body butchered right in front of me and I wasn’t horror-struck and even a little dismayed. It just seemed so normal, how can that be?’

‘If your whole life is based around the same thing, it comes normal.’

‘I guess you are right there, with my tales and my research, my life does seem to roll around murder.’

'And why do you think that is? What is that trying to tell you?'

'What do you mean?'

'Well do you think it is the same for everyone? Do you think that murder is normal to everyone?'

'No.'

'So why is it normal to you?'

'I don't know.'

'What would help you is the answer to the question.'

'Which question?'

'Did you see him?' she replied and then her boots disappeared from my sight and I heard the pounding of her running away.

'Wait!' I shouted, but there was no reply as I knew there wouldn't be. She had gone, once again still mysterious and secretive as she ever was, leaving me forever more in the dark. I looked down at my feet and the surrounding bread, this strange woman has entered my life somehow, is she a crazy woman? And if so why has she decided to cling on to me? She quite plainly cares for me, these scraps of bread tell me that is so and I also get the feeling she is trying to teach me something, I say teaching as if she was trying to tell me something she would have come out with it by now. But she doesn't, she waits, she allows me to talk and follows my line of thought and then she puts questions to me, questions I cannot answer. She is teaching me something, but to the life of me I cannot comprehend. I sat down and started chewing the bread, it was fresh and tasty, and in the back of mind I thanked her for it.

'It is true then, I could hardly believe it when I heard that you had been arrested my dear boy, and for murder no less!' said a shadow on the other side of the bars. I stopped eating the bread and without getting up I said,

'Why Charles, you have come to join me in my humble abode, what a delight! I cannot promise much but I seem to have the best room in the place, with natural sunlight and decorative mould you can't go wrong!'

The shadow moved nearer and I could see Charles's face staring at me, 'You seem to be quite jolly considering.'

'I do, I don't quite understand why, maybe it is my medication. Or shall I say the lack of it.'

'You have not taken your medication, Thomas?'

'No and I feel better for it, no nightmares, no visions. It has been just a normal day.'

'A normal day where you get arrested for murder you mean.'

'Well yes.'

'You are playing a dangerous game Thomas.'

'And why is that?'

'To come of your medication quickly will do you more harm than you seem to realise, I care for you Thomas and I worry.'

'I know Charles, but what would you have me do? For if you didn't realise I seemed to be stuck in one of the Queen's finest cells.'

'And if by magic, our friend Charles appears and you are free.'

'I am free?'

'Yes, for I told the police you were at the club with me, you saw something in the window and you went to investigate and saw the scene of poor Jimmy, through the noise you decided to wait for the police.'

'That is a lie.'

'A little white one, but one that worked,' he said with a wink. 'Now kind policeman please release my friend here for he is a wronged man!' he shouted over the Robert Abberline.

'Yes Sir, right away Sir,' he said as he fondled with his keys.

'You certainly have a powerful way about you Charles,' I said as I got up and dusted myself down.

'You cannot get anywhere without a little bit of power my lad! As soon as you learn that the better,' he replied to me. Robert rolled his eyes at me at that statement as he unlocked the barred door.

'Glad to see you out Sir, I never thought you could do such a thing,' Robert said to me as I walked passed him.

'Thank you my dear boy,' I replied as I started to follow Charles up the stairs, I got to the top and was about to open the door as Charles had already passed through when the policeman shouted,

'I can't say that about all folk though,' Robert said as he walked passed my cell, and then passed my neighbour's to get his seat again. My eyes flickered towards my neighbour's cell to see the ugly looking man staring at me in the shadows of his own cell, but strangely I knew it wasn't the whole of me he was staring at, just one part of me, my ears. I guess Robert is right with his statement, he cannot say that about all folk.

Chapter Eight

1888

The soup I was gorging on was, to put a better word for it dreadful and quite unpleasant. It seemed lumpy on the spoon but when it was inside my mouth, the morsels seemed the group together to swell and irritate my throat, the taste I cannot describe as everything tasted the same nowadays, I was always eating hot ash no matter what meal I was having but in truth I was appreciating the feeling of eating again, it had been a while since I had a cooked meal. Joseph always cooked me a meal when we got back together, him being a fish market porter meant he was able to get the best cut of fish for his famous fish pie and potatoes, sadly it tasted like hot ash to me but the heat of the meal was delightful and compared to this lumpy now quite cold soup I was now missing the fish pie and Joseph.

'You can't change the past you know,' the strange woman suddenly said to me, I looked across the room towards her with a quizzical expression of my face, could this woman read my mind as well? Before I could ask her what she meant, she carried on with her speech 'People do try of course, but it would never happen. I mean think about it, you have already chosen the past and everything that was in it so why bother thinking of what you could have done differently? It is all very careless to fritter away your time like that.'

‘How can you say that? You make a living looking into the past,’ I asked between mouthfuls.

‘It is a job, it is not something I suggest for people to do but I can’t turn them away can I? If they feel compelled to know what has happened in their lives, who am I to stop them?’

‘I understand,’ I replied.

‘I don’t, I mean anything is better that this. If you were to tell me I was the Queen of some far of land, or even a maid to the Tudor king, I would love to hear it,’ said Maria without looking at either of us.

‘Everyone is entitled to have their own opinion; the past is the past to me. The future is far more important, you can see what you do like and what you don’t and then change it. By the way, I see you were the one that changed my history books around of the shelf, I like to hear that you read one of them,’ the strange woman said to Maria.

‘You read Maria?’ I asked.

‘She taught me,’ Maria said, still looking at the bowl of soup but pointing with the spoon to the strange lady in the chair.

‘Don’t say it like that Maria, reading helps one to move on in this world.’

‘Yeah it really helps the situation I am in now doesn’t it?’ Maria said childishly.

'You never know what the future will bring Maria,' said the strange woman. As I took another mouthful of the horrid soup I wondered what I was missing, there was something going on here, something surreptitious and a little cloak and dagger for my liking. I was not meant to know something and yet it felt like this something was painful obvious to everyone except me. Was Joseph right when he shouted at me the last time we spoke 'Mary you are such a stupid girl! You will never learn anything!' Is that what I am? Just a stupid girl and that I will never learn, but maybe I will prove him wrong, prove everyone wrong. Maybe I will learn what will become of me tonight and if I don't like it, I can change it. After all everybody can change the future, can't they?

The word stupid brought me thinking back to the past, I turned to the now empty melting pot and all of a sudden I was a year younger, sitting in my now new home putting the kettle on as Kate Eddowes had just arrived.

'Is it fine to enter?' She asked standing by the door.

'Of course it is Kate, I was putting the kettle on.'

'I should change your name to Polly too then.'

'What do you mean?'

'Surely you have heard of it, 'Polly put the kettle on, Polly put the kettle on, Polly put the kettle on and we'll all have tea,' it's a sort of children's song,' she answered as she tapped her boot on the wooden flooring.

'Oh yes, of course. How stupid I am! Come, come place yourself inside Kate and warm yourself up by the fireplace,'

'Yes, yes that would be quite lovely, the winter is getting on now, and there will be snow soon no doubt. Maybe a white Christmas perhaps, I like seeing it but I do not like being out in it. The cold you see Mary, in my old age it hits me hard, so matter how much fatting is on my bones!' she said as she placed herself at top of my bed, close to the fire.

'You are not fat and you are certainly not old!' I exclaimed, as I left the water in the kettle to heat up.

'You are a sweet one, but are telling untruths.'

'Am not.'

'Am too, like you saying that you are stupid, that is quite clearly a lie,' she replied as she dusted off her apron.

'Joseph tells me I am.'

'And you believe him?'

'Why would he say that if it wasn't true?'

'So he has the power over you.'

'What do you mean?'

'I know the type when I see one; he likes to look down on people. For some reason he thinks he is better than everyone else around here, he just can't see he is one of us, a measly fish porter so to make him feel better he takes it out on you.'

'Joseph is not like that.'

'So how's your reading going?'

'Oh well, I have stopped reading, Joseph said it was a waste of time as he was here for me now and he would read to me when I wanted him too, that's how much he cares for me Kate.'

'But where is he now?'

'Gone off in a mood, because of moving he missed the early line up for jobs at the docks so he has no money to pay the rent. I have to work the streets tonight.'

'And he didn't want you to?'

'Of course not, what boyfriend would?'

'I worry for you Mary, like it or not Joseph is taking over your life. You started reading because you wanted to better yourself, Joseph could see that the only thing you actually needed him for was *dying* away so he stopped it and you, my love let him. You have to work the streets to live, but Joseph wants you to need *him* to live. It was fine, you working the streets when he found you, but now he thinks you are his, it is not fine at all.'

'You have got him wrong!'

'Oh yeah, so how comes I was told to visit you when, how did you put it? 'When Joseph leaves' Does he not like your friends because we are street walkers? Because we remind him of what you once were.'

'I thought you were my friend Kate!'

'I am Mary; you just don't see it yet. I love you as a mother loves her daughter; you are more to me than a friend Mary.'

'Then why say those horrid, horrid things?' I asked crying into my hands. Kate moved over to me and offered her handkerchief, which I slowly took.

'Because, I'm sad to say my love, that it is true and deep down inside you know it too,' Kate moved me over to the bed and allowed me to sit down, she left me for a split second crying into what was now a damp cloth, while she removed the kettle from the heat as the water was boiling so much so that the lid was moving. I watched her make the tea and said through my tears,

'Joseph always moans at me for doing that, I get distracted you see and he said that one day I will melt the spout of that kettle if I wasn't too careful.'

'You should always be careful, my love,' was her reply still with her back to me. 'Here drink some tea; I noticed you didn't have any sweet powder so I added my own. A girl always needs sweet powder,' she said as she passed me a cup. We drank our tea in silence and sat there for what seemed like ages like statues, until Kate moved to put her cup down on the side table. 'I never meant to make you cry Mary; I would never wish to do that. I forget you are thin-skinned compared to us lot, I just worry for you but I don't always express it in a way that is good for myself,' said she as she held my hand. I could feel that her hand was *deathly* cold still, even when I knew she had just spent an hour or two by my fireplace. Her cold hand seemed to wake me up a little,

'I know you are caring Kate, and I know I am lucky to have you but Joseph is all I have and I don't like being on my own,' I said rather childishly.

'I understand my love, truly I do. But wait a while, wait for the thick skin to arrive and you might realise how strong you can be without him, now I must go,' she said as she stood up from the bed and moved towards the door.

'Don't go Kate, I didn't mean to cry or get angry with you,' I cried as I stood up. Kate turned on the spot and looked at me sadly.

'Yes you did Mary, you were angry and upset because I said something you didn't like. What you did was normal, what you did was natural. You are you, and I am me, you don't have to regret the way you feel. I didn't take it to heart. And you are wrong by the way, he isn't all you have.'

'I know I got you lot,' I said wiping my nose.

'Yes you have, but that is not what I meant. You have *you*, once you realise how special you are, you will know how a pretty powerful thing that is.'

'I'm not special.'

'One day someone else will tell you that, and you will believe them. One day. Well goodbye my love,' she said as she waved, walked out of the door and I could hear her boots hitting the pavement down the alleyway and into the street. I looked towards my fireplace and instead of seeing the grate that held the kettle I saw a huge, black melting pot. I shook my head and I was sitting in the strange woman's chair once more.

'Finished your soup I see,' said the strange woman.

'Yes thank you,' I replied looking down at the now empty bowl.

'It seemed I lost you for a bit.'

'Yes, I'd rather think you did.'

1898

Charles and I were walking back home towards the Square Mile of the City in silence; I took the time to study my friend. He was in a buoyant mood as always, there even was a slight skip to his step. My friend was a man of habit; he hated dirt and grime so that he often wore *white* skin tight gloves. He also had developed a tendency of not stepping on the cracks in the pavement and if he ever did he would have to take ten steps back and start again, when he was standing still he would always put his feet tightly together, so he could stand tall and have supremacy and command over everyone he met. If he had a new pair shoes, he would buy a new pair of socks to go in them in fact I would even go as far to say he would probably buy a new suit with new white gloves, which in turn would mean a new shirt as 'a shirt should never be worn with the same suit twice' he would often tell me.

Some people found this to be a little unusual perhaps a little unnatural, but it was those trivial matters that made Charles different and separate him from the rest of the hum-drum you would come across in London. I don't know whether it was this fact alone that draws me close to him, in truth I cannot remember my life without him, he had to be somewhere near me, he has always felt not very far away from me. Maybe that is why I was having a carefree and light-hearted moment back in the cells, I mean I had been arrested for a gruesome murder but somehow I knew everything would come right in the end, Charles would save the day and I wasn't wrong was I?

'What are you thinking my dear Thomas?' He asked breaking the social silence but adding to the environmental clamour that was around us.

'That you are always there to save the day.'

'I seem to be, don't I?' he asked rather cheerfully.

'But tell me, how did you know I had been taking to a police station?' I asked. Charles stopped in front of me and turned around; he seemed to be staring intently at me as if looking into my soul.

'I asked the delivery boy,' was his reply.

'The delivery boy you say? Oh yes, I had quite forgotten about the delivery boy.'

‘I haven’t,’ he mumbled.

‘So when you heard you instantly came up with a plan then?’ I asked as my friend began to walk forward again but this time without the skip.

‘Yes I had time to come up with one.’

‘Time? You did not come as soon as you heard?’ I asked a little shocked.

‘The world does not spin around you my dear boy, I had jobs to do first and I knew you would be fine for a few hours.’

‘A few hours? You knew I was in a cell for a few hours! What important jobs did you have to do before you could get your friend out of jail?’ I shouted.

‘Calm yourself Thomas, you are making a scene. Everyone is looking at you Thomas, please calm down. See what happens when you skip a day on you medication.’

‘It is not my medication talking here!’

‘No it isn’t, and that is my point.’

‘You are full of little points aren’t you Charles! But everything you say is a lie!’ I shouted.

‘What do you mean Thomas?’ Charles creepily whispered.

‘Well, well I mean,’ I shouted as I tried scrabbling through my mind to think of something to answer what I had just said, I looked towards Charles and I don't quite understand why I said it but 'Well for instance, that shirt of yours. You have worn that shirt with that suit before I know you have and yet you say to never do that! Next you will be wearing the same white gloves twice in a row!' I shouted as I glance down at his gloves which moved quickly behind Charles's back. It was at this moment I felt everybody's eyes staring at me for I had just said something crazy and by the expression of Charles's face I had made him angry. *Very* angry in fact.

'You are sounding mad my friend!' Charles said under his breath. 'You are behaving not like the Thomas I know. *You are not Thomas*! Thomas would never have spoken to me like that, and he certainly would not have made this scene in the high street!' He furiously stated as he started to walk off at a fast pace, leaving me behind.

I felt guilty and ashamed for putting my friend in this situation so I pleaded 'I am Thomas! I am your friend!'

'Are you? How can I be sure?' Charles shouted back while stopping a placing his feet together on one entire pavement slab. He did not turn around to face me but stood with his back towards me and arms folded neatly behind his back as if he was expecting something in front of him.

'How can I prove it to you?' I beseeched.

'I do not care how you do it, or where you go for it but in God's name, take you medication!' He shouted at the top of his voice. He then hurried down the street and around the corner, leaving me alone and feeling stupid, I always hated feeling stupid, and I was indeed stupid compared to Charles. He was a better person than me; he would have never spoken in such harsh terms to me. I had humiliated him and quite possibly mortified the restrained a peaceful man that was my friend, so he had ran away as quietly as he had talked. What had I done? Would he ever forgive me? Those were all good questions but the main one that was running through my mind was, how quick could I find a cab to get me far, far away from this street and those staring eyes?

I wanted the cab to take me in the opposite direction to the way Charles and I were walking towards just a few moments ago, I told myself that I didn't want to drive passed him but the truth of the matter was, that where I needed to go was placed in the dirty slums of the East End.

'To Kingsmen,' I shouted at the driver. It was then I saw a woman in the street she was just standing there slowly shaking her head in disgusted at the mention of that place as I entered the cab but gladly I didn't have to feel self-conscious for long as the driver was quick with the whip and we soon were leaving the street.

The trip didn't last long at all; I had hardly got comfortable in my seat before I saw the changes to the surroundings happen outside my cab. It was like I was travelling in some sort of time machine going back in the past, from the freshly cut stone of the Bank of England to the filthy used pubs of the East End I passed with everything getting older and deep rooted into the streets of London.

The cab slowed as we turned the corner into the alleyway which led to the Opium den, I tapped the roof with my cane and stepped outside making sure I paid the driver well.

The night had come and the streets were foggy and unlit, I felt a feeling of dread come over me as if someone was watching me and was ready to pounce. I did not feel my normal happiness and joy I always had coming here; knowing what I was about to partake in, something had changed and that something I knew was me. I did not want the drug, I did not want the dark visions to come back to haunt me. I could not save the girl in my dreams, I know this now, and it was stupid to think I could. Why am I always being stupid?

'Ah there's my lovely,' cracked a voice within the fog, 'I had thought you had forgotten all about us,' suddenly a shadow appeared surrounded by the mist, I could tell that this figure was a woman and that she was only inches away from me as I could feel the warmness of her breath against the cold, damp night air and yet I was unable to make out her characteristics of her appearance.

'Sorry madam, I have made a mistake. I must go home,' I replied as I pulled my coat around my neck as if to protect me from the creatures of the night.

'Surely this is your home Sir, and we have been waiting for you.'

‘Waiting for me? But how did you know I was coming here tonight?’ I asked. There was something in how this woman said ‘Sir’, it was different to how she said the other words in her language and yet it was recognizable.

‘They always come back, you see Sir,’ was her replied as I felt her arm around my shoulders as she slowly pulled me along from the street and down the alleyway towards the den.

‘Do I know you?’ I asked, to which she abruptly stopped. I looked over to her shadow and it come across to me that this woman was trying to figure out how to reply.

Finally she said ‘I don’t know Sir, do you?’ as she shoved her face into mine. I had never been this close to a woman of her class before; at least I can’t remember being this close. Her face was dirty to match her dress, as if she had wiped her face with an oily rag. She smelt horrid but I used to that around here, as chances to clean oneself is few and far between in Whitechapel. Her hair was a mess and unclean, tied loosely at the back and covered in knots, she unquestionably could not afford a comb.

‘Yes I have seen you,’ I replied.

‘Is that so?’

‘Yes, you are the girl that is always sitting at the back of the den, downstairs smiling to yourself,’ she was the mummified girl; I had seem a few nights ago before all this started.

'So I am Sir, so I am,' she said as her arm gripped me tighter and shoved me along to which the den door open as if by magic and was once again I was surrounded by the sweet smell of wonder.

1888

'Right, now we all have food in our bellies, should I begin to make the forest clearer for you?' said the strange woman to me. I sat up straighter instantly in the chair, the moment had arrived I was going to see my future but before I could answer the woman, Maria stood up and said

'I will not be here for this.'

'Oh come, come Maria, it might be in your interest to stay,' replied the strange lady rather too disturbingly sinister for the type of conversation we were having, was I missing something important here? Something was telling me that I was, but what?

'No, no it's not and besides I have seen it all before, if you can remember?'

'Fine, well don't go far. I need you to be near.'

'Yes, yes I know,' Maria answered back in her now common child like way, as she walked out of the room leaving me alone with the strange woman once again.

'You seem to have a rapport with Maria,' I stated.

'She has been in my life for many years' she said shrugging her shoulders, 'It would only be *natural,* but what I mean to say, Maria is a complicated girl. She comes across this trouble-free and undemanding woman but she really is a lost girl, one of the thousands within this city. I cannot save all of them, but maybe I can *save her.'*

'You are very considerate Madam.'

'Yes well, one must do what one must do, I suppose is what they say.'

'She seems,' I started as I glance at the door, Maria walked out off just seconds before.

'She seems what?' the strange lady quickly, I turned back in my chair to see that the lady was staring at me intently.

'Awfully lonely,' I replied.

'Lonely? Yes that is perhaps the correct word for Maria, with her family one by one leaving her in some way or form and with her being so young, the youngest in fact. Now she has no one to look after her and no friends. A girl like her needs friends Mary; I mean where would you have been if it wasn't for your friends?'

I glance away from the strange lady, for she was right. Where would I have been if it wasn't for my friends? I stared at the cold, hard flooring with a sad moment as I remembered my friends had all one by one left me to face the rest of this world alone. I rocked my feet to and fro and I watched my boots moving forwards and backwards my vision got blurred, with a slight wink of my eyes I was back in the Ten Bells pub earlier within the year, talking to Mary Nichols.

'Come on Sweetie, give us a smile,' Mary said to me as she passed a drink to me across the bar.

'I don't feel like smiling.'

'It doesn't matter what you feel like doing, you have a full set of teeth, my lovely. Something many of us wish for, so smile while you can.'

'I was meant to be in Paris, I was meant to be an actress.'

'So? You had to come back.'

'Sometimes I think that maybe I could of handled it after a while.'

'You are a bonnie little thing, what would have happened to you if he kept hurting you; maybe even hurt your face? You would be like just one of us then, an ugly and obnoxious woman that is having a good day when the lowest, repulsive creatures want to pay you for a good time in a back alley because they can get no better.'

'Oh Mary, life is so horrid!' I proclaimed, how can I carry on living this way? I feel used, dirty and dilapidated.

'That's the Whitechapel way, my love,' Mary said as she took a mouthful of her drink.

'I remember being a little girl running through the fields in Ireland, my papa telling me that one day I will marry a man that will love for who I am, he would call me pretty and be proud to have me, where did it all go wrong?

I don't even have any shoes for my feet!' I said as I watched my bare, grubby and quite foul smelling feet swinging underneath me.

'And now you are a Whitechapel whore, things come and things go,' Mary said shrugging her shoulders.

'It wasn't meant to be like this, I was meant to be special.'

'Well it depends what you think special is I guess, if you are comparing yourself to every other single person in this world then no, you are not special Mary. Just a number.'

'What am I to do?' I pleaded.

'Limit your options.'

'Like my options are not limited anyway,' I said in an almost mocking fashion.

'And yet you ask for more.'

'Can you blame me? I mean have you looked around here lately?' I said as I waved my hands, pointing at our surroundings. 'What would you have me do?'

'Don't ask for more, you are what you are. And what you are as left you here, so use it.'

'I don't understand.'

'Don't be like us, be the best of what you are, be the best little street walker that Whitechapel has ever seen and then be proud of it.'

'Be happy with what I have, you mean?' I asked as I looked up at her with wide eyes.

'Yes. You can always improve on what you have, not on what you don't have,' Mary Nichols said as she jumped off her bar stool and walked towards to the door.

'Where are you going?' I asked her.

She turned on the spot to face me and said 'I am going to improve you.'

'Improve me?'

'You need boots don't ya? You are coming I take it?' She asked as she smiled back at me.

'Oh Mary,' I said as I smiled back her then I glanced down at my bare feet, it would be nice to have some boots I thought as I started swinging my feet again. Mary must really care for me I reflected, tears filled my eyes as that thought ran around in my head so I wiped them to find that my swinging bare now had a pair of old man's boots on them as I was back in the strange lady's lair once more.

Chapter Nine

1898

The woman stands in a lake, she turns slowly towards me. Her long, wet hair drips thickly down her face, but as the drip falls it stabs at her skin making it peel away, leaving behind a gruesome living skull. Her eyes stay in its sockets so she carries on staring at me but now the gaze is unnatural and haunting. The drip falls around her body detaching any piece of flesh in its way, making the lake now full of her floating skin. Her bony skeleton starts to move towards me but it could only jerk forward as it seemed to be stuck in the soiled and grimy waters. Her emaciated fingers reached out for me but I felt myself turning away at the ghastly sight to see the bloody remains of Jimmy Turner lying across a table to the left of me. As I looked at his body as if it was the first time I had seen it, the table started shifting ever so slightly. But then I noticed to my horror the table was moving at all, Jimmy's body was stirring back into life, he managed to lift his upper body up in the air and slowly his head turned towards me. It is a frightening sight to see a dead and bloodied face staring intently towards oneself, what is making it seem a more hideous spectacle is that I knew this nightmare for I knew Jimmy. In fact I was talking to him moments before he died, I was sitting upstairs in the theatre while the murderer was downstairs killing him and making his mark. At that moment the kettle started boiling again; Jimmy started pointing towards it while still looking at me. What Jimmy? What are you trying to say? What did I miss?

I awoke with a start, *what did I miss?* Was there something there I missed that would have told me who killed Jimmy? Were I really that close to finding out and I let it pass me by? As I tried to breathe slowly in and out, I realised I was lying in a pool of my own sweat. It felt sticky and cold, how long have I been here? The opium room in which I was in stunk heavily of mould and of stale smoked drugs and as soon as my thoughts registered that fact my head started to pound frantically making me scream a little with the pain.

'Are you well?' asked the room.

'What?' I replied back to it as I glanced around the room, it was only then I saw in the corner of the room sat the mysterious woman I had met before.

'Are you well?' she repeated. 'Can I help you?'

'No I am fine,' I answered and I sat up in the bed. 'Thank you.'

'That's all right my lovely as long as you are back in the world of the living and not in the world of the dead I can talk to you.'

'Are you my guarding Angel?'

'That takes me back, it's been a while since I have talked the fairy stuff.' she mysteriously answered.

'The fairy stuff you say, what do you mean by that?' I asked while I rubbed my head.

'That doesn't concern you, what should concern you is what happening around you.'

'And what is that exactly?'

'Can you not see it? Things happen around you; do you think they do by chance? Something or someone is trying to tell you what you should know, don't you get it?'

I stopped rubbing my head and stared at this strange shadow of a woman, 'Look, I have a headache, I have been released from hours spent in a horrid police cell for a grisly murder I did not do but I saw. I saw poor Jimmy dead,' I said as tears formed in my eyes, at last I could cry for him. 'He didn't deserve that, poor lad,' the shadow did not move but I could feel her eyes burning into me. 'Anyway all this would be a lot simpler it you just told who you are and what you want with me.'

'Life is not always simple, sometimes you have to work hard for the knowledge you keep.'

'What knowledge? I do not know anything.'

The lady stood up and moved across the room, I noticed then that she was dressed in black from head to foot apart from a red flower in her hat; she stopped by the doorway and turned around to face me. Her face was a ghostly white, her skin seemed old and wrinkled but there was something behind her eyes that told me that she was actually younger than she looked and the fact that there was no greying hair amongst long, brown hair agreed with that statement. 'You are wrong, you know everything. You just do not see, maybe you are not ready to see and that is why you don't see it yet.'

'I hope you don't mind me saying but, you are sounding like a crazy woman.'

'Guess it must run in the *family*,' she smiled at me; she was quite beautiful when she smiled.

'What should I be seeing?'

'You will know it when you see it, everything will make sense. Maybe you will save the girl, in the end,' she said as she turned to walk out of the door.

'Girl, what girl is that?'

'I don't know her name, you never said it but you dream of her. I could contemplate who she might be although. In some ways I am jealous of you,' she said with her back towards me.

'Jealous of me? I hardly think you would be jealous of me, not with all the things I have seen, of what I dream.'

'Tell me, what is she like? The girl in your dream I mean. Is she still a pretty little thing, with those big, wide eyes of hers?'

'No, she is dying in my dreams.'

'But she is not dead, in your dreams she is not dead,' I saw the back of head slowly nod to herself. 'That is very interesting, wouldn't you say?' she said as she pushed back the wooden beads that were hanging in front of the doorway.

'Please don't leave me, you know something I don't and for some reason I need to know it.'

'Yes I'm afraid you do, sadly.'

'Please help me.'

'I don't think I can, for you are not ready to see. I cannot force you to what I know of as the truth, I will not do that. I don't believe I should, I have never believed *anyone* should,' she said as I watched her drop her head a little at that statement.

'Can't you give me a clue?'

'People do not give clues; this is real life not a *detective story*. But you need to head back. You were so close,' she said as she slowly walked away. I stood up quickly to chase after her but suddenly I was overwhelmed and lightheaded, I remembered falling and hitting the floor, my head faced the open doorway of my opium room and for a split second I swear I saw the mummified girl that brought me here standing on the other side, looking through the wooden beads laughing at me, then all was black.

Drip, drip, drip. The cold wet drips were hitting my face No! Get away, get away you horrid drips! Stop hitting me! Stop stabbing me! Do not cut into my skin you hear me!

'Do not cut into my skin!' I shouted as I awoke to find myself outside the Billing Club in the ditch while heavily sharp rain poured on to me.

'Mr Thomas Sir, are you quite all right?' said the guard of the club as he stared down as me.

'I don't understand,' I managed to say.

'It will be all right Sir; I have called for your friend Charles to take you home. You would have to be careful Sir in weather like this, you could catch something. In fact you might have caught something from that girl.'

'Home.'

'Yes, you will be taken home Sir,' the guard said and that was all I remembered as things went black again.

I woke to find myself in my own bed out stretched, looking up at my ceiling. I suddenly sat up I have been here before, I quickly checked the outer sheets of my bed linen, Thank God there was not blood! I collapsed back on my pillow, thinking all was well as I glanced to my hands, the old cuts from the night before were trying to heal themselves, but what I couldn't understand was that my hands had blood on them, fresh blood. I removed the inner sheets to find I was bleeding on my white gown. I looked over to the wall behind my bed head; there were no more scratch marks. Why am I bleeding?

I got up and washed my hands, as I washed I noticed I had no new cuts, where was I bleeding from? Then I noticed a hole in my white gown, I took it off to see in the full length mirror a cut, running from my belly button to my lower half. Oh my God! Someone help me! I have been slashed! My head went lightheaded, and I felt very sick.

I rushed to my bedroom window; I opened it and stuck my head out the window to get some well needed air and help. Strangely the street was deserted, no one to be seen as I looked up and down. Then in the corner of my eye I noticed someone looking up at me, I turned, it was the outlandish girl I had met so much times now, my eyesight was getting blurry, she was fading from my sight. I screamed out ‘Help me’. Then all was black.

1888

The strange woman pushed the extraordinary table in between the two of us, I noticed that engraved into the wooden top were letters and two words, using a dark grey stone she covered one of the words. She then pulled a lamp nearer and lit it, but instead of turning towards me to began talking about the forest worlds and such like, she stood up a moved to the back of the room by the bookshelves and started scanning the titles.

‘What are you looking for?’ I asked.

‘Something to persuade me,’ she answered without turning around.

‘Persuade you to do what?’ I asked.

‘To change history.’

‘I thought we were changing the future.’

‘From your standing point I guess you would think that, but from a different point of view you could say we will be changing history tonight. I just need some influence to allow it to happen.’

‘Surely you don’t need anything to encourage you to do this; I mean I would find it pleasurable even enjoyable I would think to change things. It makes me wonder.’

‘Makes you wonder what?’ she asked as she picked up a black covered book and started flicking through the pages.

‘If you have this, power shall I say? Why then, live here and live like this?’ I asked looking around the cold, tarnished room.

‘My power, as you put it. Does not work for me, you forget I am just the shepherd, you are the maiden.’

‘You have said I am special, that I am a maiden. You are making out that any change to my life that you can show me, will be important.’

‘It will.’

‘How can that be so? I am a common street walker, how can anything you tell me change that?’

‘I cannot change it; I am not *trying* to change it. I can only tell you what can change if you allow it,’ she replied as she slammed the book shut and took a deep breath.

'Are you well?' I asked the strange lady to whom she promptly turned around to face me while leaning somewhat backwards against the bookcase, with the black covered book still in her hand; she was just gaping at me without saying a word as if she was trying to figure something out in her mind. I knew that was no point in asking what she was thinking about as I probably wouldn't get a straight answer so I waited for her to speak.

'Your life Mary, it is a sad one is it not?'

'What?'

'You do not like your life, you say you are just a common street walker, your partner has left you and your friends have died in a horrid way. You feel alone, you deny being special but yet you have followed me here so I take it that you want to be special and who would blame you. I know I don't, I don't blame you at all.'

'I want to change my life.'

'That I cannot do.'

'I know, I know *I* have to make the change.'

'But could you? Could you really make a change? For what I am about to tell you is haunting and unpleasant to hear, do you have the stomach to listen to me fully? To not ask questions or run away until I have finished what I need to enlighten you with? Are you strong Mary? That is what I wonder.'

I turned to the strange woman I had come to know, I looked her straight in the eyes and in quite surprisingly calm way I replied 'I am strong, I want to see this through until the end. Why am I the maiden? Why am I special? I have lost so many dear friends, you are right when you said I feel alone, it is the worse feeling anyone could have and if you can take away this feeling from me, I will stay here until you have finished.'

'So you will not run away and forget this unusual night?'

'No I will not run away, I will not forget everything you have told me tonight. You are looking out for me; I can see it now I can even feel it strange as it sounds. You want to help me, I know you do. So I will listen.'

'Then I will start,' the strange woman said as she slowly walked back over to me and sat down in her chair, she placed the book she was holding on the floor. I glanced down at it, its title was written in red, there were only three words to it, to the life of me I could not read them but there was something realizable about them. She saw me look down at the book and smiled to herself, she then turned to face the lamp, took out a green velvet bag of her other hand and emptied the contents out into the fire guard, there was a puff of smoke and the room filled with a malodorous smell. I coughed a little and through the smoke I could see a pair of flashing green eyes, looking intently at me.

'On the 9th November this year, will come the night for change, it will be your choice Mary. I will tell you what will happen that night,' she started.

1898

'What's the name?' I heard in the back of head, was someone there? Was someone asking me? Then I heard a lady's voice answer, I couldn't quite hear what she said. Then there was the sound of footsteps walking away, no! Don't leave me! I then heard a noise of someone moving next to me.

'Can you hear me love?' said the same lady's voice. 'Can you hear me?' I couldn't reply, I tried to nod, was I nodding? I couldn't tell. 'Do you understand yet?' She asked. Understand what? 'You need to let go, you need to leave this place, you need to find out why, and you need to find out whom.'

'Who?' I muttered whether it was loud enough I had no idea until she answered.

'Who put you here,' she whispered but with that, there was a loud noise and the sound of footsteps running away. Then the sound was replaced by the sound of a slower, heavier footsteps walking toward me from the other direction. The footsteps stop next to me. There are more footsteps from someone different.

'Who brought him in?' said a man voice; I recognised this voice at once as it was Charles, my friend. An unknown woman said something. 'Well that's not good enough! I want to find out whom! Let me see that paper!' There was silence. 'Not Kelly, Dunn. Thomas Dunn, don't look at me like that! The man lying before you is the celebrated author, Thomas Dunn!' with that the woman left. There was a sound of movement and I felt that Charles had sat down beside me.

'Thomas, can you hear me?' He asked in a softer tone. 'Who was that girl who brought you here?' I didn't answer. There was silence for a while until Charles said 'Oh Thomas! I had hoped you would have forgiven me, for all *I have done to you.'*

'It's not your fault,' I managed to say as I opened my eyes. The daylight hit my eye sockets so fast I had to close them again to protect them.

'Thomas!'

'Where am I?' I asked.

'In hospital, you hit your head quite hard.'

'What about the cut?' I asked.

'What cut? The nurse didn't say anything about a cut to me. '

'There is a cut from my stomach to my lower parts,' I said, it seemed as if Charles was terrified by my statement as he sat there frozen in shock. 'What? What have I said?' I asked.

'There is no cut,' was the simple reply as Charles looked down towards the floor.

'I saw a cut, I was bleeding!' I screamed.

'Calm down Thomas, you don't want your next place to be the mad houses do you?' Charles said as he looked up from the floor and straight into my eyes, the darkness was slowly reappearing around his eyes, I had angered him somehow.

'There really is no cut?'

'I promise you, you are in here because you hit your head. If I had known I would have stopped them taking you here for such a lame reason, I'm sorry I was not there for you.'

'Who are them?'

'What?'

'You said they brought me here, who's they?'

'I don't know what you are on about; I said nothing of the sort. My dear Thomas I fear you are much worse than I first thought. You must never leave my sight. You will come to live with me, I can look after you.'

'No Charles, I am here to help you.'

'What do you mean Thomas?'

'You asked me for help remember, with Ellen.'

'Oh that! You should not be bothering yourself with all that, not in your condition my dear boy!'

'But I want to help, I went to the theatre.'

'Is that what you were going there? I did wonder.'

'I thought someone might remember something.'

'And did they?'

'Well the only person who seemed to know anything, died.'

'That is unfortunate indeed! So what next can we do?' he asked me as he looked intently at me, I knew he still needed my help. I smiled a little to myself; maybe I can help him for a change. I sat up in my bed and answered him.

'I don't think it is wise for you to get involved Charles.'

'What!' he shouted.

'Listen to me Charles; you have only cared for one woman in your life. Ellen meant the world to you, do you really want to drag up the past and upset you?'

'Well if you put it like that, I know you care for me Thomas and in truth I am glad to see you more yourself.'

'I am sorry for my little outburst yesterday.'

'It was two days ago Thomas.'

‘Two days ago you say?’

‘Yes, why where have you been Thomas?’ he asked creepily.

‘I have been... away shall we say?’ I cringed.

‘Oh I see, you took your medication.’

‘Yes, now where was I? Yes I have a few thoughts on where to go next on this Ellen thing although I will admit trying to solve a murder that happened ten years is a little impossible but I will give it a try, for a friend.’

‘Thank you my dear friend, I will be honest with you Thomas, and I can be honest with you can’t I my beloved and most trusted friend?’ he asked me most sincerely.

‘I should hope so Charles.’ was my short reply.

‘Ellen’s murder has been privately bothering me. She was so beautiful; the way her lips moved when she sung was enchanting. She was special and rare; she was a vision of delight. I cared for her, I really did.’

‘I remember Charles, I truly do,’ I said as I placed my hand over his that was placed on the side of my hospital bed.

‘*Do you*? Do you remember Thomas?’ he asked as he waited for me to nod my head before he continued. ‘I loved her like no man had ever loved a woman, for she was not a woman to me, she was a priestess of the highest order.

An exquisitely attractive looking idol, for yes I did idolize her, there was nothing she could do to stop me loving her, I still love her although she is not around, I know she is dead, I know she never made it to America. I know that when she went missing I had not just lost her in this country but deep down inside I knew I had lost her in this world for she had passed on into the next,' Charles cried. It was a sad sight to see one's friend in utter despair; all my friend demons were being laid bare for me to see. I felt in a strange way, honoured to have been a part of this unpleasant incident, also I had a sensation that this was important and was going to change both our lives somehow, I didn't know how or why but I knew this moment would revolutionize the existence of two best friends.

'That makes sense Charles,' I said as I patted his hand.

'But does it? Does it really? I mean how would I know if she had died? I couldn't. I first I wouldn't believe it; I thought if I just deny it, deny the numbness I was feeling I was getting. I even denied it to her mother, my darling mother! She knew straight away her daughter was dead, I guess it was a mother's intuition, what else could it be? I claimed she was mad, I actually said that and now look at me!' he wept.

'We are all mad here,' I mumbled.

'What did you say?'

'Oh nothing really, just a passing thought. But didn't you do something nice for her?'

‘Nice for her?’ he asked as he wiped his eyes.

‘Well yes, as I recall you paid for her to leave Whitechapel,’ I said but Charles looked blankly at me which prompted to ask ‘She did leave Whitechapel didn’t she?’

‘Oh yes Thomas, oh yes.’

‘Well then, you shouldn’t worry about her mother.’

‘But worry I do.’

‘That is where I come in, I will solve the case of the disappearance of Miss Ellen Rose,’ I said proudly, I thought it would make my friend cheerful again maybe even smile but I was wrong. It made him burst out in outlandish laugh, after he had finished and seeing my face crest fallen he said,

‘I’m sorry Thomas, I meant no harm it was just I always thought that I was Sherlock Holmes and you were my Dr Watson but maybe, just maybe it has been the other way round all long!’ he said with a smile.

‘I have learned everything from you my dear fellow.’ I said with a laugh.

‘We will see Thomas, we will just see about that,’ he said as he moved away from my bed. ‘I will have to go Thomas; the nurse said you will be let out tonight, so rest now.’

'Yes, Charles. I have a deep conscious feeling I will have a busy for a few days.'

'Good. That's good Thomas, I need you to busy from a caring friend of course but I know you, you need to be busy Thomas maybe you should start picking up that pen of yours,' he said as he walked away, leaving me alone in my hospital bed.

The strange woman was right in what she said to me in the Kingsmen Opium den but it had only just hit me what she meant. I was so caught up in the death of Jimmy Turner that I forgot why I was there is the first place, I needed to speak to Jimmy about the murder of Ellen but someone stopped it. Would it be crazy to think that Jimmy was murdered because of what I was asking him? If so, then there is only one conclusion.

If Ellen was killed, like her mother first thought and like Charles thinks now then the murderer of Ellen and the murderer of Jimmy could just well be the same person. I had to think back to what Jimmy had told me before he died, for it was going to be the only way to solve this and help my best friend. Yes Charles, I will pick up my pen once more.

Chapter Ten

1888

The night is cold and damp but I must carry on. The fish supper I have just had was delightful and warm, so I am sure my stomach is warm on the inside. I turned the corner and am faced with a quiet high street; it is a little too quiet for me. I know that Jack the Ripper had scared many street walkers back in their lodgings but time had passed, Jack the Ripper had not killed for weeks. Some people were saying he had died in an asylum, others were saying he had left England on a boat heading for America but none were saying he is still around here lurking in the shadows, waiting to kill again.

For we all knew Jack the Ripper wasn't the threat anymore, he was gone. Now the ever daunting threat of the English winter with its bitter iciness was looming near and that normally means only one thing, the street walkers would be out in numbers to try to get as much gullible customers as they could before the white snow fell. As picturesque as the snow makes the streets and alleyways of Whitechapel look it stops the customers coming here, for they could get their business in whore houses that are hidden within their own clubs and societies and as for the locals well that is, as a rule the last resort.

But tonight it is all eerily quiet and silent, the only sound to be heard was the slapping swish as the wintry, frozen wind hitting the locally made flags that are hanging between gas lamps in preparation for the Lord Mayor's Day when the sun rises once again. I turn around as I swear I heard something, the wind pushes my hair in front of me so I tuck it behind my ears and try to focus my eyesight to the bottom of the road, once again all is still and undisturbed for I am alone as always.

As there are going to be no customers on the street for a while I feel I need to be in a room of people for tonight I am aware of an rather odd feeling of something sinister and evil will happen and I want no part in it so I head for The Ten Bells.

I push open the wooden doors to the pub and instantly my cheeks feel the warmth of the room within, my eyes squint a little at the well lit place and immediately I felt safe from the terrors of the outside world.

'Oh here comes you, not with your little friend tonight then?' said a boisterous woman standing by the bar with a rather large mole on her left cheek, looking straight at me.

'She's not my friend, I just seemed to have gained her through an associate,' I said trying to explain, but why I was trying to do that I had no idea.

'Oh an associate hey? That is such a big word for you, think you are better than everyone do ya?' she asked as she slowly walked up to me.

'No I never said I was,' I replied as I took a step backwards as I was feeling threatened.

'No you didn't, did ya? But she did, didn't she?' she questioned as she looked down at me.

'Who are you talking about?'

'You know who, that associate of yours. I heard what she said to you outside, that you are special and deserve to be saved. I heard it.'

'You don't know what you are talking about, you don't understand. You could never understand things that are passed your control; you don't understand the power someone could have on other people. She is caring and thoughtful, although I would admit that it doesn't come across that way at first, but you see I didn't understand. Now I do, I understand the feeling of gentle thoughtfulness of doing help for a person of some importance.'

'And you just happen to be that person of importance, I take it?'

'People are important to some other people, isn't your child important to you?'

'Well yes, one day he says he's going to be a delivery boy and take me away from Whitechapel with his wages.'

'Well that is as maybe, but he is not important to me, just like I am not important to you but my associate

thinks I'm important,' I said feeling proud of myself as the woman looked totally dumbfounded.

'You think you are clever, well you are not.'

'High praise, coming from you,' I said as I stood my ground for I wasn't going to allow this nobody to shove me around. There was a moment I felt as if she was going to hit me for her eyes were shining with hatred and her fist was clenched but something changed her mind.

'You know what? Why waste my strength on you?' She said quietly.

'Why indeed,' I answered.

'I will waste my breath though; you better watch your step Miss. After all you are alone tonight, no friends to keep you safe and I have many friends, they will not like the way you have talked to me, they will not like the way you have made me feel. You think you are clever, you think you are smart but that head of yours will mean nothing if you are dead,' she said with menace.

'I am not sacred of death, no it would be better than a life in Whitechapel, and you try to frighten me with a threat that would do me well Madam.'

'You talk strong, forceful even. But I wonder how much of what you say is true? When faced with your demise, will you not shake? Will you not look wide eyed? Will you not tremble inside? Will you not regret your life and this very moment? You are standing here in the warm Ten Bells, you are breathing, and you are alive. What I say

to you is, relish the time you have as I am sure it will end soon.'

1898

As I left the secure and cordial place that the hospital seemed I had only one thought in my mind, *what did Jimmy Turner tell me?*

I decided to walk the few yards around the corner to where, oddly some may think there was a small park. A tiny place of greenery amongst the great buildings of the financial area of the illustrious city I have the luxury to call my home. It holds two benches sitting opposite each other with trees surrounding the back of them, there was also a bronze statue of William Shakespeare placed in the middle as this was the spot he thought of his first folio.

Well if a great mind like Shakespeare can use the spot for thinking, why not me as well? After all I am a wordsmith too, of sorts.

I was correct in thinking the park would be quiet, not many people know of this place, how utterly disappointing and rather dismal of the human race not to take a few minutes to savour the beauty and inspiration of this piece of heaven within the hell of the bankers world.

All that the Rothschilds family do and have done for London, putting their money in here, there and everywhere and this area being their playground I would guess they have never noticed this place. This place that sits here ever so quietly, not making a scene or fuss is a mystery and because of that it gets unnoticed by generations. Busy, busy people running from one place to another, *not seeing what is in front of their face*. That is the City's way, how completely depressing.

As I sat there, with the birds singing their sweet tune I glance to the skies and my eyes were blurred by the light.

'Ellen's mother was a recluse,' I heard someone say, I looked back down and around me, I was on my own.

'Who said that?' I asked hopelessly.

'She spent most of the day inside her home on Courts Row, only coming out at night. So it was a shock to see her,' the voice said again. I glanced at the statue of William Shakespeare. Was I Mad? Surely William is not talking to me I thought but then in an atmosphere of spooky surroundings similar to the scene in *The Christmas Carol* where Scrooge first sees the appearance of Marley in his door knocker, the face of Mr Shakespeare changed into the ghostly image of Jimmy Turner.

'Jimmy!' I proclaimed, but the ghost didn't seem to listen to me.

'Most people thought that she belonged in Bedlam and that night, when Ellen first disappeared I mean Sir,' Jimmy said. '*Well her mother came rushing in, when we were at our busiest I might add and she screaming and carrying on, much more unnerving than when women normally carry on, I will tell you Sir.'*

'Did she go to Bedlam Jimmy? Was she that mad? What made her behave in that way? What made her leave her home that night, to tell people that her daughter was murdered? Was she trying to tell someone that might have been in the theatre?' I asked, hoping in a slight way the statue would answer me, but sadly it did not.

'All I know is she looked terrifying, her dress was torn and falling apart and her scars Sir were shocking. But the noise Sir, the noise coming out of her mouth was like the devil coming alive as I never heard a woman scream with tears so loudly since. It brought a chill to my spine Sir.'

"Her dress was torn apart Jimmy? Why would that be so? Her scars you said, they must have been huge and in a place where you could have seen them for you to mention them. How ghastly she must have looked to you Jimmy, no wonder you remembered that night. Wait. You clearly remembered that night. What if someone over heard you remembering that night? What if you saw something that night that would seem a little sinister now? If that is so, is that why you were murdered before you could talk more? Someone at the theatre knows something; someone at the theatre murdered you. But there is something I have missed I have a sensation, a rather disturbingly evil feeling I have missed something of great importance.

'*She did seem to say something, I can't remember what Sir. But I remember her face Sir; it was horrid I can tell you,'* The statue carried on.

'What did she say Jimmy? Did you remember at the last moment of your life? Is that why you have died?' I asked him.

I must find her, I must find Ellen's mother. So I need to find out where she went to and for that I must go to where I know she has been. Courts Row is where I must go. I stood up from the bench and started to walk away when I got a spine chillingly feeling that the statue was still staring at me so I turned to see the ghostly face of Jimmy Turner as it started the bleed. The flesh of his face was stripping away to the point that I could see bone mixed with blood, his face was butchered to pieces. Jimmy wasn't human anymore, the murderer didn't stop at ending his life, no, the murderer went a step further didn't he Jimmy? He killed your soul, who could have wanted you dead that badly? The image I saw before me was attention-grabbing but it was horrid, but as horrid as it was I could not turn away.

'Jimmy! Stop this!' I cried. 'Why are you haunting me like this?'

The jaw bone moved a little through the bloodied mess of muscle and tissue to utter a few collective words, he seemed to whisper it. Against my better judgement I moved a step nearer to catch the imperative words. The skull like vision give the impression he liked the idea of me moving nearer to him as he appeared to smile at me, before he talked again. *'A hot boiling kettle needs to be stopped'* was the sentence I heard.

'What are you on about?' I asked the death mask. 'I stopped the kettle from boiling over'. The statue seemed to wink at me and then cruelly and quite hauntingly laughed at me. He carried on laughing at me until his ghost disappeared into the bronzed face of William Shakespeare.

I shook myself on the spot, somehow I was getting used to seeing terrifying images that must form in my head. I don't know if that is a good thing or not but as I turned away from the statue I got another shock. Right in front of me a man was standing, his hair was a mess and face was pale and unshaven and one of his eyes was covered by a dirty patch. His clothes were of the poorest quality, he smelt bad and was missing a leg as his trouser seemed to end sharply; he was quite a modern day street bum. He had heard the conversation I have just had with who, he must have thought was William Shakespeare as he was looking at me with a questionable impression. For some unknown reason I decided that my first words to him would be 'I am not mad.'

'We are all mad here.' was his short reply.

'We?' I asked.

'Walkers of the street, for we have no homes to go to.'

'You think I am one of you?'

'I am one of everyone.'

'I am not a street bum!' I proclaimed as I was quite disgusted with that idea.

'What makes me a street bum? The way I dress? The way I look? The way I smell? Not what I have done for this country, I know that. I fought with my soul for this country, I risked my life, and I risked my leg. I am a soldier. I managed to come home alive, but the come home to a hero's welcome? No, I come home to find I have no home, I have no job, and I have no life! I am a nobody and nobody notices me, I can move around these streets and alleyway without being seen for I am no one, just a street bum. But what have you done? What have you done that is important? You say you are not one of me, you say you are not a street bum, but have you looked at yourself lately? You face is pale, you are unshaven, you have not washed for days, you have a dirty bandage around your head and you smell of a certain scent I remember from the East End dens. I see you talking to a statue and your first phrase to me is 'you are not mad,' when quite clearly you are. I will tell you now your existence is unimportant, it is meaningless.'

'Thank you for those kind words Sir but I must be on my way.' I said as I moved past him. As I did he grabbed my arm and pulled me nearer so that he could whisper something chillingly in my ear.

'Does Jacky say hello before he kills?'

1888

I laughed heartily at her comment and walked away from the loud-mouthed woman and sat down at the back of the public house.

'Why so lonely Sweetie?' a manly voice asked me.

'My friends are somewhere else tonight,' was my reply, without looking up.

'In heaven or in hell?' was his creepy answer; I glance up at him to find I was face to face with a vicar. He was tall and rather old looking, he was wearing an enormous black hat that covered his face and cast a shadow of his footsteps, all his other clothing was set in black too. He was somewhat large around the waist but thin everywhere else.

'I am sorry; I didn't notice I was talking to a man of the cloth.' I mentioned.

'Would it have mattered?' he asked as he sat down beside me and removed his hat.

'Probably not,' I said as took the moment to steal a quick glance at his face, he seemed friendly enough. He was a little portly in the face just enough to hold his circular glasses on his rosy cheeks. He had whiting hair but his eyebrows were still very dark, it made his appearance a little amusing.

'I had thought that would have been the case, you know the Lord is always with you. If you embrace him you will never be lonely.'

'Thank you Father, but your words are wasted on me.'

'Because you are a street walker, you mean?'

'No, your words are wasted because I don't have faith in a higher being, we are our own god. We chose our destiny.'

'Interesting.'

'That a street walker can have views of this world like any other, you mean?'

'You think there are other worlds?' He asked, looking a little surprised.

'Do you know, in your heart of hearts that there are not other worlds Father?'

'A question with a question, I can tell you what I know and what I know is the simple fact that you interest me, very much so I might add.'

'Do I interest you enough to buy me a drink?' I said with a smile.

'Two rums coming up,' he answered as he waved his hand in the air to catch the attention of the bartender, within a few minutes there was two drinks in front of us.

'I thought a religious man can't drink,' I pointed out.

'I am not, they are both for you.'

'Why do that?' I asked.

'Well you seem special and I thought maybe you need or may want two.'

'Special, what is with that word? What is it that makes it seem so less special now? That word is used far too much, it is so important and so powerful that people don't realise what they are playing with by using it. It has the same meaning as faith, people believe in it, people will do anything for it and yet it is only one single word, uttered carelessly.'

'You are correct in what say there, words are powerful and intense. My religion is based on influential words, people can read the word of God and have faith that he is there for them. People can follow the Lord through his words.'

'Yes well, I follow my future that is all.'

'Do you believe you can change it?' He asked as he noticed I had finished one of the drinks so pushed the other glass towards me. 'Would you want to change it?'

'Change it? Now there is a thought!' I laughed.

'What is so funny?' he asked.

'Something you would probably not wish to understand.'

'Oh?'

'What if I was to tell you that I was given the power to change what would have happened to me on this very night, by a caring although a little strange woman?'

'I would ask how many drinks you have had tonight.'

'I thought so, but you see it is true, every word. My future will change tonight.'

'So you have decided to sit in here on your changeable destiny moment? I find that hard to believe.'

'Believe what you will, but I have to be here. I had to talk to that woman over there,' I said pointing to the back of the boisterous woman with who I had a heated conversation with only a few minutes before. 'I had to talk to you, I had to explain this to you, all this I knew was going to happen because I have already been told it was going to happen. The change has not happened yet.'

'So when does the great change happen then?'

'Sometime tonight, when it happens is not important. What is more important is another point.'

'And what is this very important point?' he questioned with a slight laugh. He is laughing because he does not understand. He does not understand the meaning of tonight, the meaning of his conversation with me, he does not understand at all. But it does not matter, it will never matter. His thoughts and feelings does not change things, does not change what is going to happen. He does not know that he will always remember this night, this conversation for he will always remember me.

'The very important point is the fact that you will *<u>not</u>* *be reading about me tomorrow morning in the local*

newspapers,' I mysteriously replied as I finished the last of my second drink, got up from my seat and moved towards the door. When I got to the door I pulled it open and took a moment to glance back at my talkative vicar. He was still looking at me with a questionable expression, I winked at him. You said Father that I was interesting, well you didn't know how truly interesting I really am did you? My dear preacher man, I pity you I thought to myself as I walked out of The Ten Bells public house and into the freshly cold night's air and on into my future.

1898

It was a least ten minutes of running at a fast pace before I felt I was a safe distance away from the rather creepy and strange man. It was true in what they say, *strange things happen to the sanest of people at war.* I had no time to worry about the odd and crippled man; I have a murder to solve and a killer to catch. The night was getting dark, so I had a decision to make, do I go home and get a good night's sleep now or do I head for Courts Row? Well, what is waiting for me at home? Nothing, so to the east I go.

I managed my way through the streets and alleyways towards Court Row to find an enclosed street packed with houses from one end to the other, which number do I knock at? I will start at the very beginning I guess.

Knock, knock. The door opens, 'Hello, my name is Thomas' the door shuts, I try the next door. *Knock, knock.* The door slowly opens 'I was wondering whether you could help me' the door shuts. *Knock, knock,* the door opens and shuts before I speak. After hours of doors being slammed in my face I was coming to the end of my tether and was about to give up when out of the shadows came a figure, a figure I had seen before, a figure of a delivery boy.

'I hear, with my ears like, that you want to know about the old crazy woman that lived at the bottom of this street, am I right Jack?' he cheekily asked.

'Yes I am, wait. Why did you call me Jack?'

'Oh, would you prefer Mr Ripper then? Although I am unsure where the '*the'* comes in though.'

'I told you, I am not Jack the Ripper.'

'Yeah, yeah not the killer and what not' he casually said 'So what do I call ya then?'

'Dunn.'

'You've done what?'

'No, my name is Thomas Dunn. I am a writer.'

'Oh I writer you say, fancy. Although in truth I found you more interesting as the legendary murderer, oh well. I guess you have prepared me for a lifetime of disappointments,' he said acting sad.

'You are a cheeky lad aren't you?'

'As cheeky as they come.'

'Well, can you help an uninteresting writer?'

‘Depends.’

‘Depends on what, may I ask?’

‘Will you write me into one of your stories?’

‘I always have room for a mischievous and jovial little character.’

‘In that case, I will take you to my home and tell you all about the poor crazy woman.’

The delivery boy’s home wasn’t that far away from Courts Row so it took only a short while before I was sitting in a single room that was a bathroom, kitchen, dining area and sleeping quarters all in one.

‘Where is your mother?’ I asked while I sat down at what looked like a piece of wood but was being used as a table with three legs.

‘My mother you say? How do you know that I don’t live on my own? I mean I could you know, I work and get paid so I have money of my own.’

‘I don’t doubt it, but unless you have taken to wearing women’s undergarments from time to time I would take the guess that you live with your mother,’ I said pointing to the undergarments in question that were lying across the floor in one corner of the room.

‘You are one of these clever types aren’t you?’ the boy asked after looking at where I was pointing to ‘I heard of people like you.’

‘People like me hey? Do explain yourself, I am all ears.’

‘Well you know, the type that lives on his own in a posh area of London, say like Baker Street for example. You go around solving crimes and making friends with an irregular,’ he said pointing to himself. ‘You see the meaning of things that no one else does.’

‘That is an apt description of me.’

‘You even talk like that Holmes fella too!’ the boy laughed ‘Do you know him? Have you seen his brother or even Dr Watson?’

‘Sherlock Holmes is not real; he is just a character in a book.’

‘How do you know what is real and what isn’t? Aren’t we all just characters in books? And if you are not then that is only because the book hasn’t been written yet, don’t you think Tom the writer?’

‘That is very witty of you; I am a little taken back by what you said there. You are quite a rare find aren’t you?’

‘You thought I was just a regular Artful Dodger didn’t you?’

‘You quote me Dickens as well! I am amazed and bow in your honour,’ I said as I stood to give a mock bow towards him, to which he gave a mock salute back towards me. I sat back down and said ‘Now you said I have made friends with you but you have not answered my first question.'

'I haven't?'

'Your mother, where she is tonight?'

'She works at night; she is a street walker of sorts. But if I am honest she is too old for all that larking about, but she won't listen. She says that she will be too old when she is laying in a coffin, oh well.'

'That is a rather shocking thing to say to her son.'

'You don't live in Whitechapel do ya Tom?' he laughed.

'Well no I don't but I don't see what that has got to do with it.'

'You wouldn't I guess. Nothing can shock me Tom, not even I would-be murderer like you.'

'I have said that I'm not murderer.'

'Yes you have, but I can't help picturing you as the murderer in this story of ours, you look the type and around Whitechapel I see a lot!'

'The devil's playground some people say, and I glad I fit in.'

'Smelling the way you do, and looking the way you do I would say so!' he laughed again.

'Yes, well I have not been home for a while and I guess I do smell a little,' I said sniffing myself.

'Like the Thames Tom! You look very different from when I saw you at the theatre; you were very smart looking, and a right Toff we say. You and that other guy, very fancy white shirts,' he said but then he looked gloomy 'but I guess I noticed the bloodied mess more.'

'Quite,' I said reaching over and patting him on the shoulder.

'Who was he Tom?'

'Jimmy Turner, a bartender at the theatre.'

'But why Tom? Why did he have to die?' he said in a way for the time I saw him as the age he was.

'That is what I want to know.'

'You think there is a connection between the crazy woman and the death of Jimmy?'

'In a long twisted way, you see the crazy woman was the mother to an actress at the theatre and I was going to talk to Jimmy about her but.'

'A murderer got in the way,' the boy butted in.

'Yes, you could say that. I want to find out about her because she thought her daughter, the actress, had been murdered.'

'A lot of that going around,' the boy laughed despondently.

'Sadly you are right there.'

'Well I remember my mother telling to not play in Courts Row as there is a crazy woman there, and she would eat me.'

'It is a fairy tale.'

'Yes, but me being me I went there once. I was curious you see,' he said quite proudly.

'I can imagine.'

'And I saw her; she was sitting at a window of the house at the bottom of the street on the top floor, just staring blankly out. I tried to wave at her, but she took no notice. She didn't look crazy, just sad and lonely even.'

'She was mourning for her daughter.'

'I guess you are right Tom, although I didn't know that I just knew I felt very sorry for her, I was not scared of her at all. I was going to knock on her door when a man moved across the window and blocked her from my view so I thought better of it.'

'Do you know where she moved to?'

'Moved to Tom? Well I don't know Tom I thought she was still in there, I have seen no coffin or anything.'

'It was just after her daughter died, a gentleman paid for her to leave Whitechapel.' I said, but why I said gentleman and not Charles's name I don't know.

'I don't think she did Tom, I would have heard of it.'

'Well you were very young.'

'Even so Tom, I think she is *still there*.'

This conversation was getting us no where so I decided to change it. 'Anyway you mentioned you saw a man at the window when you last saw her, could you describe him?' I asked as this may be a clue.

'Well, no Tom. I'm sorry I can't, it was so long ago.'

'It is alright,' I said a little disappointingly.

'But it is funny, we are talking about him as I am sure I have seen him again recently, well that is what I thought but I could have been mistaken.'

'When was that?' I asked.

'Well it was the same day I saw you, Tom. Funny how things fit together isn't it Tom?'

Chapter Eleven

1888

The wind was still blowing its devilishly cold air though the streets of Whitechapel with a now added partner, the rain. The watery drops were light and almost frothily wispy in nature but the amount of them were still drowning me so much so that all my layers of clothing were clinging to me. The mischievous sprite, evil in his nature was compelling me to go to the lodgings to feel to warmth of the fire place, I laugh at your endeavour, I smile at your attempt but you fail to realise the strength I have to earn funds to live. I know you would rather me die tonight but it will not happen for I am not going to the lodgings, I am not heading in peril, I will not be your play thing, to do what you wish. I am my own person with my own destiny and I will change it as the virtuous Spirits are on my side tonight. I am feeling so righteous evil one that I may spoil you, I will head towards Miller's Court and tempt my fate a little further for I have every reason to do so I thought to myself as I moved away from the Ten Bells public house turning left and crossing the street.

'Fancy seeing you here and on this night of all nights,' said a shadow of a woman standing at the top of the alleyway leading into Miller's Court, I recognized the voice instantly as it was my newly made friend that I met

only a few weeks ago in strange surroundings. 'I thought you were changing your destiny tonight and all that.'

'You joke well, considering,' I replied.

'That is nothing to consider, there is nothing to think of, there is nothing to regret and there is nothing to be in fear of,' was her overpowering answer.

'You truly believe that? Or is it your famous Whitechapel charm coming out?' I asked as I moved nearer to her, I could sense she was shaking but was it because of the cold weather? I wonder or was there something else on her mind? Something was telling the latter was so.

'My famous Whitechapel charm hey? Well maybe not so famous yet, my dear friend.'

'I wanted to see you tonight, something was telling me too, silly as it sounds,' I said as I patted her on her wet shoulder, which made a slapping sound.

'Maybe it was that strange woman we both know, I would hate to think of what powers she truly has. I would imagine we have only seen half of the wonders and delights she has to play with.'

'I don't know about that, but all I do know it that I don't want to talk of her tonight, not with you anyway.'

'So what do you want to talk about then? Why are you here?' she asked me and in truth I had no idea how to answer it as I didn't understand myself why I was here, why I was standing at this point. Why was I tempting fate? What

was I trying to prove? That I am better and more intelligent than the devil, it is silly so think so, it is silly to act so, so why I am doing it? I asked myself. I glanced at her and I saw what she stood for, what her meaning was and yet here I was laughing at the keeper of sins. I suddenly felt guilty, why didn't I feel guilty before? But I feel remorseful and embarrassed at the way I have been behaving, I almost felt accountable for things that have been done and for things still yet to come. I needed to change the subject a little.

'You seem cold tonight.'

'It is windy and raining my love, if you hadn't noticed.'

'Cold in nature, I meant.'

'Oh I see, well I find it hard to feel happy these days. It's not like I have anything to look forward too.'

'I don't know what to say.'

'Does anyone? Would anyone understand?'

'I guess not, it is complicated to explain the situation we have found our self's in.'

'Quite.'

'Is there anything I can do?' I asked hopelessly.

'That is not how things work is it? We can't help each other, not now. I guess I can go home now hey?'

'Yes, I am planning to stay out a little longer before I go in.'

'That is nice to know but I would suggest leaving rather sharply as Billy Bo has been standing outside the Ten Bells glancing our way.'

'Billy Bo?' I asked, glancing behind myself towards the gas lamps that stood outside the public house. It was the first time I saw a mysterious dark figure, with one foot resting on the step leading into the drinking hole. His head lying low, his flat cap placed a little too forward on his head so that his face was anonymous to me. He was standing there as casual as he could, cleaning his nails but he had no real need to as the state of his clothing proved he had no care for upkeep of his appearance. He occasionally glanced at his foot on the step but he wasn't fooling anyone as his attention was firmly on me, I could not see his eyes but I could speculate that they were glowing red with hatred and desire to do me harm, or was that my dreams talking?

'You might know of his wife Maud?' she asked as I looked blankly around at her she carried on describing 'A rather loud woman with a mole on her left cheek, she likes to pick on lonely women within in the pub to make herself feel better about her life with Billy and her son Will. If anyone bites on her words, well she sends her fella to sort them out afterwards, since you have just left the pub and Billy Bo is so very interested in you I will take the guess that you, shall we say...bit.'

'I did have a little disagreement with a lady fitting that description I will say it was very entertaining way to a pass an hour or so.'

'Then I would move along promptly, as I have been on the other end of Billy Bo's punches before.'

'Thank you for the advice,' I said as I past by her.

'Helpful I am,' she shouted back at me, as I glanced back at her, her shadow disappeared into the night while Billy Bo's ghostly figure followed my footsteps. I must get away from here and from him.

1898

The boy finished making some tea for us both, it was quite a delight to drink something warm but the taste was a little to be desired but the boy was quite proud of his work so I didn't mention my true feelings.

'You have not told me your name?' I asked the boy.

'What does a name matter, would a rose smell so sweet if it was called any other name?' the boy said as egotistical as I have never seen anyone be.

'Shakespeare? You have an unending amount of knowledge don't you?' I asked.

'You have to read to get ahead, that's what my father used to say. Although I had often wondered what my father wanted with that part of the body never the less my father had many books for me to read.'

'Your father is not with you now?'

'My father is always with me, but no he is not in this living world. He was a boxer, the famous 'Billy Bo' and he died in the ring,' he said staring into his cup.

'I am sorry to hear that.'

'Don't know why you should be sorry Tom, you didn't know him. In truth not many people did, they just thought he was a brute and handy with his fists but that wasn't the real him. He really did not want to hurt a fly in the early years, but something changed in him. I saw it even though I was young, he stopped reading and he just stopped caring. He was always a dirty man but then everybody is around Whitechapel aren't they?' he asked pointing towards me.

'Quite.'

'Anyway, he used to follow my mother into the pubs to make sure she didn't get into trouble because he was worried about her. She always managed to get into an arguments and fights, she still does now to be honest with ya, I don't know how she does it, and maybe it is just in her nature. But it was him coming back one night, later than normal that was different he wasn't himself and he was never the same again.'

'Oh that sounds dreadful.'

'I have always wondered what happened that night.'

'So you didn't ask him?'

'No, we don't do that ya see. Never butt your nose into other people's problems; it's kind of unwritten law around here. I never knew what happen but I sensed it was something wrong, something evil in nature and the funny thing is I think my mother knows, I think she always has known but never said anything about it. But I guess I have never asked her, so why would she tell?'

'Maybe this thing that happen was so shocking she thinks it is wrong to tell you, you have a great love for your father I can see that, so maybe telling you might change that.'

'You think my father did something wrong?' he said quietly.

'I don't know what happened, I am sorry if I have offended you and your father, sometimes my mind carries away with me.'

'You can't offend me Tom, am I the cheeky chappie that all your readers will fall in love with and bless me from the bottoms of their hearts.'

'A character that needs a name, I can't keep calling you 'the delivery boy' can I now?'

'Very true Tom, I would say that 'delivery boy' although is a description of sorts for me, I would rather see my name in print. It would make me happy.'

'And your father, your true father,' I said as I patted him on the shoulder.

'Yes, you are quite right. It's Will, my name is Will,' he said as he smiled ever so sweetly at me.

'Well Will,' I started to say, just when there was an almighty bang and the door burst opened causing a strong gust of cold air to enter the room. I turned to look and there was two burly men standing side by side in the open door frame. As quick as a flash of lightning one of the men grabbed hold of Will where he screamed and struggled. I moved over to him, but something must have hit me on the back of my head as I felt a sharp pain and then everything went black.

When I awoke I was face down on the floor of Will's one single room, as objects come into focus I heard a woman weeping in the corner and I saw a pair of men's shoes facing me with a pair of legs sticking out from them, then those shoes started talking and they were talking to me, calling me by name. 'Well Mr Dunn, we meet again like I thought we would' I slowly moved my head upwards to see the face of Inspector Foresight staring down and I tried to speak but it sounded mumbled. 'What was that Mr Dunn? Could you repeat yourself?' the Inspector asked me.

'Where is Will?' I managed to say.

'I am sorry to say Mr Dunn, that Master William Jenkins is dead. Murdered I would say,' the Inspector replied to the screams of a woman in the corner, everything went light and blurrily again as I lose the ability to hold my face up any longer so I hit the floor again. 'Officer, pick this man up at once! He needs help!' I heard the Inspector say and then I felt someone grab hold of me and I was lifted into a chair, Will's chair. 'Are you alright to talk Mr Dunn?' was the question put forward to me.

'I feel unwell.'

'You do get through some scraps Mr Dunn that I can tell you but I think you will be alright.'

'What happened to Will?' I asked as I felt the back of my head which left dry blood crumbs in the palm of my hand.

'It was terrible Mr Dunn, seeing a young boy's body in that bloodied mess,' he started as the woman in the corner started hailing again. 'Take her out of here would you officer, she is acting like a mad woman!' As the woman was being lifted out of the room the Inspector said to me 'Poor woman really, mother to the lad she is. To be honest with you Mr Dunn I always thought she was a little fruity in the head to start with, what with her fella dying in the ring and all that.'

'She was the one that found us, wasn't she?'

'Yes, I bet this is going to it for her now, no one to live for you see, sad really.'

'It's all so sad.'

'So what has happened to you since I last saw you?' he asked pointing to me.

'I have had a few experiences.'

'That as lead you to be in another murder scene.'

'I am not the murderer.'

'No, this time I don't believe you are. But you fascinate me all the same; I believe you are the thread that is holding all these murders together.'

'So you don't believe I am the murderer just the cause behind them.'

'A very apt description.'

'I don't know which description I would prefer.'

<u>1888</u>

I picked up my pace and turned down a few alleyways looking behind me all the way, I thought once I had got away from Billy Bo but within seconds he was back behind me. I feels like I have been running for ages, I feel lost and disoriented I had run to parts of the East End I have never been before, my heart was pounding and I was feeling panicked.

'Stop running girl,' came a gruff voice from behind. 'You don't know where you are headed.'

'Please leave me alone!' I screamed as I ran a little further ahead

'I can't do that love.'

'Please, I never meant to have an argument with your wife. She started it anyway,' I said.

'You don't understand love,' he shouted back as I felt the ground underneath me fade away and I fell on wet, cold mud. I looked around me a little confused at what has just happened to find that I was on the homelands of the Mud Larks for I was on the shores of the Thames. I struggled to stand up in the thick layers of mud and as I did so I noticed that the level of mud was above my ankles but below my knees, mud covered my dress and my left arm, I tried to move away quickly but was failing miserably. 'You don't listen, do ya love,' said Billy Bo as he was now standing above me on the stoned wall that I had fallen off from.

'Please leave me.'

'I can't,' he said as he jumped down from the wall into the mud.

'So you want to beat me up,' I said as I gave up moving away from him, I was going to get a beating tonight, yes I would have bruises and it will hurt but at least I will be alive.

'No.'

'No? But isn't that what you do? Beat up anyone who has words with you wife.'

'Yes it is,' he said quietly as he moved nearer to me.

'So why not me?'

'Because you are special,' he replied as he was so close to me I could feel his breath on my face, he smelt bad.

'Oh yeah? In what way?' I asked in the flirtiest way possible, maybe I could cheekily get my way out of this situation.

'Strip.'

'What?' I asked a little taken back.

'I said strip, now,' he said menacingly. I stood once step back from him and started to slowly slip my dress of my cold shoulders, looking at him with questionable expression. 'Faster!' he shouted. I jumped at the loudness of his voice and took of my dress; it felt heavy in my arms. 'Now give it to me!'

'You want my dress?' I asked.

'No, I just don't want you to have it, now pass it over!' he shouted. So I threw my dress over and tried to cover parts of me with my muddy hands. 'I wouldn't bother trying to cover yourself up, I have seen it all before and no doubt half the neighbourhood as well,' he laughed a little.

'I don't find this funny, you are a sad little man that likes to have power over women, I have met your type before.'

'You are wrong. There is no one quite like me,' he said as threw my dress to the side of him. It made a thudding sound as all the layers fell like a stone into the mud.

'Yes that would be right, you are so impressive. Look at you, the big powerful man,' I said as I glanced

away from the dress to Billy Bo, I was feeling angry, how dare he treat me like this, he is no better than I, why does he have the right to do this?

'You should not play with me misses.'

'Why not? I thought I was special.'

'You are, but not good special.'

'Not good special,' I mumbled to myself. Are there different types of special? I have never thought about that before, I thought the word special was meant for good, am I not good? I am a bad person. As if Billy Bo heard my thoughts he said

'You are bad, rotten to the core. You are the bad kind of special.'

'What are you going to do with me? If you are not going to punch me with those famous fists of yours, then what is the meaning of this? Of all this' I asked looking around me. As I stood before him, naked, shaking with the cold, covered in mud and damp with the rain, the wind was pushing my long hair in front of me, so I brushed it behind my ears like I have always done leaving me showing all my body to him. He glanced briefly at me, with his intimidating and quite chilling eyes.

They say the eyes are the gateway to someone's soul, if that is true this brute's soul has been burnt to cinders. He stands there in front of me like any other man on the street, he would be invisible, with his well flat cap, his dirty white shirt, and the sleeves were rolled up passed his elbows, his brown waistcoat and grubby trousers. All was normal, all was the same as anyone else and yet here he was staring at me, staring at my naked body which was shuddering and quivering in this cold winter wind on the shores of the river that lead its way through our city meaning to do my harm. He made sure he stared at every part of me in such a creepy way, I had never met such an evil man, I was standing before the devil but I was not mocking him now. I repeated myself, 'What are you going to do with me?'

'What am I going to do with you? Let me think about that quite foolish question.'

'From where I am standing I don't think it is such a daft question, I mean look at me, look at what you have done.'

'It is true in what you say, from where you are standing maybe knowing what will happen to you might help your mind, maybe you think it will put your mind at ease. If so, then you are dim-witted as look around you misses, what do you think is going to happen love?'

'I am hoping you are just trying to scare me and then you will let me go, leave this place to never to return.'

'Am I?'

'Are you what?'

'Am I scaring you?'

'Yes, very much so.'

'I am glad, I like to see the fear in my opponent eyes, and it brings delight to me before I bring the final punch. But I am sorry I cannot let you go.'

'But I will not repeat this to anyone I promise and you have won. I know that, you know that. Can't we just let that be?'

'No,' he said quietly.

'But why?' I asked pleadingly.

'Because my love, I am going to kill you,' he simply said.

Chapter Twelve

1898

'So could you tell me, how you came to be lying on a floor of a slum in the East End in a small puddle of your own blood?' Inspector Foresight asked.

'It is a rather long story.'

'I thought nothing less from you.'

'I was in Courts Row.'

'Courts Row, you say. What would you be doing there?'

'I was investigating a murder that happened over ten years ago.'

'Of course you were,' he said sarcastically. I laughed a little at his statement it did sound hard to believe I admit but then I thought occurred to me, he is a policeman he might have known about the murder of Ellen and he might know something I don't, why didn't I think of that before?

'You might have heard of her, Ellen Rose,' I said

‘Ah, the singing Nightingale from the Willow and the Owl you mean, I was still a sergeant then. Wait, is that why you were really in the theatre?’

‘Yes, I wanted to talk to Jimmy about her but I was greeted with the same scene you saw.’

‘Interesting.’

‘Yes, yes it all linked through me I get it.’

‘That’s not what is interesting me now, but it now all fits into place for me.’

‘If I could get back to Ellen, do you think she was murdered?’

‘Yes.’

‘You said that rather quickly Inspector,’ I said as I had a momentary look across the table at him. He was sunk down low in his chair with a quite sad expression of his face.

‘I suppose time has passed now, that was information we had to hold back from the public, information that told me that she was murdered in no doubt,’ he said without looking up at me.

‘What was the information?’

‘As well as her throat being cut there was something else. There was an organ missing, god bless her soul. She looked terrible, my wife and I often went to the theatre to see the singing nightingale, she was so beautiful but to see her like that, it wasn't right.'

'What organ was missing?'

'Her heart.'

'My god!' I proclaimed in horror, I can't believe what I was hearing. So Ellen was murdered, her mother and Charles was right after all. How do I tell Charles, he will be inconsolable.

'Yes I remember now, her mother lives in Court Row, hence why you were visiting I see it now.'

'Well Jimmy managed to say that her mother thought she was murdered so I thought I would visit her neighbours as she has moved on.'

'Moved on? She is still there as far as I know. And I make note of where all the loonies are on my patch.'

'But Charles gave her money to leave Whitechapel.'

'He did, did he? Well she didn't take it; it was probably what that argument was at Miss Turner's funeral. It was not very nice I can tell you, but she is still there.'

'In Courts Row?' I asked.

'Yes, she has never moved,' suddenly I thought popped into to mind, I dark most evil thought so I asked,

'Tell me Inspector when was the last time you saw Ellen's mother?'

‘Well it was actually quite a while ago.’

‘Come Inspector, and take two of your men with us. I feel there is another dreadful sight install for us yet!’

‘Surely you don’t mean.’

‘Yes Inspector Foresight, I believe Ellen’s mother is no longer of this world,’ I said as I stood up and moved towards the door, I heard the small footsteps of the Inspector following behind while shouting at two of his biggest and cumbersome officers to tag along with us to Courts Row.

When we hit the Row I let the Inspector get ahead as he knew which house she lived in, it was a rather sorry looking house that sat on its own and the end of the street. All the love seemed to have left it some time ago, the windows and doors were boarded up with some kind of cheap wood. ‘You are sure she is still in there?’ I asked the Inspector.

‘Yes, the wood on the door is too keep people away, but isn’t pinned the door really. But what is bothering me is that the wood on the windows is newer,’ he said as he glanced at me, waiting for me to realise what he truly meant. Within seconds I understood the gravity of his words. The new wood was shielding something evil that lay within the upstairs rooms. ‘Too new for my liking’ he carried on. ‘Right guys, I need you to rip through the door. But let us go in first, everyone got that.’

'Yes, Sir,' the two officers said together. They were as big as they were strong because within seconds the wooden door was ripped open and torn apart. The Inspector tapped me on the shoulder to follow and that is what I did. The house was haunting and dark when we entered, the smell was something I had never met before, the repugnant and vulgar stench clung to my nostrils, and I almost turned away in disgust. I followed the Inspector as he slowly walked upstairs with every creak of the every step we took.

'Stay close to me,' the Inspector said.

'Do you like Edgar Allen Poe's stories Inspector?'

'The ghost stories you mean, why do you ask?'

'Because I think we are in one.'

'Yes I understand you, whatever is up here will be quite ghastly and we should prepare ourselves for that at least.' As we reached the top of the stairs, turned left and stood by a wooden door the Inspector asked 'So Mr Dunn are you prepared?' as he started to push open the door.

1888

'You are going to kill me?' I shouted through the bitterly cold wind.

'You have learned at last to listen, but it won't help you now I'm afraid,' he said as he reached in his back pocket to show his shiny knife.

'You can't kill me!' I shouted back at him. He can't scare me, I am not meant to die tonight I believe it, I

believe in everything that happened that night. She was right, she let me know that I was going to be killed tonight but if I stayed away from the lodgings I would be safe. I have stayed away, I will be safe. I will live, it cannot end this way. 'What right do you have to kill me? You are nothing, you are so mundane that you can't handle it, so you make this scene, you try your best to frighten me to make yourself better, but you won't win.'

'Why because you are special you mean? Don't make me laugh. You are standing there covered in mud, naked on the seashore; I think in fact I know I have already won. But what interests me, you have always said you are not special, why do you believe it now?'

'Well I believe in her.'

'Ah, her. Tell me, why do you always think of her as strange? Why do you describe her as strange? Why whenever you think of her the word strange pops into your mind? Tell me why that is? Maybe because she is simply as fruity as a cake and yet you believe in her, you believe her so much that you think I can not kill you.'

'You can't,' I wept knowing all the while that he could.

'I think you will find I can. Why are you so shocked?' he asked me.

'Shocked? I am more than shocked!'

'I don't know why you are, I mean surely you knew. You must have known all along that you were going to die

on this night, this night was always going to be your end in some way or form, you cannot run away from your destiny, you cannot change it. You were always meant to die, but it was your choosing how you were to die.'

'My choosing?'

'Yes, do I have to explain everything to you? Are you that dumb? You could have gone home, you could have been famous, everyone would have known your name because of your death, because of him but you didn't, you stayed out. You met my wife, you said that thing, you ran here and you met me. You are standing there, naked on the shores of the Thames waiting for me to kill you as I have told you I would because you are a nobody, you will be forever a nobody. I will kill you tonight, I will slit your throat and when the last drop of blood pours out of your neck I will get to work. I will cut your arms off, I will cut your legs off, and finally I will cut your head off. I will bury your torso on the grounds of Scotland Yard for they will never catch me. I will throw your legs out at sea because at sea you have no need to walk. I will wrap your arms up in cloth as you will have no more need to hold and your head? Well your head I will keep, as your head makes you who you are, it identifies you. If there is no head then you are just parts of a body, you will have no name, no one will remember you. It was your choice, and you chose badly.'

'Are you mad?'

'We are all mad here, don't you think.'

'You are sick, this is all sick!'

'So sick, it's quite delightful. Quite delightfully sick, I would say. I don't know what you have got to complain about; at least I have put thought into killing you. That was the bonus of you running for so long; it allowed me time to think about what I would do to you.'

'Are you asking me to thank you for killing me?' I laughed madly, as I had now lost my mind.

'That would be polite, I mean after all the effort I have put in, I will not just slit your throat and run like that Jack the Ripper fella.'

'Jack the Ripper! Don't you mention his name.'

'Oh yes, I see. It was quite daring of me wasn't it? Taunting you with the person you were meant to meet tonight, I wonder what he would have looked like. Would he have been taller than me? Would I have known him? Would you have known him? Now there is a question. Would you, the old special you know Jack the Ripper? I could just see crowds of people whispering at that question, would she have known her murderer? Now that's quite a mouth-watering question don't you think?' he said smiling like the Cheshire Cat.

'You seem to know a lot about me.'

'I do, isn't it interesting? Isn't all very interesting?' he said as he snorted out a chuckle.

'How do you know?' I beseeched.

'How do I know what missy?' he said as he turned a little to look out into the Thames, there was a small boat passing along and I guess Billy Bo was staring at it.

'How do you know, who I am? Who I am meant to be?' I screamed.

'But you are not now are you? You are just a body, a soon to be dead body,' he said still looking at across the water's edge.

'Then what are you waiting for? You are not planning to go through with it!'

'You think I am waiting because I am doubting what I am meant to do?' he asked.

'What you are meant to do? You were told to kill me?'

'Yes.'

'Who told you to kill me?' I asked.

'You did,' he said as he turned around to face me, he was able to move around in mud more better than I for I was sinking forever within the slimy ground. 'Now I believe it is almost morning,' he said glancing to the skies. The dark night was given away for the coldness of the morning light. The rain had stopped, leaving a fresh feeling to the surroundings, but the iciness was still as fierce as ever. 'I do believe it is the right time' he said as he glanced down at me 'Time to die,' he sang to me.

'All this because I have I had a row with your wife?'

'No, it was never about that. If you just had a row with my wife, I would not have chased you this far as I would not have cared. Many people have had rows with my wife it is her nature you see. No, you were different, you were special.'

'What did I do that was so special?'

'You mentioned my son and by doing so you made your choice, you will meet your maker tonight.'

1898

As the door opened with a ghostly screech, the smell that drifted from the room to us was as inferior to anything I had ever sniffed before, so distinctly I reached for my handkerchief from my pocket and placed it to my nose as I tried to register the scene sited before my eyes.

The sight before us was disturbingly and in truth quite alarmingly familiar to me, but it was more horrendous than I could have seen in my darkest of nightmares. It was as if I was seeing my hallucination ten years after it had happened, the room was covered in inches of dust, there was a fireplace that was crumbling away to one corner. The room had only one table with a chair underneath it inches away from the door and to the left of me, running length ways. The Royal Purple fabric on the chair had been ripped to shreds; it was like a gigantic hound had somehow entered this building and made a play thing of the chair.

The table itself was of sturdy oak, full of wood knots but without its varnish, there was ginger beer bottles lying on top, some had been knocked over and its reddish contents had spilled out into the floor at some point, leaving a sticky messy puddle. A slight scent was coming from these bottles, not of ginger beer but of something more deadly, something chemical in nature but sadly I could not refine the scent as the odour that had filled this whole house and the smell the Inspector and I had both whiffed as we had entered was coming from something entirely different.

The most horrifying part that lay before us was the figure floating in the middle of the floor, her back was facing us but we knew she was dead as she was hanging from a well used rope. Her body or shall I say what was left of her body after years of slowly rotting away, had been soaked to the bone, her long hair was wet and knotted and below her swinging bare feet was a pool of her own blood, which had been bleeding for some time and had dried. From where I was standing I could see a patch of open soars running below her ear, to around her neck and down her shoulders nested a very sickening family of larva and maggots that were chewing their way to the bone. I moved forward but the Inspector held me back. 'There is nothing you can do for her now' he said to me.

'Who would have done such a thing?'

'The devil, evil has set foot in this house.'

'How very religious of you Inspector,' I said still staring at the remains of the mother of Ellen Rose.

'Religion does not enter into it Mr Dunn, if you have been in the job as long as I have, you see things, things you should not be able to see. You get to observe the dark side to this world. All the madness, all the malevolence and sin in this life time can shake a common man to his core, I can tell you and Mr Dunn I have been shaken on too many of occasions.'

'She must have been hanging here for years,' I said as I leaned against the door frame, watching the Inspector moving forward and around her body to face her.

'I would say she has been here, like this for more than five years by the state of her. She is in an awful condition.'

'A condition? I don't understand Inspector I can see she has been hanged.'

'And the rest, Mr Dunn and the rest,' he said shaking his head with sadness. 'She has been butchered and then hung, hence the blood on the floor and the blood over in the corner behind that table you are standing by,' I glanced over to where the Inspector was meaning to find that through the light covering of dust was indeed black marks that splattered across the wooden floor and some had splashed up against the wall. This was where she had been hacked to pieces and dragged over half of the distance of the room to be hanged as I was able to follow the blood line from the point of murder to the point of hanging. It was all so carelessly done, the poor woman must have faced iniquity like she had never known. 'And by the look of her tongue that is dangling out and the blackness in colour I would say that she was poisoned first, then butchered and then hanged.'

'Poisoned?' I asked as I saw the Inspector tapped the woman slightly that made her swing.

'The murderer went out of his way to kill this woman, poisoning was not enough, hacking her to pieces did not do it for him, so hanging was the final blow. Was he happy then? Leaving her to look like a criminal, hanging for crimes she had committed, did he believe she was I wonder? And if so what were those crimes?' He asked to himself as he followed the blood line from the body to the table but stopping half way to pick up a small wooden stick that had been lying in the dust. 'What do we have here then?' I thought again he was talking to himself but at that point he turned on the spot and faced me with his eyebrows raised.

'It looks like a small stick,' I replied.

'From where you are it probably does.'

'What does it look like to you?'

'The thorns tell me it is a stem from a rose flower, rose are a very expensive flower wouldn't you say Mr Dunn?'

'Yes I would.'

'So what would a woman such as her that lives in a place such as this be doing with a rose? One single rose.'

'I would imagine she wouldn't own it.'

'So, what are you saying Mr Dunn?'

'The murderer brought it with him.'

'That is a rather strange thing for the murderer to do isn't it Mr Dunn?' The Inspector asked as he rolled the stem between his second finger and thumb while marvelling at it.

'It is rather strange, yes. But what does that tell us?' I asked.

'Either our murderer is a mighty fine gardener or we are dealing with a Doctor Jekyll and Mr Hyde.'

'From the book you mean?'

'Of sorts, our murderer has the ability to murder someone in cold hard blood and then feel sorry about it and be full of remorse afterwards, two characters one person equals a massive headache for me and a mammoth task in head for the force,' he said has he placed the stem in the inside of his long coat and moved over to the table but to the bottles on the table especially, then he started to smell them.

'Ah success! Here is the culprit,' he said as held one bottle up in his hands.

'I can't believe she was poisoned!'

'I would guess she knew her murderer and if I am correct our murderer has left a footprint, a rather sticky footprint,' he said as bend over the puddle of the bottle contents on the floor. 'I was guess that the murderer would have a dirty and stained shoe. Oh and what is this I spy on the floor? Well this murderer took his sweet time that is for sure, he smoked at least two cigars, a cool character indeed.'

'It was the same murderer of her daughter, I can sense it.'

'A gut instinct, have you ever thought of becoming a policeman?' he asked as he turned to face me.

'A policeman? No, I will stick to things that happen in my head, not to the things that happen in real life,' I said pointing to the poor image of Ellen's mother.

'Why don't you write about what has happened?'

'People won't believe it.'

'Ah, too true, too true, but does it really matter if it is a classic? For it will have a history of its own,' he asked as he patted my shoulder to leave the room 'I will let all the right people deal with that scene, you need to go home. Have a rest maybe get away from London and what not.'

'A rest would be nice,' I said as I rubbed my forehead as I had a headache.

'Oh Mr Dunn, you seem to have dropped your handkerchief,' The Inspector said from the landing as I glanced up from the stairs to look at him, feeling a little unsteady as I did so, I said.

'No Inspector, I have my handkerchief here with me,' and I waved it at him as I had got used to the smell of the poor woman's rotting flesh.

'Oh? But I saw it fall out of your pocket when we entered the room,' he said as he wave a white cloth back at me 'But come to mention it, now I can look at it, it looks more like a piece of white material,' he said as he threw it down to me. As I grabbed it, I glanced at it. It was indeed a piece of material, a piece of material I recognized but from where?

'I don't know where I got this from Inspector.'

'Strange things will happen in the house of horrors,' was his reply as he walked back into the murder room. I shook my head with disbelief, placed the white material back inside my pocket and took a slow walk home.

1888

I awoke from my dreams, sunk down in the strange woman's chair, the smoke was gone and so was the woman. I glanced around the bizarre room; it seemed more threatening now than when I first entered it. 'Is anyone there?' I asked but no one was there to answer me.

I felt sick to the stomach, what did that dream mean? Was I meant to die at the hands of Jack the Ripper like all my friends? Is that why I am the maiden, the special one because I am going to die in a horrid and most disguising way? I feel lost, like my world has turned upside down, what way do I go? What way do I stay? I am going to be one of Jack the Ripper's victims, my god! And what did that dream mean? If I am to run away from Jack the Ripper do I die anyway? Do I met Billy Bo and he kills me instead on the shores of the Thames? Does he cut my throat and then cut my body into pieces? Throwing parts of me around London where no one knows where I am, so no one can mourn for me. I will be *a nobody*. What does this all mean for me, for my life?

I cried heavily in the chair for what seemed like hours until I was so tired I couldn't force out any more watery tears. I thought this night was going to be wonderful and full of delight, full of hope for the future but my future is going to be death, whatever way I am to look at it. My future will not be at all and what is the most chilling and quite disturbing thing is that I was alone; I thought I had made a friend. Yes the woman was strange but wasn't we all around here?

The strange woman seemed kind, thoughtful almost motherly, and it had been such a long time since I felt the love of a mother, but she lied to me. She made me believe I was special and that things would be alright, but how could anything be alright after what I know now, is this what I really needed to know? Why would she do this to me? And where is she now?

I stood up and walked up and down the room for I was feeling panicked and my father always told me, 'go for a walk Mary, that's a good girl, walk off your troubles, things will seem better after a good walk sweetheart.' But father how can I walk off death? How can I walk off Jack the Ripper or Billy Bo? I felt like giving up there and then, when suddenly a consciousness of someone by my side stirred up inside of me so I rotated around to see the strange woman's bookcase crumble away and a dark coloured grave stone rose from the ground, the ceiling had gone and what was left was a brilliant clear sky, I felt a slight wind over my shoulders as I was transported back a few months ago when I decided to see the grave of my friend Mary Nicholls.

'You had the same idea then?' came a voice from behind me and the reason for the creepy feeling; I spin around to see Annie standing a few inches away from me, holding a cheap brunch of flowers. She followed my eye line and said 'Yeah, they were all I could afford to nick' waving the flowers at me.

'They are very colourful.'

'Yeah, I always thought Polly needed some colour in her life,' Annie said as she walked passed me and laid her flowers down on the stone square.

'I miss her,' I said as I turned back around to face the grave stone.

'We all miss her Mary,' she said standing up but still looking at the grave. 'It's wrong that they wrote that on the grave.'

'What have they put?' I asked quietly.

Annie looked over to me with a questionable look, 'I thought you were learning to read.'

‘I have Joseph to read for me now.’

‘Oh yeah? Carry him around in a little bag do ya? Where is he now to read the grave for ya?’

‘Don’t argue Annie, not on top of Polly.’

‘Yes, yes. It wouldn’t be right. It says Mary Ann Nicholls, victim of Jack the Ripper.’

‘That is wrong.’

‘But also sadly true.’

‘Who is this Jack the Ripper? Do you think we know him?’

‘Would you really want to know?’ Annie asked me.

‘Are you saying you don’t?’

‘Of course I don’t, what would be the point in that? Would that save us from him? I don’t think so and who would we tell? Who would believe us Mary? We are nobodies, just people to be used and thrown away, that’s all we are Mary. We will have no meaning, we will not change anything. We are like rats, everyone knows we are here but does nothing about us, what would knowing who this Jack the Ripper is do for us?’ Annie asked as she glanced back at the grave ‘It certainly didn’t help Polly,’ we both stood there for a while in silence looking over the last resting place of our friend Polly, the wind picked up a little so I placed my shawl up higher so it was covering my shoulders.

‘Someone will save us,’ I whispered.

‘You can get that silly idea out of your head, no one is going to save us because nobody cares, and they never will Mary. If you want to be saved you will have to save yourself and I am sorry but I don’t see you doing that.’

‘I don’t believe you, one day people will care for us.’

‘By then it will be too late, we would have all been murdered by Jack the Ripper.’

‘How can you say that? The police will catch him, and we will all be safe’

‘If you believe that, you will believe anything,’ Annie said as she walked away from the grave ‘You mark my words Mary, we are all goners,’ I turned to argue my point when Annie disappeared from my sight, the grass around my feet turned to wood and the other grave stones faded away to show the strange woman’s chair and mine placed by the fireplace, for I was back within the strange woman’s lair.

Annie was right; in the end Annie was always right. There will be no one to save us, no knight in shining armour, if I am going to saved it would be off my own back, not anyone else’s. I must find a way of saving me. A sudden urge to look at the book the strange woman dropped by the side of her chair came over me. What was the importance of it? I glance over to the chair, the book was gone, had she put it back in the bookshelf? I moved to the bookshelf there was no space, she must have put it back.

I looked quickly at the titles of the books, oh what is the use in looking? I asked myself for I cannot read. How would I know what to look for? How would it help me in the situation I am in? I was about to move away when a book caught my eye, it wasn't the book itself but the fact that there were not dust lying on it or around it, it had been moved recently.

This was the book I was after; this was the book the strange woman had to read first before letting me know the fate that is waiting for me, what is this book with three words for a title? I rolled my fingers around it, feeling the texture of the book, it felt shiny and new, and I breathe in deeply as I took the courage to grab a little tighter around the book edge when I felt the sensation of someone behind me.

'I thought you don't read much,' said Maria. I turned quickly around to see her standing there holding a book.

'Where is?' I started to ask when Maria finished the question for me.

'The strange woman who brought you here? Oh well she is a little sick at the moment. She asked if I could take you home.'

'Oh, it was probably the smoke.'

'Probably, oh and she said I should give you this.' she said as she handed me a book.

'I can only read a little.'

'Nevertheless she wanted me to give it to you.'

'What is the title say? Who is the author?' I said as I took the book.

'You ask a lot of questions don't you? It's an old book, the woman read it to me ages ago, rather scary but I liked it. The author seems to have a unique way of writing.'

'Unique you say, in what way?' I asked.

'Well he writes differently, he's not a Dickens or a Doyle. He is not even a Collins, he a little bit of all and none, silly as that sounds.'

'I have heard of Dickens and of course Doyle but Collins?'

'He wrote a story, about stone and some poppies, I can't remember it now,' Maria huffed in a childish way.

'Oh I see, well if this author isn't any of them and all of them at the same time, what is he?'

'He's special, that is the word I would use for him.'

'Well that would be different, being 'special,' I said sarcastically. Maria laughed a little and then it seemed as if she had done something wrong and instantly changed her expression to something more ridged.

'It's called '*the coffin bell rings,'* by Thomas Dunn'

'Is this Mr Dunn any good?'

'*You* tell me,' she said as she shrugged her shoulders, 'so you want to show me where you live then?' She asked as she began to walk away from me and out of the room. I glanced back at the bookshelf and at the book I almost had within my grasp. I had a spit second to decide, so I decided. I quickly grabbed the book and placed it under a layer of my shirts and followed Maria out of the door, for it will be my safety I just know it.

Chapter Thirteen

1898

The morning light was breaking through the clouds; I could see the rays of sunlight at every gap between the tall modern buildings that had been built recently around where I live, soon London will be bigger and more congested than I have ever known it to be. Most of the peers at the Billing Club were quite delighted with the idea of their great city being swarming with more people like themselves but something was telling me this could all end erroneously as they didn't see the vast picture that lay before them. They didn't know or I should say pretended not to know about the problems in the East, they only think of themselves and what they need, not thinking that the East could help as it is a blueprint of things that could happen elsewhere, elsewhere being within their precious City Square Mile and the aristocratic surrounding areas.

The diseases, children dying or not reaching past the age of five, the disgusting and quite revolting smell were all because of overcrowding, and the West isn't that far behind it in truth. Take away our large windows, our grand front doors, our expensive decoration in every room and you will find more and more buildings expanding and extending, houses that we call homes swell under the want of space. Leaving what exactly? Where is all the greenery gone? Where is the nature that had stuck its foot in the ground years before we did? Yes, we have parks, manmade parks but for how long? How long will it be until these parks are gone because of the essential need to house the ever growing population? Will people regret losing this part of history? Would we even notice or care?

'A penny for your thoughts,' said a voice beside me; I glanced to the side of me and noticed the same working's man boots I have seen so many times now, walking in tune with my shoes. How long had she been walking along beside me? I didn't have a single clue; I hadn't sensed her at all.

'You best leave me be,' I replied, rather mournfully. The thought of William lying dead on some mortuary stab, what did the Inspector say? 'A bloodied mess' as I recall. What if the fate of Jimmy Turner has fell on the shoulders of poor Will too? Fell on a set of or rather small shoulders at that, he was so young. He didn't deserve to die; he had his life laid before him, why did he die and not me? Why did I survive? When it was my fault that he has left this world to go on into the next, years too early, it was my fault his mother now has no one, I have made a mess of everything. For some reason the devil is following me at every turn, is it so wrong to solve the murder of Ellen Rose? What am I not suppose to know?

'Oh? How come?' she asked as her sweet voice entered my head.

'Everyone around me seems to be dying; I have almost died a fair few times. I am not a lucky person to be around; my horseshoe must be placed upside down.'

‘What makes you think it is you that has the bad luck? Maybe it is the people you hang around with, the people that have died might of have their own share of this bad luck and you just happen to be there when the evil angel lands by their side, although it is odd,’ she replied still walking in link with me.

‘I try my best not to hang around with anyone.’

‘You like to be on your own, do ya?’

‘Well at this precise moment, I would like to be on my own. I have seen things, that maybe I shouldn’t have seen. Things someone could only dream of in their worst nightmares.’

‘And how’s that going for you? Being on your own I mean,’ she said as if she wasn’t listening to a word of what I have just said.

‘I don’t quite know what you mean.’

‘You never do lately.’

‘I do know that I feel I am living through a course of Grimm Fairy tales, seeing the bogey man and catching a glimpse of what he does.’

‘Have you seen him?’

‘Who? The bogey man you mean? Don’t make me laugh, he is an imaginary fiend that adults use to scare their children to behave, there is no such thing that eats children!’

'At yet you feel you have seen him.'

'It was a figure of speech that is all.'

'How sure are you about that?' she asked me inexplicably.

'Look is there something you want from me?' I said as I stopped walking and turned to her. My life is too painfully complicated for this strange woman and her strange ways of talking. I would do anything for something simple to happen, something without secrets and codes, something without meaning and if I can stop one, then I feel I would be on my way to lose this dark cloud of headache I have been under for the last few months.

'Yes.'

'What is it then?' I asked as was losing my patience and knew I was only a few yards from my own front door.

'Moment in time, a moment in your past, I would like to have that, if you would allow me.'

'A moment in time, you ask. What a rather strange thing to ask for as none of us have the power of time, time runs on. We can't control it, so why ask for it? What has happened in my past that you would like to have?'

'You do not remember because maybe time has run on like you say,' she said sadly.

'If I do not remember the moment, how can I give it to you?' I asked.

'Dreams then, I would like to have your dreams.'

'You want my dreams?' I asked shocked, why would someone want someone else's dreams? Those are the most personal of things, why would someone take that away? More importantly why does this strange and quite interestingly middle aged woman want mine? What could they do for her?

'Do you want to keep them, then?' she asked sharply back towards me, as she stared at me with those wide interesting and almost memorable eyes.

'If there was a way for me to give you my dreams I would, for I don't ever want to keep them.'

'I thought not somehow, why do you want to get rid of your dreams I wonder?'

'But you just said you wanted them.'

'And you said you give them away, I wonder why? And I wonder why *you* haven't wondered why? Don't you find it unusual for someone like you to want to give your dreams away? I mean I can only imagine what your dreams hold for you, surely they would help you.'

'Help me? You think my dreams can help me?'

'Well in the line of work you are in, surely a writer needs dreams, for dreams are imagination are they not?'

'Sometimes I speculate against that.'

'Oh? Your dreams are more than that to you, aren't they?'

'I am beginning to think so.'

'That is interesting, don't you think?' she asked as something caught her attention because she glanced over my shoulder into my home. 'I have to be on my way,' she said quickly turning away from me, I grabbed hold of her arm. It felt cold.

'Wait, don't leave. I need to know what is going on here.' I whispered.

'I don't think you are quite ready yet, you are almost there but not quite.'

'Is this it? Is this all I get to know from you?'

'You want me to tell you something then? Something that would be important to you?' she asked.

'Yes, for God's sake Yes!' I shouted, for I felt like finally I was getting somewhere, maybe I will lose this headache after all, but her answer was nothing better than I had ever got from her before. Her answer did not make me understand anything that has happened, I did not understand her or what she wanted from me better at all because she said

'Beware of the company you keep,' she said nodding towards my home. I dropped my arm to turn around to see in the window of my home the maid was spying on us in the corner behind the curtains.

'The maid you mean?' I asked as I turned back to face the mysterious woman that has entered my life lately, but she was gone again.

1888

The morning was dawning, it feels like I have seen too many mornings rise despairingly over the lodgings and slums that my eyes have forlornly and some may say, unluckily come accustom to. My mind has often wondered how it could be, that divinity's eyes were shining ever so beautifully from a high off heaven setting with every morning's break, over this hell like surroundings. Was God, in all his power taunting us as he glanced down? The way the light is not white, but full of different colours as it bounced on the rooftops had given me a kind of hope, faith if you will that things will be alright in the end. As there will always be this light shining upon me, all I had to do was to wait until night become day again to see it.

I often thought many people may think I jest when I mention these thoughts, how can such a low class creature like me have such dreamy and wistful outlook upon life? But they don't understand that I am one of them. If they think they are extraordinary, then I am extraordinary, for I am no different to anyone.

Maybe I will be remembered as such, would there be anything wrong with that? Does someone have to be special and unique? Can a person not just pass away quietly, to whence they came? Never to be bothered with, or thought about again, how very peaceful that would be for me now. I have always wanted more from the magical present that is life; I wanted to be famous, to be spoke of on the lips of all people from young children to ageing soldiers I have seen littering the streets of the place I call home.

Now God has granted me everything I wanted, I do not want it anymore; I do not want to be famous for my death, for the way I leave this world. God is as clever as he is wicked.

The streets were starting to become busy of market and fish porters, butchers and bakers all having been awaken by the light from heaven to leave their homes and are going to work. All getting on with their lives, something I am finding hard to do.

'Maria,' I said quietly.

'Yes,' she answered in her carefree way.

'I need to go down to the river.'

'What now?'

'Yes, now,' I mumbled.

'But why Mary? I thought you would have been tired, you haven't slept.'

'I need to see something.'

'I don't know about this,' she answered, while looking at the cracks in the pavement and rolling her left foot from side to side.

'You don't have to come with me.'

'Yes, I do.'

'Well come on, then,' I said as I started walking in the opposite direction, I was in no mood to waste a moment of time, for *time runs on and we are powerless to stop it*. We began trotting along through the alleyways and side streets in an eerily silence. I wondered what was wrong with Maria; she seemed so upset about going to the river so much so that I didn't quite understand why. After all I hadn't asked her to come with me, she could have gone away, but she hasn't she decided to follow me. This girl was becoming as strange as the woman in her lair.

'How old are you Mary?' she suddenly asked me.

'Older than I was last night,' was my reply, to which Maria smiled.

'She has that effect on everyone.'

'How many has there been?'

'What do you mean?' she requested still looking towards the cracked pavement to which we were walking on.

'How many people go to her for past lives or future lives?' I asked.

'A few,' was an uncomfortable reply.

'Did they leave happy?'

'Not all,' she said sadly but still not looking at me.

'Why did you ask me, how old I was?'

'I was curious.'

'You know what that did for the cat, don't you?' I mocked although how I could not be serious at this moment I wasn't sure I could explain.

'Yes, let's not talk of all that.'

'I guess I will be talking to myself then,' I said as we headed to an end of a road and stopped on the stone wall that stood tall above the muddy shores.

'You have been here before, haven't you?'

'No.'

'But you seemed to know your way here?'

'I saw the way in my dreams, in the dream I had last night.'

'My God, my God!' Maria screamed at me which made me turn from looking out across the river sideways to look at her. She was standing a few feet behind me, as hard and cold as a stone. She grasped her mouth with her hand and squeezed tightly, to the point that her cheeks were becoming red and sore around her fingertips, *she was a ghost of her former self.*

'What is the matter with you?' I asked, to which she removed her hand away from her mouth leaving her finger marks on her cheek bone and she stared at me. I had never seen anyone stared at me the way Maria did that morning and I knew from the moment I saw it I would never forget it. For it was more than fear, more that fright for it was terror, sheer terror was what I saw in her eyes. 'Maria what is wrong?' I asked again as I moved closer to her, but she backed away from me. Was it I that had scared her so? What had I done?

'Take me away from here!' Maria shouted as she turned away from the shore and from me. She was in a state, she was panicking I could tell from her breathing.

'Maria, I do not understand,' I said.

'Why take me here? Oh why oh why? Why be so cruel to me? I need not to have seen this place; I need not to have known of this place! What a cruel thing to do!' Maria cried out to anyone that would have heard her, as she fell to her knees on the cold, hard cobbled stones. I bent down to try to pick her up but she pushed me away. 'Leave me be! Leave me be I say! You do not understand how could you? You do not know the pain I am in being here!' she shouted.

'What has made you so angry Maria? It is just the river, I wanted to see if it was here in the way I thought it would be, I only wanted to see the river,' I tried to explain, as I watched her roll around the street crying and behaving quite like a child of three, maybe that is what she is, just a child. A child lost in this underbelly of London, like I was. She has no body to look after her, I had my friends.

God, are you giving me a chance to do some good before I am due to leave? Is this why I was destined to meet that strange woman in her strange lair? Are you giving me the chance to become one of your angels, to sit beside you as you look down upon this land? I must look after this lost girl, she needs me too.

'It is more than a river, it is devil and it is hell, for it is the worse place of all!

'Come, come Maria. Let's go home, you were right in what you had said, I am tired and could do with some sleep, I just wanted to see the river but I should have gone home.'

'You were meant to have gone home,' she whispered.

'I know, I know let's go home now and if you want it could be your home.'

'You mean that?'

'Well, yes. I don't see why not.'

'But I see who not.'

'What?'

'Well wouldn't that fella you said you were with mind me living with you?'

'Joseph has left me, it is up to me what I do now and it is my place. I have to pay the rent, so why can't I have a nice girl like you stay with me? It makes sense, that way neither of us will be alone. Besides Joseph doesn't mean everything to me anymore, there is more important things going on, like looking after you.'

'Interesting,' Maria mumbled.

I am sorry I brought you here,' I managed to say, for she had stopped rolling around and started to wipe her eyes and nose, I moved nearer to her and she allowed me to pick her up this time.

'I am sorry too,' she whispered to me.

'I know you are,' I said in a motherly tone.

'Mary?' she asked as we began to move away from the shore and back amongst the smelly alleyways.

'What Maria?'

'We must never speak of this, of what just happened. Promise me that we won't,' she said pleadingly.

'If you don't want to talk of it, then we won't.'

'Promise?' she asked again.

'A sister's promise,' I said as I held out my pinkie finger, to which Maria hugged it with hers.

1898

I find myself shaking from head to toe, to the point I could imagine my brain sloshing from side to side inside my head, maybe that was why I could not think further than the sound I hear from my teeth has they rattle to their own tune and rhythm. I am feeling chilly and wondering if I had ever been colder than I was right now, there was talk in the Billing Club of a group of people travelling to the North

Pole and South Pole and whether 'the armchair sitters' thought all that fuss was worth the money or not because 'once you seen one load of the white snow substance you have seen them all'. All I know now is that I feel as if I had foolishly taken the mission myself, alone and was now there between my friends the ice and the snow. But saying that, there is also a distant feeling inside of my soul that was hot and slowly burning as if my organs were churning up and melting, I wonder, is this the start of another famous fever? I hope not, another fever would be the end of me I know it, I am weaken and would never admit this out loud but I am frail, I feel tried most of the time and although I know I am only middle aged I feel as if I have lived through many lives and situations, that I am old on the inside.

I am wrestling with a material that felt too close against my skin; it was making me experience the touch of death, slowly strangling me. As I move around I can sense the hairs on my legs and arms moving with me causing an itching irritation. Something is telling me I am wet all over, that I am having the sensation of swimming in a puddle, was it my own sweat? Again I hope not. I started tapping my neck for my throat had closed up so much that I am finding it hard to breathe, and I do so like to breathe.

I suppose I should explain what is happening to me and how I come to be in this state from walking through my front door. On the contrary to what I am now used to I don't think I am having a horrific hallucination, I do not feel as if I am in a trance or cannot understand what has happened to me so no, I do not believe I am in a dream this time.

I will try to remind myself of what has occurred as it may help my brain to focus on the situation at present. I was confused by the strange woman that had disappeared, leaving me alone on the pavement outside my house. I remember staring around up and down the now busy street seeing a number of normal things like coaches and their horses, a newspaper boy shouting about a crime, ladies walking in twos laughing and joking, gentlemen walking in harmony with their walking sticks but I was still feeling stumped and a little perplexed.

How does she manage to disappear and reappear so brilliantly, was she controlled by magic? How does she know me? And what is even stranger is that I feel I know her, not her now but her before, when she was young. I can't even understand myself at the best of times, how can I begin understand her? I remember giving up looking for her so I turned around and walked up the marble stairs to my front door and seeing the door move and open on its own account. I remember seeing the maid, standing there on the fresh hold of my home looking annoyed and irritated, I could swear if I could see her teeth they would be gnashing against each other. I moved pass her and handed her my quite soiled coat to which she took a distaste too and using the smallest part of her fingers to hold it.

'I have been worried Sir,' she said strongly as she took her eyes from what she would be classing as a rag to me.

'Didn't Charles tell you I was in the hospital?' I asked her.

'Yes he did Sir but you were meant to come home last night Sir and now it is late morning, almost afternoon.'

'I had some thinking to do.'

'You do realise, what you look like Sir don't you? ' she questioned.

'Yes, I find the 'down and out' look, quite appealing if you must know,' I said bowing at her.

'I don't find anything amusing Sir,' she said moodily.

'No, I guess you wouldn't.' I said sadly.

'Right Sir, you are not quite yourself, that is plain to see, now that I have you. I will look after you,' she said as she placed my coat on the chair and moved towards me.

'I am fine.'

'No, you are not!' she shouted, as she pushed me towards the stairs. So standing behind me all the way I was bundled up the stairs, along the landing and into the bathroom, where I was quickly stripped, off all my clothing and placed in the cast iron bath. I was told to stay put as the maid went off to get some ice for I was about to have a cold wash. She tipped the white cubes into the bath; I remember watching them fall from the rose wood bucket into the bath and on me. The pain I felt was annoying and I remember arguing that fact to her, but she was listening. So with me lying against sharp cubes of ice the maid went off the fill the bucket with cold water to which she tipped over my shoulders, the coldness hurt and shocked my body system, I started shivering straight away and I recall shouting at the maid at the top of my voice to no affect of the maid's actions at all. But it affected my voice and my throat closed.

At last I was placed in my bed, but I was not quite dry enough and had the quilt tucked tightly around my naked body, the material cling to my body and it felt as if I was being strangled. Too tired and in pain to move from the bed, that is where I find myself. I am feeling exposed and angry with being put like this and I am finding it hard to sleep, which was all I wanted to do moments before I walked through my own front door.

'Finding it hard to sleep, my dear boy?' boomed a voice from over the quilt. I moved it away from my head to see my good friend Charles sitting beside my bedstead, like he did at the hospital.

'I didn't hear you come in,' I whispered.

'No, I guess you didn't.'

'That maid, needs to be gone.'

'Oh come, come Thomas. Don't be too harsh on her; she cares for you that is rare to find in a maid.'

'She didn't listen to me.'

'Her emotions took over, that is all. It is quite common in women, something us men have to live with I suppose,' he said as he lit his cigar and lent back on the chair.

'How long have you smoked for Charles?'

'Why my dear boy, don't you remember? I have always smoked. Can't really do anything without my cigars' he said waving his open cigar case, with five brown, thin cigars all lined up at me. 'You don't remember that?' he asked.

'No, I can't recall seeing you smoke.'

'You must be ill Thomas.'

'Before you say it, I will take my medication tonight,' I butted in.

'That is reassuring, but I was going to mention having a break at my home in Kent, I know you wanted to solve Ellen's murder for me and that is very nice of you. But I feel I am losing a friend over it and I don't want to.'

'I failed you Charles,' I whispered.

'You failed me? Surely it is the other way round, my dear boy!'

'No, no. Listen to me, I was sure I could solve her murder so you could get on with your life for she was murdered Charles that I am sure. But everywhere I turn leads to a dead end, a very dead end,' I cried.

'Come, come Thomas. Don't get yourself in a state, it cannot be helped, you tried. That means a lot to me, honestly it does but I feel we should leave Ellen and all her business to rest, I feel I can do that Thomas now, but please do me this one favour. Please leave London for Blissful Hill in Kent,' And that was that, I did not argue with Charles as he was only thinking of me as any best friend would and so my living quarters were moved to the place in which he suggested, Blissful Hill.

Chapter Fourteen

1888

It was a cold November morning, when I was making my way home from The Ten Bells public house. It had been a rather successful night by all accounts, I managed to have four clients, one of which I administered a cheeky snatch of the gentleman's wallet and another I charged double the normal price as he seemed new to that type of thing, plus he seemed rather taken with me. He didn't say so, but a woman can always tell.

My last days had been to a certain extent quite blissful, Maria and I had become firm friends spending most of our time together, either working the streets or being at home we are always together. In fact the only reason why I walking around the streets of Whitechapel on my own this morning was that I few nights ago Maria must have caught something, as she was terribly ill, being sick everywhere. I have been quite worried and it brought forward the motherly feeling I always thought I had, so I told her to stay home last night. I had just got to my door when I felt a sensation of someone staring at me. I turned to face the small alleyway I had just walked down to see Joseph standing there as broad as day; I did not want him to bother Maria in the state she was in so I began to walk towards him.

I took my time to get to him as I was unsure how I was going to deal with him. His stance was a little abnormal for his legs were further apart than they would naturally be; his hands were curled in the shape of a fist and were lying on his hips. His flat cap was placed firmly on his head pushing the sides down to cover the tips of his ears; this made it hard for me to see his eyes. Whether he did this on purpose as he knew I liked to see people's eyes as they told me so much about how a person was feeling, I don't know but in truth I wouldn't have put that passed him.

I have always loved this man I was walking towards, I loved him so much that I saw passed on the malicious and brutal elements of his character for the moments of sweetness and the feeling of being mutually together with him, but now things have changed for all I can see is the wickedness and the horrid vices in him. His white shirt was somewhat clean, for the fish guts were faded. Who cleaned his shirt I wonder? It certainly wasn't me, so he had been playing away again, why I am not surprised? How many times had he made an argument out of nothing just so he could leave and live with someone else? Too many times for me to count and yet I always took him back, what a fool I was! No wonder he felt as if he could use me, silly young Mary will always take him back, I bet that is what he is thinking right now as he watches me walk up to him, well not this time Jo.

He was two different people really that is how I can describe his nature, one would be mean and insulting towards me the other would be a real gent, always caring and thoughtful, always saying the right things. Jo was always good at saying the right things, he could fool most people into thinking he was always nice and compassionate, and he managed to fool me.

Even when he had hit me, blaming me for him being out of work, he always made it out to be my fault, he had me saying sorry most nights. He claimed he didn't want me working the streets because I was better than that, but when I tried to better myself he wouldn't have it. He stopped me learning to read because he felt as if he was in control of me if he read to me. I don't even know if he was reading the truth to me or whether he was trying to scare me off the streets, with detailed descriptions of what Jack the Ripper was doing to my friends.

He used to laugh at the throat slicing, saying 'well that will sure shut Annie up!' and he seemed to actually praise him for the work he was doing as 'they all are dirty little whores' and he didn't want me to be part of that life. Even though I was a streetwalker before I was with him and actually that is why I met him, for he was my client. I wonder what he will say about Jack the Ripper when in a few days time he will kill again. Will he be full of regret? Or will the good old Jo charm come out once more, to captivate and mesmerize an audience, making himself out to be the weeping widower? Somehow I can just see that happening.

I would be asking too much for someone, somewhere, maybe in years to come to find out what Jo was really like, to see through the lies that no doubt he will tell for his moment in the limelight. I laugh to myself as I think of this actually happening, to think of someone finding out the truth behind him that they may even think that Jo was Jack the Ripper all along. I say I laugh at the thought of this but there is a lump in my throat and icily sensation when I think that Jo could well be Jack, for it is not hard to imagine. Could Jo really kill me? Is that why I will be another victim of Jack the Ripper? Because I will find out of that night that I have known who Jack the Ripper really is, a haunting thought and what is as scary to think of is that I might be walking towards Jack the Ripper right now, if that is so he a little too early I will be safe today.

'I am guessing you want to talk to me.' I said.

'You could say that,' was his moodily reply.

'What do you want?' I huffed.

'Oh come, come. Where is the Mary love? Normally because you haven't seen me for a while you would have ran up that alleyway and jumped into my arms.'

'To watch you drop me, and laugh at me while I lay on the floor you mean.'

'You've changed.'

'Are you saying that wouldn't have happened?'

'No, of course it would. But who are you to stop me laughing at you.'

'You can be quite cruel Jo.'

'It never bothered you before.'

'It does now Jo, I have managed to cope with my life without you in it and to be honest I haven't been happier.'

'A woman can do that for ya,' he mumbled, as he looked away from me towards the pavement.

'What do you mean?'

Jo looked up at me sternly as he replied 'I heard all about it Mary, don't try and deny it. You are living with another woman.'

'So? What has that got to do with you or anyone else in fact?'

'You don't even deny it!' he shouted as he looked ruthlessly at me. A few months ago that look would have scared me to a shaking mess but not now, not today. He was just too pointless a person to think of in the larger scheme of things.

'Why should I deny it, it is true. I am looking after a young girl that has no one to turn to.'

'But you go everywhere with her.'

'So? Jo please come to your point quickly, I am in need of some sleep,' I said as suddenly I felt a pair of hands around my throat and I was being lifted up and across a little way until my back hit the sharp, hard wall of number 26 Dorset Street.

‘She is living in my home!’ he shouted with his face inches for mine. His face was all screwed up and his jaw was clinched, he looked as if he was one of those mad dogs I have seen stropping around.

‘No, she is living in my home, you left remember. You left me alone,’ I squeaked out as I struggled to pull his hand away, as I did so he released me and I dropped to the floor grasping for breath.

‘Well you seem to have done well for yourself.’

‘Did you think I would crack up and go to Bedlam because you left me Jo? Well I can tell you that will not happen,’ I said as I pushed myself up slowly using the wall to stabilize myself to which made Jo burst out laughing, but it was a different kind of laugh. He wasn’t mocking me this time, there actually sounded as if there was some respect in that laugh. It made me feel better about myself.

‘I like the new you Mary.’

‘Yeah well you are not the only one,’ I said as I began to walk back through the alleyway.

‘Wait!’ Joseph shouted.

‘What now?’ I asked without turning to face him.

‘I want you back Mary.’

'You always do Jo, but I wouldn't, not now. Goodbye Jo,' was my sad reply, as I carried on walking to door, as I opened my door I took the chance to look back at where Joseph was standing to see he had disappeared. I don't know if my words had hurt him or not but I had a feeling I may have caused myself more trouble. But in truth I do not care, for how much trouble could he really do to me when there is someone else out there more deadly and evil than he would ever be.

1898

Being in Kent is lovely and quite exquisite, being just outside London and all it quirks. I hear birds singing loudly and of a very proud cockerel that sits on the fence in front of the large manor house, he wakes me every morning with his delightful noise. It seems a world away from the busy streets on London and I am enjoying every second of it. I feel as if I have been released from the chains of hell to arrive in the beautiful surroundings of heaven. I have taken to enjoy long evening walks around the countryside in which I watch the sun fall, leaving the sky and every cloud that's in it turning a golden colour. I have learnt to paint, and catch to beautifulness that this life has to give us. I have even taken to leaving my flask behind.

Charles meanwhile isn't around that much, but he has all his servants write reports about what I do from one day to the next. I don't mind that much; for I am quite enjoying my break and learning new skills. One morning I had taken the opportunity to walk along the county roads to the nearest town. Clostchester was an old shipping town that has one side against the sea of the channel; it is enchanting to walk along the stony beaches, smelling to sweet delightful scent of fresh salt water fish, seeing the stream boats floating along the watery waves. Everybody has a smile on their faces, there are poor mixed with the rich but nobody seems to mind, everyone is in the same boat as they say. This is my kind of town, and I began wondering if I could ever think of moving here from the City, to become the writer I had always wanted to be and maybe if I became good enough to draw my own illustrations, not to rely on anyone else's interruptions of my words.

I had placed myself with my easel on the stony beach that morning and began to sketch a corroded boat that was lying almost abandoned a few feet from the shore line when from behind me I heard a voice, 'Hello there, I say hello!' I turned to see the vicar of this parish, standing on the pavement that leads onto the beach. 'I would come over to you, but my poor feet cannot stand on the pebbles that move in whatever way they wish!' I folded down my easel and stood up; I began to move gingerly across the stones towards the vicar, when I was near enough he spoke again. 'You are a smashing gentleman by leaving what you were doing to come and talk to little old me.'

'I do try my best to be polite.'

'And polite you are Sir, I hope you don't mind me disturbing me like this, but I do like to get to know everybody in my parish. You are the new boy from the big smoke aren't you?'

'Well I wouldn't call myself a boy now but yes I am from London.'

'Here for a little break are we?'

'Yes, I have been somewhat ill of late and my friend thought a little trip to your pretty town would do me wonders.'

'And so it shall Sir, so it shall! I have often wondered what living in London would be like, must be quite appealing hanging with all those famous people and what not. But do tell are you famous?' he asked, to which I couldn't help myself but laugh, to which he laughed back.

'I am perhaps not as famous as I should be.'

'I am sorry for my choice of words; I have a habit of getting myself into trouble.'

'I don't mind, you are a breath of fresh air to the types of people I meet in London. My name is Thomas Dunn and I am a writer.'

'Thomas Dunn, I can't say I have ever read one of your books.'

'No, I don't believe it is to your taste. I am a horror writer.'

'Horror? Well you are quite right in what you say then; horror is not to my taste, I am sorry to say. I don't know whether you will get any spooky goings on here.'

'I am pleased to hear that.'

'I guess you would be, the only slightly moody peck in this great town is the house on the hill.'

'The house on the hill?'

'Oh yes, it is down the county road, it a big manor house, it more sad than anything.'

'Are you talking of Blissful Hill manor house?'

'Ah you have heard of it I see, yes that's the place. The name should be changed, poor thing it was.'

'What happened?'

'Murder Sir.'

'Murder?'

'Oh yes, it was certainly murder, one of the cruellest murders, you could imagine Sir. It was I would say about fifty years ago. I had just come to this town and the family in Blissful Hill was very friendly towards me, and I began to visit them on the odd occasion. Now let me see, there was the father George, he worked in London most of the time, some business I don't know about, trained to be a doctor but went in politics instead, seemed to be quite harsh with everyone he met, and some say with his wife Charlotte. There was a disgrace in London, something involving him and that's why they moved down here, to start a fresh one would say I guess. Well his wife on the other hand was quite lovely, caring and the kind of grace to carry of any indignity. She was quite a life of any party, and many parties they had too.'

'Sounds like you got to know her very well.'

'Indeed I did so, she was quite taken with religion, forgive and forget that sort of thing. She seemed quite devoted to her husband, even though he didn't show the same emotion towards her; she always had a good word to say about him. There was a little girl, I only saw her a few times she seemed different to her mother, there was a look of sadness in her eyes and she spent most of the time with a maid they had picked up in London. The maid I found to be a little cold and distant, she did not seem happy at all, I never understood why, there was some scandal with her becoming pregnant with a boy but I never listen to such talk.'

'Of course you don't,' I said sarcastically, but the vicar didn't seem to notice as he carried on.

'Well anyway I must get to the point, on a certain night, can't remember the date of hand there was fire, very bright it was, could see it for miles. When the town got there to help there found the house empty, all part from the lady of the house. She was found lying on her bed, her skin burned off leaving the bones on show.'

'Oh my!'

'Yes it was ghastly, I have never seen such a thing and she was so beautiful but to see her like that, it still haunts me.'

'Where was everyone else?'

‘Well that is the strangest thing, the father was away in London as always but the maid and the girl was gone, never to return.’

‘You said it was murder.’

‘Yes, it turns out that before the fire started the lady of the house was poisoned, sadly the police came to the thinking the master of the house poisoned her and when back to work.’

‘Could he have done it?’

‘I don’t believe so, but then I am no detective.’

‘What a haunting story, I would never have thought something so seedy would have occurred here.’

‘Like I say, Blissful Hill is a sad little peck on our landscape, but I am glad someone is living in that big old place now, it looked so gloomy and depressing standing there on the hill as I reminder of the things that have happened.’

‘Yes, my friend Charles must have brought it at a rock bottom price.’

‘Oh I see, you are a friend of Charles’s, why didn’t you say? A jolly nice fella always gives to the church you know.’

‘Yes Charles has always been friendly.’

‘Where did you meet him?’

'Well it was, I don't know really. I feel like I have known him for a lifetime.'

'I quite understand, well I must be off, things to do and what not, see you on Sunday I hope.'

'Yes on the dot of the bells ringing.'

'Good show Thomas! Good show!' and with that he was gone, waving to many people as he went. Harmless old fella that one, quite cheerful but with a horrid story to tell, I thought to myself. That really shocked me to hear of such a thing happening in my class of heaven, but I guess murder happens everywhere, everywhere that I am anyway.

1888

As I walked through my own door the stale and disgusting scent of long-standing sick hit me hard in the face, the room was very dark and almost bleak in feeling. If it hadn't been for the sight movement of the bed I would have never known that Maria was still here. She was lying flat on her back, her head facing towards the wall, her legs raised up and one arm was placed under her head while the other flopped over the edge of the cast iron bed. She made slight noises of pain while she breathed in her sleep, the bucket I had placed by the bed was almost full, the tea I left was not touched and either was the scraps of food. She is clearly unwell, I am seriously wondering if I will lose her soon. As I stood over her, considering what my life would have been like without her, she must of sense me as she stirred.

‘I am alright Mary,’ she managed to say through her dry, cracked lips.

‘Well I can quite clearly see that,’ I said as I turned from her to the small wash basin and filled a ginger bottle up with water and passed it to her.

‘Thank you,’ she said after she had drunk from the bottle.

‘I think we need to talk.’

‘Oh? What about? If I didn’t already know’ she said as she slowly pulled herself up and swung her legs around so that they were placed on the floor, beside the bucket. I placed myself beside her and said,

‘I am out of my depth here Maria; I don’t know what to do with you. You are plainly ill and need to see a doctor but I cannot afford it.’

‘I know.’

‘The only person I can think of is.’

‘No, not her.’

‘She seemed to care for you the last time I saw you both together, maybe she will know something that could help.’

‘I said not her. I am not ready to see her again.’

'I still don't understand why you stopped seeing her, but you may need her, I don't want to lose you and I am feeling like I am Maria.'

'You care for me; I can see that but please think of something else,' she said pleadingly.

'I can get a nurse, there is a nurse living on the Whitechapel Road that owns me a favour, I can get her,' I said to which Maria's eyes brightened for the first time in days.

'Yes, Mary. Do that then,' she said as she lay back down on the bed and turned away from me.

'I will not be long,' I said as I stood up and made my way to the door, Maria made a noise of goodbye and I left, shutting the door behind me.

I hated lying to her, but I needed to do something to help her and the strange woman is the only answer I can think of. So I retraced my footsteps back to the strange woman's lair, hoping against everything that she was in. I reached Montague Street, it was quite unlike the last time I had ventured along this old and acrimonious road, it felt as if it had altered somewhat, whether it was seeing it in daylight that was giving it an anonymous undertone or whether it is simply an perplexing street I have no idea but where else would a strange lady live but a queer street in a curious city?

I can see her house instantly; the red paint was shining ever so brightly in the morning sun. I drew myself nearer and tapped on the door, but my face saddens with the no answer I got. I started to move the door and was about to step inside when a voice shouted out from behind me.

'Oi! What yer game?' I turned to see a portly, big breasted lady standing with her hands on her hips, staring hard-heartedly at me from the starting of the strange woman pathway.

'I was seeing whether the lady was in,' was my blunt answer. The female's expression changed as she started to laugh,

'Well I haven't heard her being called a lady before! Good friends are you?'

'No, I met her more than a month ago and was wondering if she could help me.'

'Her help you! Well I don't know who you are but you should be on stage with that act, you are having me in hysterics!'

'I don't understand.'

'I can see that my love, where she is she can't help anyone.'

'She has died?'

'Worse love, she is in Newgate.'

'She is in prison!'

'Yes, although we all thought Bedlam would be the place she would end up.'

'Quite I can understand that, but why Newgate?'

'She was found covered in blood, screaming murder in Courts Row.'

'She had murdered someone in Court's Row?'

'That's what we all think, although no one can make out what she was screaming about, but to who she murdered we have no idea.'

'There was no body?'

'No, but the blood must have come from somewhere.'

'True,' I said as I walked towards the lady, 'well that was a little bit of a shock, I can tell you, well thank you for the information,' as mentioned as I walked passed her. Instead of saying goodbye to me as I thought she would she once again shouted

'Oi!' I turned to face her again when she asked, 'You don't like cats do you?'

'I am sorry?' I questioned.

'Cats. You like them?'

'I love them, but I can't have one.'

'Why is that?'

'I am not going to be here for very long,' I said sadly.

'Oh, right you are then. I just found this ginger cat, hanging around here. So I took it home, but she is causing all sorts of *mischief*.'

'What did you say?' I asked, something the lady had just said rang a bell with me.

'Well I was just saying she is a bit of a handful, that's all. But if I am honest she is such a sweet little thing and good company too.'

'I think she will answer to the name of Mischief.'

'Oh? Why do you think that?'

'Something in my waters is telling me so,' I said as I turned away from the lady for the last time. The strange woman wasn't mad when she was talking of a Mischief; she was talking about her cat. Maybe she is not mad at all. But I must find out what has happened to her, I must go to Newgate if my feet can manage to carry me there.

Chapter Fifteen

1898

I decided to head back towards Blissful Hill rather than go back to my art work on the beach, the story the vicar had just told me had caught my attention and curiosity and I could not stop thinking about it, so the creative feeling I once had, had disappeared. Maybe there was something in the house still that might hold the solvable answer to the dreadful murder that happened so long ago.

I entered the manor house through the large gothic styled hallway, placed my cane in its rose wood and brass stand and walked through the second set of half glass doors into a very grand sitting area. Its white marbled fireplace dominated the whole room, with its quite ghastly looking faces carved into the marble top, there was heavy dark wood panelling everywhere you looked which was very much in style as few years back and there was a set a large American guns hanging across each other on the wall, a closer look would show they had not been used so just a decorated piece, maybe a gift. There was two rather large portraits in the room either side of the fireplace, one of a man holding an account book, leaning on a wooden cabinet that held a number of hospital based equipment. With an interesting clock behind him, as I looked at the clock a odd sensation came over me, for I had not seen a clock like this one before but I knew the name of the maker. It was a name

I have become accustom to for it was my own, it was a Dunn Clock.

The man was staring quite forcefully at the onlooker, who chose to glance at him almost as if it was wrong to do so, this clearly was George, the business man who spent most of his time in London. It stroke me that it was rather odd to still see the old master of the house, hanging pride of place in the entrance room for all to see, when the last moments of his life he was casted as a murderer.

But it was the other portrait that hanged almost lonely in thought that captured my heart; it was of a woman sitting on chair looking down at a wicker cradle that was lying at her feet. I get the feeling that this should be a lovely motherly moment incarcerated in paint, but there is something in the eyes of this woman that tells me this is not the case, she looks almost heartbreakingly sad but why would that be so? I wondered to myself just when I felt a presence behind me; I turned to see an old man, with a scar running across his right eye, he was white in hair and black in suit. He stood with one of his ivory gloved hands by his side and the other holding a white glove that was no doubly was one of Charles's. His shiny, waxed black shoes were tightly pressed together as he stood there, I would not be so surprised if this gentleman was in the army in his early years.

'You are looking at Charlotte Sir, the last lady of this house,' he sternly stated.

'She was very beautiful.'

'That she was Sir, I quite agree with you there.'

'Did you know of her?'

'Yes Sir, she was very kind to me. I was let out of the army early, due to my blindness,' he stated as he pointed to his right eye with his only free hand 'I didn't think I would be able to work again but the lady took me on and I have been a butler here ever since.'

'Surely when the house became empty of its master and lady, you had to leave.'

'No Sir, I am a part of this house it has never been empty to me.'

'What do you mean by that?' I asked a little perplexed at his reply.

'Do you believe in ghosts Sir?' he asked back at me.

'Do you?'

'When I first came here, I would have laughed at the thought of it. After all I had seen in the war, I thought that once you die that was it.'

'But now you think differently?'

'Yes Sir, don't get me wrong I have not taken leave of my senses for it is true in what I say. I have seen a ghost.'

'A ghost of who may I ask?'

'Charlotte Sir, at least I thought it was her Sir.'

'But you are unsure?'

'Yes and no Sir, at the time I saw her I was so very sure it was her, she looked so beautiful Sir, but the master, your friend said I was mad and if I don't forget what I have seen he would ask me to leave. I don't want to leave Sir, I love it here, I have been here for so long,' he paused almost as a second thought he said 'You will not tell him, what I have said to you will you? It will make him angry that I am still thinking of it, but you see I pass that portrait everyday Sir and I can't forget it.'

'I will not mention a word of it, I know how Charles can get sometimes, but it sounds as if you had seen this ghost recently is that not so?'

'Yes Sir, it was a few days ago, just before you arrived Sir.'

'And Charles was not happy with you mentioning it to him?'

'No Sir, he was not happy at all.'

'Interesting, does Charles know of the late master and lady?'

'I would say so Sir, but I do not understand why. It was mentioned that he went out of his way to buy this place because he knew of the sad history.'

'Why would he have done such a thing?' I asked almost to myself but the butler answered.

'Like I have said Sir, I have no idea; it was such a sad ending to a lovely family.'

'I have heard that to be the case.'

'Is that why you were looking at the lady Sir?'

'Yes, there is something quite eye-catching about her, almost as if I know her,' I said as I glanced back at the portrait.

'She had a certain appeal to many people who met her Sir; she was very motherly by nature.'

'Which doesn't explain this portrait,' I said still facing the picture in question. I suddenly felt the butler move beside me to look at it with me.

'You are quite right Sir, I have never noticed it before but she has been quite clever as she always was.'

'Clever you say?'

'Why yes Sir, you see she never wanted her portrait painted, she hated the idea of it. But the master, he was very powerful and she dared not disobey his wishes.'

'You said she had been clever.'

'Well it came at a time, when she had given birth to a girl.'

'So she should be happy, but clearly she is not.'

'Well you see Sir, a few years before the birth of the girl; the lady had lost a child in late pregnancy. I don't want to say anything bad about the master Sir but he had one of his rages and pushed her down the stairs.'

'My god!'

'Quite Sir, she lost the child after that. The master told everyone not to mention it again to anyone. Although I think enough time has passed for me to tell you, the lady was not even allowed to morn for it Sir, I guess the master did not wish to feel guilty.'

'So Charlotte had used the fact that she had given birth to a girl to put a cradle in the picture, but the cradle means the other child but she didn't want her husband to know and that is why she is sad, is that what you are guessing at?' I asked.

'It is not a guess Sir, the sheeting in the cradle is pink Sir, not blue.'

'That is odd is it not? For pink is the common colour for boys, it means to be strong and powerful, blue is the colour for girls. Although I think pink will suit girls far better, it seems a cuter colour for little girls.'

'That is as maybe Sir, but the child she had lost was going to be a boy.'

1888

The clouds were gathering together under one blanket of dark grey mass giving the surroundings an even more depressing atmosphere as if it really needed any more discouraging sentiment, for I standing within yards of the most smoulderingly motionless stone built building I have ever had to stand amongst. Newgate Prison had a reputation for sucking the life and soul out of anyone, the cells smelt of dead rotting bodies of the past and the recent toilet mess that was covered in straw. There was always one barred window in every chamber but no one ever looked out of it because of the way the prison was built, all the cells faces the same terrible sight. The sight of the hangman's noose, being able to see what will be the last moment in their lives could be very haunting, something I am now becoming aware of everything time I pass through my front door.

I moved in and was greeted by a sad little scene of which a man was being dragged by two burly looking prison officers to the cells, the man was trying with all his might to pull back so he could spend more precious seconds with his wife and children, the wife was crying and the children were screaming but at last the officers got their way and the man was pulled away causing the mother to hug her children as her husband disappeared out of her sight. There was another official looking gentleman standing in the room, he looked mean and cruel. Those descriptions were very apt as he moved over to the mother and children and said 'If you do not stop crying, I will not you allow to see your Jim until he is being hanged!'

'Please Sir, my children are upset they love their father so,' the mother tried to explain.

'Well their love is misplaced, loving a villain is not the wisest of things to do, and neither is the noise in which they are making.'

'They will stop Sir, please allow me to see my husband.'

'Don't be long about it!' he shouted as he signalled her to follow where her husband disappeared to.

'You wait here, you two. Be nice to the gentleman and no more crying,' the mother said to both her children, as good as her word the children stopped crying and sat down on the floor. I took the moment of silence to walk up to the officer.

'Please Sir; is it true you have a woman in the cells you picked up from Courts Row?'

'What is it to you?' was his gruff reply.

'I believe she is my mother,' at this statement he decided to look at me, he paused before replying to look me up and down and I could tell he liked what he saw.

'Well I must say miss that would be very interesting.'

'Oh and why would that be?' I asked in a flirty way.

'She is quite mad you know, and you don't take me as the mad sort.'

'No?' I said as I moved closer. 'What sort am I?'

'You are the pretty sort.'

'What a kind gentleman you are, now can you let a pretty sort in to see her mother?'

'I should not.'

'I won't tell, if you don't,' I said, I could see that he was thinking it over until he finally said.

'Alright, it is the cells down the hall, and then you turn left; follow one of my officers.'

'Thank you,' I said as I moved away to which he grabbed my arm

'What do I get for my troubles?' he seedily asked.

'I will let you know when I come back.'

'Right you are then, don't be too long,' he nauseatingly mentioned as he released my arm and I moved down the smelly stone hallway, following one of his burly men. I moved along the cells not seeing one woman in any of them, I am beginning to wonder if this all a big trick being played on me, but then in the last cell, there she was lying flat down on the straw.

'Wake up you dirty tramp! Your daughter is here to see you!' the guard shouted to which the strange woman moved a little, 'Good luck getting anything sensible out of her!' the guard mentioned as he left us alone to talk through the bars. The woman moved a little more but without turning to face me she calmly asked,

‘What are you doing here Maria?’

‘It is not Maria,’ I replied, to which she turned sharply and looked shocked at me.

‘Mary?’

‘It is.’

‘I am sorry; I thought when the guard said daughter that Maria might use that as an excuse to see me.’

‘I see, well she is unable to do anything.’

‘She is unwell?’

‘Yes, that is why I am here, she needs help,’ I pleaded, to which she moved to the stone bed and sat down picking out all the straw pieces that were still attached to her soiled clothing.

‘I have done all I can for her.’

‘Look, I understand something has gone on between you too, but she needs your help.’

‘She has asked for my help?’

‘No she does not know I am here, I am really worried.’

‘You care for her, like I knew you would,’ was her strange reply.

‘Are you going to help?’ I asked impatiently.

'Not if she has not asked for it,' she said as she lay back down. 'Now you can go, you have done all you could, now go I need to think.'

'Think about what?' I asked in a raised tone for I was quite annoyed with the uncaring feeling I was getting from the strange woman.

'All of what I have seen,' was her spooky reply.

'Why are you in here?' I asked, to which her eyes opened and stared at me.

'I am in here because of what I have seen.'

'What have you seen?'

'Murder, I seen murder,' was her simple reply, at the word of murder I jumped a little and thoughts of the dream I had at the strange woman's lair ran through my head so I quickly wanted to change the subject.

'Please help me with Maria for I believe she is dying!' I screamed at her.

'Dying? What makes you believe that?' she said as she bolted up for the stone bed.

'Well, for she is being constantly sick and is too weak to eat.'

'Is she bleeding?'

'I have seen no blood.'

'No womanly blood?'

‘No, none of that either.’

‘She needs a hot bath.’

‘I don’t think a wash can help.’

‘Very hot, the hottest you can make it and if you can get one, a midwife.’

‘A midwife?’ I asked placing my hand around the bars of the cell.

‘Yes a midwife, for Maria is pregnant.’

1898

I looked towards the dismal painting that had been the focus of the butler and mine’s conversation. It is quite an adroit and ingenious piece of art, which showed the hidden character of this woman. As well as her natural beauty that shined ever so brightly even in this sad circumstance and the dullness because of the age of this artwork, her concealed and clandestine temperament was one of great shrewdness and dexterity. I am in awe of the lady before me and the fact I am beginning to have such a high regard for unknown female, saddens me when the thoughts of her life and the way she had to live it enters my head. She had such a miserable existence, how she had the vivacity to keep calm and carry on I cannot imagine.

‘Would you like a drink Sir?’ the elderly butler questioned as I sat down in one of luxurious chairs that stood within the splendid sitting room.

'A port would be nice,' I said, still trying to figure out what I had just heard, as I was passed the drink in which I asked for I said 'This master of the house sounds like a bad lot.'

'I don't like talking of the master,' the butler said as he stood opposite me.

'And yet his portrait is still hanging there,' I said as I took a sip from the glass.

'It wasn't always Sir; in fact it was the new master who put it back up.'

'Charles put it up? But you said he knows the story of the late master and his lady.'

'That he does Sir.'

'Sometimes my friend confuses me.'

'He does have the ability to be two different people that is for sure,' the butler mentioned, in truth although I heard his words I was in some kind of buoyant dream and didn't quite take notice of them. I took another sip of my glass and sat back in the chair, it was then that I become aware of the butler was itching to leave and carry on with his duties, probably thinking of the unknown time Charles would enter wanting whatever is wrong with his gloves to be fixed.

'You have a duty to do,' I mentioned.

'Yes Sir, I was meant to have done it a few days ago but with the shock of the ghost and making sure you are settled well here, I forgot and I never know when the master is due back.'

'He does not write on ahead then.'

'No, I mean he did to mention you were going to stay and should be watched upon.'

'I thought I was being watched somehow.'

'The master worries about you.'

'Yes well, what is wrong with Charles's famous white gloves?' I asked.

'He has caught them on something, something he could not remember at the time Sir and ripped a small piece of their material Sir, has you can see,' the butler said as he bowed slightly to display the one glove with missing material. I glance at it only for a short time as I had not real interest in them.

'I see, well I will not hold you any longer then, my dear man. Thank you for telling more of the story of the ghosts that live here.'

'Very well Sir, but it will not be repeated to the master of the house?' he asked cautiously.

'You have already had my word on that subject, but perhaps you will allow a writer's imaginings to mix some fact with a lot of fiction when some time has passed, would you not say so?'

'That would be agreeable, but perhaps you could make me a little warm for the readers, and maybe not mention my name.'

'That I can do,' I said as I watched the nameless butler walk out of the room. For how long I sat in this chair I had no idea for I was lost in a world of past lives. There must be some more information about this rather strange family, but where to look I wonder? The butler mention that Charles knew all about their sad history maybe he would have the information in his study, the door to his study had always been closed since I have been here, and normally I would not like to pry into other people's belongings but I am sure Charles will not mind, for he did say to make myself at home. I placed the glass on the small round table and moved across the room to the other end and positioned my hand over the gold coloured brass handle when I heard,

'I think you will find that door to be off bounds to the likes of you,' said a rather formidable womanly voice from behind me, I glanced down at the brass knob to see in the reflection a woman standing behind me dressed in black.

'So you are the one that is watching me are you?' I said without turning around to face the rather rude woman.

'I am the one that is doing I have been told if that is what you mean.'

'You have taken a dislike to me that I can tell. Although why you have I cannot explain.'

'It is simple.'

'Is it?' I asked as I pulled my head straight to face the wooden panelling, but still without turning around to face the horrid little woman. It was rather a strange feeling being so close to a closed door, so close in fact I could every knot in the wood work.

'I think you will find it is, you are not my master, and yet you walk around this place as if you are him.'

'I was told to make myself at home.'

'I do not care what you were told; when the master is away you are under my control.'

'Your control you say?'

'That is what I was told.'

'Well in that case, I will repeat you words back to you for I do not care for what you were told,' to which she huffed and walked away for the sight in the brass handle, far away enough to end the conservation but too far away to leave me on my own in this relatively large room. From that moment on I decided that something quite strange and mysterious was going on around the manor house called Blissful Hill and I was only inches away from discovering what it could be. I decided to walk away from the study door under the watchful eye of who I would take it to be the maid; for I knew I would be back when the steady eyeballs of the discourteous and quite bad-mannered member of staff that dressed as dark as her nature were not watching me.

Chapter Sixteen

1888

I left the vulgar stone build Newgate Prison feeling a little shocked and to be honest a little impure, you would think I would get used to exploiting my body for certain means but the reality is that you never get used to the feeling of being manipulated by the worse of all the male creatures in this City.

After what I had to do just to walk out of the incarceration I had to be truthful and quite frank with myself by saying I was feeling rather low, but the shocked feeling comes in when I think of what I have just heard from the lips of the strange woman. Maria was pregnant, why didn't I think of that before? I thought that because Maria had only been working the streets for a month I wouldn't have to think of things of that nature, but I presume she is young and fertile. I must get back to her as soon as possible, after of course I find a local midwife. Although the streets of Whitechapel do not seem to have any 'local' nurses as they all appear as if the poor class of hospital staff have come across the waters from Russia, wherever Russia is. I have only heard of the word Russia, from bits and pieces of conservations between the working men in the public houses. Apparently all these Russian families are coming across from their hometown filling our streets and our homes and what seems to be most important, they were filling our jobs with cheap labour and that hasn't gone down too well in the good hearted nature of our local lads.

Anyway I know of this Russian woman that lives in an alleyway of Whitechapel Road, she seems a little odd in nature but compare to the strange lady I had just left in that prison she isn't half as bad. Most people class her as odd because of the way she looks, she wore her long knotted limp, brown hair parted in the middle and tied in a rather large bun. She is always dressed in the same light brown dress that has, what was once white lace but now had turned a light yellow sitting around the neck line. Her face is very unusual as the shape of her eyes are rather too large, her nose is very manly and long and there is two substantial strain teeth permanently on show through her two fat lips.

When the play of Dr Jekyll and Mr Hyde came out a few months ago, in a theatre not that far away from Buck's Row they had said that the look of Edward Hyde was taken from this Russian woman who is only known as Jill. Even though I knew all this, when I finally reached the door of this out of the ordinary looking woman and she answered, I had the overwhelming feeling of queasiness and found myself looking instantly towards the flooring that was inside her house.

'Yes? What do you want?' was her stern introduction to me said in broken English.

'My friend is unwell.'

'So?' she asked as she shrugged her shoulders.

'I was wondering whether you could help,' I replied in a nervous way.

'You want me to help you? Don't make me laugh,' she said in a parsimonious manner.

'What is wrong with me asking help from you?' I asked.

'Well for a start, you have not been able to look at me in the eyes,' she calmly said, to which I bolt upright and I managed to glance at her. 'That is no point trying to look at me now, I know your type, think you can look down at me because of the way I look and now you want me to help your friend! You disgust me!' she began to shout as she went to shut the door, but I was quick and managed to fit my foot in between the gap in the door stopping her from doing so.

'I am truly sorry for the way I have behave towards you miss, I have heard the words of other people and I acted on them badly I will admit to you. You are not a monster, you are not some person to look down upon, you are a lady and most of all you are a woman, a woman who must care to show that spirit on the outset.'

'Well I.' Jill stammered.

'I thought so,' I butted in. 'Well is makes me wonder if this caring woman can care for another young girl that badly needs her help, can you?' I asked as I continued to stare at her.

‘You care for this girl I can see,’ she almost whispered.

‘She has no one else, she can go to,’ I quickly retorted.

‘She is young is she not?’

‘She is very young.’

‘Been working the streets?’

‘Only for a short while.’

‘But you believe her to be pregnant?’

‘I believe so,’ I answered then it was her turn to look away as she thought about the situation.

‘Can she not come here? I do not like going out, you see. People are so cruel and they laugh at the sight of me, the children are the worse. Mrs Hyde they call me. At first I didn’t understand for I hadn’t read the works of Mr Stevenson, but I manage to leave my house at night and went to the theatre on one of those nights, the sight of that Edward Hyde character was quite gruesome and unsettling, to think that anyone could think I could marry a man like him makes me quite depressed when I think of it.’

‘I am sorry to hear that but I feel I will not be able to move her.’

‘She is being that unwell?’

'She is very unwell; otherwise I would not have bothered you.'

'So she is being sick.'

'Sick by the bucket loads.'

'I see, wait a few minute while I get my scarf,' she said as she left her door and disappeared inside her house, I took that opportunity to move my foot out of the door way so I could stand more naturally. Within minutes Jill was back at the door with her black scarf placed somewhat in an odd manner as the scarf was not placed around her neck but over most of her face. 'We have to be quick,' she said as she shut her own door, it was then I first realised she had a Gladstone bag with her.

'What is that for?' I asked as I pointed to the bag as she walked briefly along the Whitechapel Road.

'They are my tools of my trade,' she plainly stated.

'Are there many tools for this situation?' I asked her.

'Depends,' she answered as she looked from side to side, studying everyone she could see.

'Depends on what?'

'On how bloody the situation gets,' was her quite sinister and in truth spine-chillingly answer.

1898

Things are starting to not feel quite a lovely as I had first thought, and the longer I stay here the more I noticed it. Two of Charles's servants were not allowing me out of their sight; I had no real idea why. The maid seems as unpleasant as ever to me no matter what I do or what I say, something about me she does not like and there is nothing I can do to ever change her feelings towards me. Although I have taken notice of a little chink in her strong, forceful armour and that is in the shape of the young man servant who worked mainly in the fields that surrounded the manor house. I have caught her on many of occasion staring lovingly at the sight of this young boy, this chink might sound harmless enough to most people but you never know when you can use a piece of information to get what you need, I just need to think of how I could use it.

My pleasant walks were being overrun by this young man servant constant talking of the years of history that was in Blissful Hill that he recently learned from the butler. It was delightful but a little annoying as I liked my own space.

'I hope you don't mind me asking, but why have you for the past few days, walked with me? I am quite well and able to walk by myself.' I said to him on one of these walks in question.

'Well I, I need the walk the master's dog don't I?' The young man servant said.

I stopped. 'Look boy, what's your name?'

'My name you ask Sir? It's Johnny,' he said as he put the lead on the old dog.

'Look, John. Can I be honest with you? And I hope you will be honest with me. I like to walk alone, I enjoy it that way and although I have been immersing myself in your enchanting discussions about this lovely place. The time has come for me to ask why I am not aloud out of anyone's sight. And don't try to say you need to walk the dog, because I take my walks when the mood takes me, not at set times like a dog would.'

'I don't know Sir, what I mean to say is Sir, I don't know about all that Sir.'

'You don't know why I am not aloud out of anyone's sight or you don't know if you should answer me?'

'Sir I can't talk of it.'

'I had thought so, Charles told you didn't he? It's like he's keeping me caged! Why? Why am I caged John?'

'The master, he worries about your health.'

'Why isn't he here then? What is he up to?' I asked.

'The master just told me to watch your every move and make sure you don't return home.'

'Why can I not return home? What is he up to?'

'Please don't make this task hard for me Sir; I don't want to make the master angry.'

‘Charles has never been angry the whole time I have known him.’

‘As you put it, to be honest with you Sir, you haven’t know Charles for that long and in truth haven’t seen his darker side.’

‘Of course I have known Charles for a...’ I stopped, why do I have to think about how long I have known Charles? Surely I should know I thought to myself. ‘Well I have known him since, oh I can’t remember. Anyway his darker side you say? Charles doesn’t have a darker side, I’m sure of it.’

‘I have said too much don’t repeat this to anyone Sir, Please!’

‘No I will not, only if you do me a favour.’

‘What’s that, Sir?’ Johnny said, as he was struggling with the dog, who was old but young at heart.

‘Take the young servant girl out for lunch; tell her I am well mediated, and sleeping. I need to be alone for an hour or two.’

The man servant did as he was told and I was able to walk around Charles’s home and study without the preying eyes and writing notepads. Charles had put a lot of trust in his servants as he had left his study unlocked, he must have known that I would never be in the study alone. Why did he so trust his servants? What other secrets have they known? I opened the door and walked around, the room was decorated in just Charles’s way, and everything had a place. There was book case full of different books from medical to the great classics of the day. It is funny, what important papers people leave around when they are old and the people forget their importance. I came across such important papers and things started to make sense to me. I was holding the deeds to my home! How can this be? What is my friend doing with my deeds? It was then I noticed movement in the sitting room that this study was adjacent to. I glanced at the open doorway to see the butler staring back at me.

'I don't think you should be in here Sir,' he said.

'I know, I know but I wanted to know what is going on around here, without everyone watching me.'

'I am not watching you Sir, I told Charles I wouldn't as you seem quite well to me Sir and I feel you do not really need your medication.'

'I know you are not watching but everyone else is, but wait! Charles told you to give me medication?'

'Yes Sir, he told me not to tell you as you would have argued with me, but just to have a word with the cook and she can place it in your food.'

I was very shocked to hear this, so shocked that I dropped my deeds on the floor and fell back in the desk chair. 'I cannot believe this! Charles wanted you to poison my food, but why!'

'Do not get unwell Sir over what I have said, I would feel so guilty.'

'Has anyone else followed Charles's wishes?' I asked taking no notice of what the butler had just said.

'The maid wanted to follow the master's wishes, but I told her not too, she was not very happy with me and I am sure that once word reaches the master I will be out on my ear,' It was that comment that shook me out of my astonishment and for the first time I saw through the butler's outfit and saw the man behind it, he was old and had seen many things I could guess but there was a feeling of friendship and loyalty within his eyes. What he had done for me was very important to his life and mine, he had save me from my dreams because no doubt the medication would have brought them flooding back to me, he had done this by the risk of his own job, a job he never wanted to leave.

'You have risked your job by not doing as you are told.'

'I know that Sir, but you see the master hasn't been quite right for ages Sir and I didn't believe that drugging you without your knowledge was the correct thing to do.'

'You may have saved my life, you do understand that don't you?'

'Do you understand what you have just said Sir?'

'Understand what?'

'If I have saved your life, there must have been a risk to it and if that is to be the case, who has put a risk to it?'

'Charles.'

'Exactly Sir, do you understand now?' said the butler as his words floated around in my head as the last four words reminded me of someone else I had become acquainted with of late.

My thoughts ran back to London, the busy streets, and the noise I was back in the place I thought was my home. I was leaving my house, heading for my favourite place, the Kingsmen Opium Den once again, but this time I stop dead on the pavement, I turn I see my best friend Charles coming up, dodging the cracks in the pavement as he as always done. I can feel my legs move to the other side of the pavement near the buildings; I slip myself into a shadowy alleyway entrance and watch my friend walk by. I have a choice I think to myself I can follow my friend and began this story again or I could go home, never to have known the dark side to my friend, the strange lady that keeps trying to tell me something about myself, the mortuary keeper, Jimmy Turner, Ellen's Mother or even Will. Poor, poor Will, if I turn and go home I can save you Will for you would never have met me or I you, and you can live on looking after your mother. I felt my legs move again and I found myself walking back home, trying to find another story to write about to solve my debts.

If only that was all possible I thought, as things went quickly black.

1888

The sight that greeted both Jill and I was one that could have turned anyone's stomach, the sick bucket was overflowing and there was a thick liquid puddle with rather large chunky pieces floating within it lying all across the floor leaving a few dry patches for us to stand in, the smell is revolting and almost unspeakable as I am finding it very hard to breathe and as I look across to Jill I saw most of her scarf was now covering her nose. She was busying herself with the items in the room.

'You have your own tin bath, this is good,' she managed to say through her scarf.

'Yes Joseph always wanted his own bath,' I began to say.

'I do not care for this Joseph,' she said rather quickly 'Your friend is far more worse than I thought, I must work fast. You fill the bath with hot water, I noticed you have a local bath along the road, get hot water there. I will leave the tin bath outside for you to fill; you are not allowed to come back in.'

'I am not allowed to come back into my own home?' I questioned.

'Do you want me to help your friend or not?' she asked back as she stared at me through the only gap in her scarf.

'Yes.'

'Well then, let me do my job,' it was then that Maria started to move.

'Maria.' I whispered.

'Mary.' she mouthed through her dry lips.

'This is the nurse I was talking to you about, remember?' I asked to which she nodded 'She is going to help you, it might hurt but it will make you feel better alright?' I asked her to whom Maria nodded again, she was too weak to fight anything I was saying to her, and I could sense it. I was tempted to mention the strange woman at the prison for I hated lying to her but I could feel that Jill wanted to get to work, whatever work would mean but to be honest I didn't want to think about it, I moved away from Maria but Jill grabbed hold of my arm.

'I thought you wanted to get to work,' I said to her, to which she removed her scarf for the first time since she had left her home.

'You might need to say Goodbye,' she simply said.

'Why?'

'Some do not survive,' she whispered.

'Oh I see,' I replied, I moved back towards Maria and quietly whispered in her ear 'Things will be alright, you wait and see. I will see you soon, goodbye Maria.'

'Goodbye,' was her reply, to which I left the room.

Once outside, the cold air slapped into my face it felt fresh and refreshing, it awoke my inner being for I was feeling ever so tired. Not just tired because I hadn't slept since yesterday afternoon, but tired of life itself. I had decided to stay in Whitechapel and not run away from the not so distant doom that awaits me in a few days time, some might think I am mad and should go to Bedlam but they don't understand and in truth I don't expect them too. I don't expect anyone too, for I have come to terms with knowing what will become of me. I will not run from that night, only to bump into Billy Bo and have him kill me, for you see I have always wanted to be famous, to be known. I tried in Paris and that didn't end too well, for I ended up whoring in a different country, where was the fun in that?

Now I am to be killed by Jack the Ripper, no one will ever forget him so why would they forget his victims? Everyone will know the name Mary Kelly; they might learn of my life, they might even feel sorry that they did not know me in person. I will not know of the things that will happen because of my death but it will not go unnoticed and I would not be in parts buried all over this City. I will have a grave, people can come and mourn for me, I will be forever in their minds. There will be books, stories about the most famous killer of our time and they will not be able to talk of him without mentioning me. If I am to die, of course I want to be remembered not just for being another whore who lived in Whitechapel but for being someone *special* for I will be Mary Kelly.

I headed for the Ten Bells once again to warm the cockles of my heart and because I didn't want to renter my home too early.

'Rum if you please landlord,' I cheerily said.

'Back again Mary, why I thought you would need your forty winks,' was his reply as he filled my glass.

'I can sleep plenty when I dead,' I said, for he did not know how true I was being.

'Right you are then, hey by the way, where's that little spawn? That follows you around.'

'She's not my spawn but she little busy at the moment.'

'Busy you say? Well I suppose she is very pretty, caught my eye she has. A little like you when you first came here, but now.'

'What do you mean 'now'?' I said as I took a sip from my glass.

'Well pardon me saying like, but I won't beat about the bush with you. You have been around a bit; you are becoming one of the others, nothing special about you no more.'

'How nice of you to say landlord, but I think you will find that opinion of me that you have will change in a few days time.'

'Oh yeah, you know something I don't then?' he said as he leant on the bar.

'I know a lot of things you don't.' I mumbled.

'Care to whisper it, in my ear hole my chance?'

I leant over the bar myself at this point and whispered in his ear 'Well let's just say, in a few days time I will be famous, so famous that the newspapers will have me on the front page.' I leant back onto my stool when the landlord replied.

'Well it must be exceptionally good to knock that Jack the Ripper fella of the front page.'

'You could say so.'

Chapter Seventeen

1898

The night is cold and wet, I can smell the dampness in the air, I look down to see my shiny shoes hitting the hard cobbled stones of the pavement for I was running, but why I was running I could not understand. I could not understand until I reached my destination, for I suddenly felt as if I knew the surroundings from a time before, a time when everything was simple and understood. I felt as if I was home again, it had been such a long time since I felt like I was home and at home with my soul.

The gas lamps were giving off a small amount of lighting for they were covered in soot and have not been cleaned for weeks, but it did not matter as I knew my way, for I always known my way really I just couldn't see it, I couldn't sense it but tonight I sense it, tonight I understand. I understand where I am and why I am here, for I am meant to be here. It is my destiny, my fate if you will, I belong here. Although the streets are empty I do not feel alone for I am at peace with myself.

I walk pass the dizzy lights of an open public house, a part of me wishes I can go in and wet my whistle but there is somewhere I am meant to be tonight and nothing is going to prevent me from getting there. Although I hear the loud voices from the people within the public house, all laughing and joking I do not stop to join in the merriment, but I do savour the moment of noise of hilarity and enjoyment as times are hard and moments of pleasure come few and far between.

I cross the street to the other side, I don't even look to see if there are any carts of coaches travelling along this road, and it wouldn't matter if there was, because nobody notices me. I move in the shadows, I move like the dust, everybody knows that the dust is there and that the dust moves in the winds but no one ever takes a moment to look at the dust in the face. No one realises that the dust is a huge factor in their surroundings so much more than they are. So the dust carries on, and goes about its business unknown. I am the dust.

My pace decides to decrease once I place myself on the other side of the road, something I do not comprehend why I do so, but I allow my brain to control my body for it knows what is best for me. Now at a walking pace I can appreciate the ambience of such an amiable place. Many people look down at this area, seeing the dirt and the grime but in truth Whitechapel is so much more than that. The interesting characters, the foreign species and tastes you can try, the remarkable buildings that litter the streets and alleyways, yes there is overcrowding but one day I can imagine the East becoming a part of the West. One day people will see the wonders of this place and they will all want to live here.

Suddenly my pace slows even more, making me come to a full stop. For a second I wonder why I have stopped here, there is nothing special about this peculiar space. But wait, I turn to my left and I notice I am standing before an entrance of an alleyway, there are plenty of alleyways around here but this one is different, this one is singular. Yes to an untrained eye it might look identical to any other alleyway you may come across in this area, but this one is special I can feel it. I feel the cooling sensation running through my whole body has I look down it, there is something unique at the end of this alleyway and my curious nature starts to raise its ugly head.

I can feel my body tip toe it's self along the wall of the alleyway, my fingers and poised and the tips of them skirt over the sharp damp stones that have built it. I look down towards the pavement, there are hundreds of cracks within the slabs, each crack being filled with moss and weeds that are forever reaching for the chance of more rain and fresh air, a feeling comes over me that is quite creepy I imagine the moss growing fast and attaching itself to one of my shoes, I imagine seeing the whole of my shoe being covered in a green mess of moss. It tugs on hard and I am unable to move, the moss keeps growing up my leg and around my chest, I imagine I start to find it hard to breathe, then with my last breath the moss floods inside my mouth and attaches itself to my organs on the inside until at last I become one with the alleyway wall. I must dodge the cracks I think to myself, just in case what I can imagine comes true.

My minds turns back to the mission the has laid itself before me, for I must see what is so special around the end house to this alleyway and what is drawing me ever closer to it, I move again and place myself outside the window, the window is disgustingly dirty and one of its panels has been smashed. As I slowly move nearer I can feel heat escaping through this smashed glass, I decide to peer in to see...

‘Don’t you think it is about time for you to wake up Sir?’ said a voice from within my dream. ‘Sir, can you hear me?’ the voice speaks again. I open my eyes and there is a woman looking down at me, a woman with kind features, a woman I have come to admire, a woman I know of. My throat is dry, so I am unable to many words but I do manage to say one word before my head fills with darkness again, and that one word was,

‘Charlotte.’

1888

This peculiar night was not as glorious as I thought it would be, although tonight was the eighth of November it was just as normal as any other night, the weather was still as miserable as ever, the people and clients were just as mean and cruel. Why don’t people realise how important this night will become? Can’t people sense it? Jack the Ripper will strike again tonight and on their own doorsteps, this will be a night to remember. I decide to go home a little early than I need to but I don’t see any point in delaying the future any longer than need be, for I have said my goodbyes to myself. I wish I was able to tell someone goodbye to their face but I know I can’t, it would be right would it?

I move of the bar stand and head towards the door, everything is a little hazy but I was used to that, many a night of heavy drinking has prepared me for the slight dizziness I am getting and in truth I have become fond of the way Whitechapel looks in this manner. I get outside and the damp air hits me hard and I instantly feel more awake, the hazy surroundings become clearer to me so I move on quickly.

'You wouldn't be running away from me Mary, would you?' came a voice from behind. I turned to see that the voice was attached to John McCartney, my land lord. He really is one of the kindest old men left in Whitechapel; I have felt quite sorry for him at times when his wife barks at him with her orders, for he is quite under the thumb.

'How could you think that of me John? For you know how much I care for you.'

'Well you are six weeks behind on your rent.'

'Oh come on John, you know Maria has been ill and I can't do the work of two.'

'My misses don't care for that, she only cares for money.'

'I can quite believe that, but surely you care about us don't you?'

'You know I care for you Mary,' he whispered as he drew nearer to me.

'Well then,' I said as I started to move away from him.

'I do need the rent Mary!' he shouted at me, not in a mean way more in a desperate plea.

'I'll tell you what, you come knocking for the rent in the morning and I'm sure I will give you a big surprise,' I said trying to sound a little flirty.

'You best not be lying this time Mary!' he said as he nodded his head towards me.

'This time I swear I am not lying to you,' I said but he didn't understand how sadly true I was being to him.

He allowed me to go home without paying his rent, he had no idea that he would never get it, and he will probably be in trouble with his misses because of it. I opened my door and closed it behind me; the room was empty because I had sent Maria out tonight. I made some argument that now she was feeling better, she should work double as hard to earn to money she lost from being ill. A little mean, I know but I didn't want her home tonight, I didn't want her to see the devil known as Jack the Ripper and I couldn't tell the truthful reason. She looked sad but she did not want to disappoint me that fact I could plainly see, so out into the cold she went.

I sat for a while on the bed, my mind going mad with anticipation. It is an odd feeling for one to wait for their own death, I tried to pretend I was not scared but that was silly of me, I can't imagine anyone being able to not be frightened of the end even when they know it is going to happen. My head was filling up with all the different ways Jack the Ripper can kill me, of course he will slit my throat because that is what he does. Wait, he will slit my throat! There will be blood, my blood around this room, I can't breathe, and I begin to feel dizzy and light. I have to get out of here! I have changed my mind; I don't want to die at the hand of Jack the Ripper! I want to die an old lady, a nobody! I ran outside and down the alleyway and back into the street, I slow my breathing down and now I see her coming out of the pub. There is my Maria, she can't see me like this so I lean on the wall at the entrance of our alleyway and wait for her to come up to me.

'Fancy seeing you here and on this night of all nights,' I say to her as she gets near enough to hear me.

'You joke well, considering,' she replied, I wonder if she know what tonight is for me. If that is true I want to tell her that I am alright about it even when I am not, so I say

'That is nothing to consider, there is nothing to think of, there is nothing to regret and there is nothing to be in fear of.'

'You truly believe that? Or is it your famous Whitechapel charm coming out?' she asks me, as I notice that she is staring at me. I wonder if she can see me shaking. But it is cold out, maybe she will think it is the weather making me shake; at least I hope that to be the case.

'My famous Whitechapel charm hey? Well maybe not so famous yet, my dear friend,' I say for I know I will be famous tonight in the end.

'I wanted to see you tonight, something was telling me too, silly as it sounds,' she said as she patted me on my wet shoulder, which made a slapping sound. I didn't even notice it was raining.

'Maybe it was that strange woman we both know, I would hate to think of what powers she truly has. I would imagine we have only seen half of the wonders and delights she has to play with.'

'I don't know about that, but all I do know it that I don't want to talk of her tonight, not with you anyway,' she mysteriously replied, what did she mean by that I speculate for a second or two.

'So what do you want to talk about then? Why are you here?' I asked her for I didn't truly understand why she had come home early, but she seemed to want to change to the subject as she said,

'You seem cold tonight.'

'It is windy and raining my love, if you hadn't noticed,' I replied.

'Cold in nature, I meant.'

'Oh I see, well I find it hard to feel happy these days. It's not like I have anything to look forward too.'

'I don't know what to say.'

'Does anyone? Would anyone understand?'

'I guess not, it is complicated to explain the situation we have found our self's in.'

'Quite.'

'Is there anything I can do?' she asked hopelessly.

'That is not how things work is it? We can't help each other, not now. I guess I can go home now hey?'

'Yes, I am planning to stay out a little longer before I go in.'

'That is nice to know but I would suggest leaving rather sharply as Billy Bo has been standing outside the Ten Bells glancing our way.'

'Billy Bo?' she asked, glancing behind herself towards the gas lamps that stood outside the public house. It must have been the first time she saw a mysterious dark figure, with one foot resting on the step leading into the drinking hole. His head lying low, his flat cap placed a little too forward on his head so that his face was anonymous to us. He was standing there as casual as he could, cleaning his nails but he had no real need to as the state of his clothing proved he had no care for upkeep of his appearance. He occasionally glanced at his foot of the step but he wasn't fooling anyone as his attention was firmly on Maria, I could not see his eyes but I could

speculate that they were glowing red with hatred and desire to do her harm, or was that my mind talking?

'You might know of his wife Maud?' I asked as she looked blankly around at me, I carried on describing 'A rather loud woman with a mole on her left cheek, she likes to pick on lonely women within in the pub to make herself feel better about her life with Billy and her son Will. If anyone bites on her words, well she sends her fella to sort them out afterwards, since you have just left the pub and Billy Bo is so very interested in you I will take the guess that you... bit.'

'I did have a little disagreement with a lady fitting that description I will say it was a very entertaining way to pass an hour or so.'

'Then I would move along promptly, as I have been on the other end of Billy Bo's punches before.'

'Thank you for the advice,' she said as she ran past by me.

'Helpful I am,' I shouted back at me, as she glanced back at me, I disappeared into the alleyway while Billy Bo's ghostly figure followed her footsteps. I hope she gets away from here and from him I think to myself. It is quite curious how being involved in one scene or another can change your whole point of view isn't it? I was already to run away from my fate, from my death but seeing Maria come out of that pub and walk towards me had altered my mind once again. It had reminded me that as I may not be a mother in giving birth, I am a mother in a caring sense, it is

not just about me anymore it is about Maria. She will need to mourn for me somewhere; I need to give her a grave to do so. It is the very last thing I can do for her. It is amazing the power of motherhood, what one would do for their daughter is to face the death of Jack the Ripper.

1898

'Help me Thomas! Please help me, I have changed my mind yet again, I know it is foolish of me to beg you now it the state that we have found ourselves, but please don't allow me to die, I don't want to die Thomas! You are the only one that can help me now; it is too late for anyone else. It is the game Thomas! The game I say! Can't you remember how important you are to me and I to you? Without me there are no you, you must save me Thomas! Save me for only you can, you have the power too if only you can remember why.

Please remember Thomas, remember why I am here, and please remember why you are there just outside my grasp. You need to realise the whole story that you are living in, it is too late for me if you don't. Remember who I am to you Thomas,' screamed the lady within the bloodied lake. Her eyes were piecing and beautiful, that is something I recognize it them, something I have always known. I am the last things she sees and her throat is slit and she dies once more.

I could not save her as she wished for she did not truly understand, she had to die it was her fate; it was my fate for we are entwined.

‘Thomas, Thomas can you hear me yet?’ said a strong, forceful voice I remember for it was the voice of my friend, Charles. I had decided that I could play the dim-witted friend I have become to be, I will play the Watson to Charles’s Sherlock but I am unknown to him I have started to become quite a detective myself. I open my eyes to see Charles’s face looking down at me. ‘There you are my dear boy; I thought I had lost you too.’

‘I am made of harder stuff.’

‘So you are Thomas! So you are,’ he replied as he took his attention of me and placed it on the bedroom door as if he was waiting for it to open.

‘You seem a little on edge Charles, what is the matter?’

‘What! Oh there has been much of a do-to here while I have been away.’

‘Has there been?’ I asked unintelligently.

‘Oh yes, quite a do-to. But of course you could not have known that.’

‘No?’ I asked.

‘Well you were having one of your famous fevers at the time, so I was told. You were found lying on the chaise longue in the sitting room, mumbling some rubbish. Whereas the butler on the other hand...’

'What has happened to the butler?' I said as I suddenly bolted up from my holiday bed.

'Calm yourself Thomas,' Charles said as he pushed at my chest so I leaned back on my pillows 'Are you alright? Maybe I should not mention it just now.'

'No, I am fine,' I said as I rearranged my pillows so that I was sitting a little further up. 'Please tell me what has happened to the butler.'

'Well if you are sure you are alright.'

'I am quite sure, my friend.'

'Well in that case I will sit myself down,' he said as he pulled a chair nearer to the bed. 'He was found half in and half out of my study, although what he was going in my study I cannot think, as my study is out of bounds,' he said looking quite cruelly. Whether he was being cruel to me I could not judge.

'When you say 'found' Charles, do you mean he was found dead?'

'Why yes Thomas, he is quite dead, quite dead indeed,' he said without a care as he lit his cigar.

'What happened to him?'

'I have no idea Thomas, in truth we were hoping you would be able to tell us, what has been going on here. I come home to find my maid out with the boy servant on some kind of date, my butler is dead lying in the doorway of the only room that should be closed and the study itself is ransacked. To be honest I am feeling a little at a loss within my own home.'

'I have no idea what had happened Charles, suddenly things went blank, I was talking to the butler and then something transpired but I do not understand what.'

'That is rather sad to hear Thomas, what were you talking to the butler about?' he asked as he leaned forwards, towards me.

'I can't remember.'

'Can't or won't remember?'

'What do you mean Charles?'

'You called your maid, Charlotte.'

'Did I? I don't remember that.'

'You were in a fever Thomas, why call her Charlotte Thomas? Why did you do that?'

'I don't understand why you are asking me these things Charles; I didn't even know that my maid was here!' I shouted.

'There is no need to get angry with me Thomas, I brought your maid with me when I heard that my home had been burgled with you inside, I had no idea you were in such a state and that my butler had been murdered.'

'Sorry Charles, I just don't understand what has gone on here. Wait, you say the butler has been murdered?'

'Oh yes, the bloodied puddle lying by his head tells me that murder is the crime. The police have been and gone, impractical brunch of dim-witted men I must say. All focusing on the butler but no mention of the burglary, I am disgusted with the way I am treated here, back in London I am treated far more devotedly I can tell you!'

'What is missing?'

'Some old documents.'

'Anything important?'

'Everything in my study is important in one way or another Thomas.'

'I could imagine that to be the case Charles,' I said as I wondered what else was lying in his study. What other documents does he hold? But I guess I would never find out now, for if it is true that the house had be burgled I could not see those documents again, I would not see my deeds to my house again. But there was a feeling in the back of my head that something sinister was going on here as the butler was the only member of staff to be friendly towards me, he helped with clues to the mystery of the past family who lived here but he is the only one to die? The friendly old man is the only one to die, that is quite painfully hard to understand and why when I saw documents that would need answering the house get burgled? It all sounds a little unlikely to me, but I guess I do not have proof anymore to question what has happened.

I glanced over to my friend as he was looking at his smoking cigar; I wondered to myself, what other secrets do you hold Charles?

Chapter Eighteen

1888

I awoke from my dream, my head hurt as I must have fallen asleep at the bar of the Ten Bells pub. I started rubbing my cheek, the pub itself was empty and was missing its land lord, and he must have allowed me to sleep here, bless his heart. I always thought he had a soft spot of me. What was that dream about? I had placed myself in the role of Maria from my hallucination from the strange woman's lair, what was the meaning behind that?

Suddenly as I was getting my wits together the door opened and some bright light came flooding in, blinding me. I shielded my eyes while trying to see who had entered the drinking hole, and I have got to be honest when I say I was not expecting to see this person, free and from prison.

'How did you get out?' I asked the strange woman.

'The same way you got in, I would imagine,' she said as she sat down beside me.

'I don't know where the barman is,' I started to say when she butted in by saying,

'I wasn't looking for a drink.'

‘Oh? Then you have come to the wrong place,’ I said as I started to rub my cheek again.

‘No, I was looking for you.’

‘Are you going to tell me that I am too special?’

‘You have come to terms with what I have already told you, that I can see.’

‘I don’t have a choice but to.’

‘But I came here on a different matter.’

‘Maria?’

‘No, she will be alright. I need to tell you why I was in prison.’

‘No, I don’t think you do for I do not care.’

‘You might when you hear it, for you will be able to blackmail someone, someone that has money.’

‘I have no need for money where I am going.’

‘But Maria might.’

‘You want me to blackmail someone for Maria?’

‘Yes, if you like.’

‘You do care for her, don’t you?’

‘More than you could ever understand,’ it was at that moment I understood everything I had seen before. I decided to listen to the strange woman one last time, so I allowed her to tell me her story.

It was a few days ago I saw her, I don't have many friends you see Mary. So the ones I do have I try my best to look after them. I thought I would go and see her as not many people do. They all think she is crazy but she is really kind and only acts abnormally out of the love for her daughter Ellen.

Her daughter had died last year, in mysterious circumstances. I remember thinking at the time that her death was an odd state of affairs, however I thought nothing else of it but it was a few months later after the funeral, Martha came up to me to express her feelings about her daughter's death. She said she felt horrid to think such a thing but she believed her daughter was murdered and if that is to be the case, she believed she knew who the murderer was.

Her daughter was a troublemaker of the worst kind; she played with the hearts of many men she came in contact with to better her life and her career for her daughter was a street walker like you Mary, but she wanted to be a actress and singer on stage. She wanted to leave Whitechapel, but she was finding it hard to do so, for she needed money to change her look to something more in fashion and that is when she met the doctor. He was young, rich and in love with her, so she led him on. He paid for her new look, he gave her a new name, so 'the singing nightingale' she became and she started working in the Willow and the Owl theatre in the West End of London.

This doctor was happy and for a while she was too, but then she met another business man, he was some kind of duke of something, who could take her to his home country, America. So she dumped the doctor, this Martha believed was her down fall as this doctor had a clandestine dark side, he hid it well but a dark side he most indisputably had.

This surreptitious doctor took the whole situation hard and was not best pleased with the singing nightingale, he started harmlessly enough or so Martha first thought. He turned up at the theatre every night to watch her sing, then one night Ellen complained he had followed her home, Ellen said that she believed this doctor was telling everyone that they were still lovers and that he was so proud of what she had become. Which at the time Ellen thought was satisfactory as she was been talked about, and she always loved being talked about but then he sent her death threats a few days before her murder, her mother knew this doctor had because she had seen them and asked her daughter about them. Her daughter just laughed at them, saying that this doctor was a feeble and pathetic man and that he would never hurt her for he loved her too much, but her mother wasn't so sure.

When her daughter died, the duplicitous doctor played the grieving lover and paid for the whole funeral, which helped as her mother did not have the money but there was an argument between her and the hypocritical doctor for Martha didn't believe his grieving was genuine for there was something in his eyes she said, it was like looking at the devil in the face.

Martha was in need of help, she had no food and she was becoming ill. She couldn't afford the normal doctor so in her last hitched attempt to survive, Martha went to the doctor she dreaded. He looked down his nose at her, he thought he owned her now and could control her. He gave her food that was poisoned, poisoned Mary! He gave her ginger beer that had acid in it; she was so thirsty she drank it.

She had told me once, she had the strength the spit the acid back towards the doctor, missing him but hitting his shoes, he was so angry with her that he beat her, and used a hot poker across her face. She was gruesomely scarred, he laughed at her. She tried many times to run away from him, he ripped her clothes, but she still believed he killed her daughter and that was the most important thing to her, for he could do anything to her now.

Martha got away once, she tried to get back to her daughter's back stage room in the theatre for that was where she had last seen the death threats, but didn't get too far with it and was dragged back outside by the doctor, he was saying she was crazy, that she did not understand the relationship he had with her daughter, for if she did she would realise just how much they had truly loved each other. But she wasn't crazy Mary, she was more sane than most.

I hadn't seen her for a while, so a few days ago I go to her house don't I? The door was open, so I walked in to see a hooded man on the stairs; he bumped into me as he made for the door for he was now running. I climbed the stairs, and went into her room. The sight I saw was shocking and ghastly, I will not describe it to you as the thought of it still brings lumps in my throat. She was dead Mary and that man that I had bumped into me had killed her, I knew then that the hooded man was the same rich, young doctor I had been hearing about, for there was a smell to the room, a chemical smell Mary coming from the ginger beer bottles, he had poisoned her I knew.

Blood was everywhere, I hadn't realised I was covered in her blood until I was running outside after the doctor and the peelers caught me. The rest you know Mary.

'What do you want me to do with that information?' I asked.

'Here is the hooded doctor's name,' she said as she passed a piece of paper with one single name on it. 'He likes street walkers young and easy to get, you can meet him outside the Billing Club in the West End.'

1898

Days had felt like they had slipped by, I had gained my strength to move around the house again, the servants had felt I was capable to be on my own again so I could walk around mostly unnoticed and Charles had gone back to London on an important mission of sorts but so important he couldn't tell me anything about it. But I did not mind as I wanted to use the opportunity of him being away to investigate a little more into the interesting character my friend has become.

I managed to work my way down the stairs and back into the gothic sitting room, a had tinged of sadness as I walked past the spot that the butler must have taken his last breath in. I moved over to the chaise longue that I was found in and laid down, my mind was wondering once again. Why was I found out here, when clearly the last moment I remember I was sitting in Charles's study talking to the butler? The butler must have placed me here, but why? He did not want people to find me in his master's study, he knew I was going to be found and Charles will not like it. If that is so, was he undertaking his master's wishes or saving me from harm, a harm that he had faced instead?

I would like to wish the latter to be the case as he was a caring man and had seemed to have taken a shine to me. But if that was what really happened it means that Charles could really have this dark side to his character, something I found hard to shallow for he had been my friend of mine for ages, for longer than I can remember. So could he have killed his own butler because he saved me? Or maybe it was because the butler had told me something he shouldn't have. Instantly my eyes fell to the painting that was hanging on the wall in line with me as that thought processed in my mind.

'You said Charlotte Thomas,' Charles had said to me. Did I really say that? I remember I thought I saw her, I thought I heard her talking to me. My eyes were transfixed on the sad last lady of the house and then they followed her gaze to the baby's cradle on the floor, how very heartbreaking the whole story was. As my gaze fell from

the painting I noticed something was not right, the bottom of the painting was slightly sticking out from the wall, there was something white behind it. I sat up and moved over to it, it was a small white envelope that had just one word on it, and that word was my name.

I quickly looked about me, there was no one around so I swiftly opened the envelope and a piece of white material fell out of the note that was written inside, I picked up the material for it seemed familiar to me, the letter stated;

My god, I hope this reaches you Thomas.

It is too late for me now and if this falls into the wrong hands, you Thomas will never get to know the truth, time is sadly running out for me for I know the end is almost here. I had to do something to help, because Thomas you do need help for you do not understand the true danger you are in.

It is dangerous knowing the truth, as I think my ending will prove to you. But you do need to know it; I hope I am doing the right thing for if you were to die because of what I am doing now I would never forgive myself.

Charles is on his way, I have made the study look like a mess for I am hoping he will think there has been a burglary, I have left you outside the study with no proof that you were ever in it, I will leave you facing this note and hope that you will see it and understand. I did not mean to hurt you when I hit you over the head while you

seemed to be in a dream, but it was the only way of getting you out of there in time without having to explain, what I am trying to explain now to you.

If Charles asks me if you have been in the study I will stand my ground and say no, even if it costs me my life as you have a kind soul and are not like your friend at all. You may think that the documents you held are gone and I hope to god that you are still wrong; for I took them, as well as other documents that may help you write that novel.

Go to my room Thomas, floorboard three, 24312 and there the truth will be laid out for you to see.

The white material you will hopefully see with this letter is one of two things, the first is that you might recognize it for it was on your person and the second is that it is the missing part of your friend's glove. The reason I have highlighted this to you is because I do not understand why you are carrying around with you the missing part of your friend's glove, but something is telling me that it is significant to your case. I only hope you remember where you found it for that might be the answer for both of us.

One last thing Thomas, please remember this kind, old man and remember your promise to make me a forever lasting character for I know this is Goodbye.

From the old butler now at peace... at long last.

1888

I had left the strange woman sitting in the Ten Bells, thinking over everything she had seen. She looked pale and ill so I knew she was speaking the truth of the story of her friend Martha, it must have been quite a fright seeing her friend lifeless with blood everywhere. It must be quite distressing knowing who had killed her but still having to say nothing to the police for people like us, do not get listened to. For we are scrum in the eyes of the law, and if this name is correct not only is he a doctor he is also a 'Sir'.

I thought I would go and see if Maria is alright, but in truth I did not want to find out the worse not just yet, so I headed west into the City boundaries to find this Billing Club that holds gentlemen of a higher class than the likes of me. Sometimes I wish I could change, change my life in every possible way. I wonder every now and then, what my life would have been like if I was born differently, born in another class.

Maybe I could have been like one of these gentlemen sitting in a club with nothing better to do. Maybe I could have riches, a manor house and a maid but don't truly understand why I have them, my profession could be somewhat important to the class that I would be in, a playwright maybe or an artist, no I would be a writer. A classic writer of our time, my name will grow with age for I will be the best of what I write about. I often wonder if anyone could have the power to change history and if so, what would they do?

I would be a gentleman, a writer, something special and different to what I am now, but I can never think of a name for myself.

I reached to busy streets of the city and I feel so out of place and I felt as if everyone was looking at me. I needed to be strong for it is essential I get directions. I reached the window of a shop that drew me curiously towards it for it sold clocks of various sizes and shapes. I pressed my nose up against the glass and watched to hands of the clocks tick around, time was moving forward while I would like it to move backwards. I know I was being silly but as I glanced at the hands I forcefully tried to turn them back through the power in my eyes, for a second the hands seemed to stop all together but it is probably my mind playing tricks on me.

I decided to ask for directions from the proprietor of this shop, so I walked in to see two people inside. One of which I could tell was the vendor, for he was wearing a brown leather apron. He seemed older than he probably was, years of working here no doubt. There was flecks of greying hair showing underneath his cap which he had pushed up to revealed his rather large forehead and judging by the dirty handkerchief that was screwed up in his left hand; he had used it often to wipe his brow.

The other person was rather different, it was a woman. She stood straight making her seem a little taller than the man she was talking to. I could tell because of the lace cap that sat perfectly on the back of her head that her profession was of some importance either a nurse or a maid. I moved nearer and could hear their conversation.

‘Thomas you know this will not do!’ she said to him.

‘Like I said to Sir Charles, his clock is more damaged than we first thought; if he wants the job well done he is going to have to wait.’

‘My master will not like your attitude and you do not want to make him angry.’

‘Sir Charles’s Dunn clock is very hypersensitive and precise it needs time to be finely tuned back into shape.’

‘Thomas, this Dunn Clock is very important to my master is came from his father and my master hates being away from it,’ she said sternly.

‘I will work on it right now; tell your master he will have it within the next day.’ Thomas said.

‘See that you do,’ was her ungrateful reply, as she turned from him and for the first time she saw me, there was a moment of shock but then she turned back to the stern look I can imagine she always has, for a second I caught in a trance of looking intently at her for I was sure I had seen her before or at least known of her. She looked me up and down with disgusted and walked out of the door.

I moved over to the clock maker and before I could say anything he said to me

'Keep your hands to yourself, I have been watching you.'

'I do not wish to make trouble for you Sir, I can see that you are under some stress from a gentleman and his maid, I only came in because I saw a kind soul in you and thought I could ask directions,' I said as sympathetically as I could, hoping he would see me not as a thief but as just another woman. It seemed to work as he replied,

'I am sorry miss, I have been having a bad day and seeing that maid of Sir Charles's didn't help the mood I am in.'

'I could see she is a force to be reckoned with.'

'Yes, from someone so young is it quite shocking but I suppose you would have to be like that to work for him.'

'Yes this Sir Charles, he seems a little strong in nature.'

'You could say so, anyway I am sorry to class you as a thief I am not normally that vindictive.'

'That is quite alright I am used to it, now I would like directions to the Billing Club.'

'Full of surprises aren't you?' he asked me.

'Oh why is that?'

'The Billing Club is a new club run by Sir Charles, and well the likes of you are hardly allowed in the front door.'

'Is there a back door?' I joked.

'I wouldn't be surprised with Sir Charles,' he said before he gave me directions to the said club. I said my thank you to him and walked out of the shop, as I got a few yards away I released my hand to see a small watch on a gold chain I had slipped from inside my sleeve to my palm. As I let the chain run in-between my fingers I thought to myself I hate people thinking I am a thief but if there is an opportunity to steal I will take it. I will remember you Thomas; through this watch I will remember you and your Dunn clocks I thought to myself.

Chapter Nineteen

1898

Inside the butler's room, sitting on the butler's single and rather hard bed tapping my right foot on the floor, a feeling of sadness came over me. This room will no longer be lived in, this bed will no longer be slept in for the owner is no longer among the living, he had faced his death because of his short lived friendship with me in which he was willing to lay down his life for the documents he had in his procession, the documents that laid under floorboard three in this very room but more importantly the floorboard under my right tapping foot.

I tapped a little harder on the wood and it moved up a little and slid back down as I released my foot, the butler has been true to his word. I just hope I am the only second person to see what lies underneath. I placed myself on my knees coming face to face with a pair of empty walking shoes, I took the moment to say I few words for my departed friend before I placed my fingertips around the edge of floorboard three and lifted it up and placed in on the bed.

Within in the hole in the floor I came across some letters of the butler's earlier life and happy times he had shared with the lady of Blissful Hill. I placed them carefully to one side as I saw what I was looking for in a black box. I lifted the black box out of the hole, where I saw a brass number coded plate. I let my fingers roll over the numbers until at last they spelt out 24312, I heard a click and the box lid open slightly.

I opened it more and in there, once again my eyes fell on my deeds to my house, I took the time to read in through and I was in for a shock for it wasn't my home, it was Charles's! And my lovely maid, who I don't remember knowing has been working for Charles! I sat back on the butler's bed, shaking. I was used to shaking now, as I was slowly stopping my need for my habit. I looked out of the butler's only window to the lovely countryside. What does this all mean?

I carried on looking through the black box to find a different letter, written on a blue piece of paper it was a letter from Charlotte to her sister, it was a sad but a beautiful read.

Dear Lizzie,

It has been such a long time since I last spoke to you or even seen you and I know that is a bad show on my part, for I miss you dearly young sister. But time has moved on I guess and we have grown, we are not those sweet little darlings that used to run around pretending to be princesses anymore are we?

I feel I need to pick up the pen once more and write to you for a purely selfish reason and for that I feel so very sorry about as I don't want you to feel burdened with my troubles but I have no one else I can talk to, let

alone trust. Although the butler here, he seems to care for me greatly and for that I am truly thankful for otherwise I swear I would have gone mad.

Sometimes I believe I am mad Lizzie, mad for staying with him, mad for leaving London and you for this place. Do you know he has named this place Blissful Hill? How can that be? How can he jest like that? It is hardly blissful here sister, it is the worst kind of hell. But I did not want to be alone Lizzie, as forceful and cruel as my husband can be I did not want to be without him but as I look back now I know I have made a terrible mistake for he does not love me, after all I have done and put up with he still does not love me.

I asked him once if he could let that maid go, in spite of everything she has done to me but he just laughed at me. He said I should forget his little indiscretions, for that is what a good wife should do. He actually laughed at me Lizzie, which made me so mad!

As you know I lost my baby boy, my darling boy something I am still very upset about only to find my husband in bed with that maid weeks after and to see her give birth to his child and to found out it is a boy! Well I had to send him away, I just had to. I had nothing against the boy but to see him made my heart break every time, and we have weak hearts don't we Lizzie?

I wanted to send the maid with her son, I would have paid for them to live together for the rest of their lives but my husband wanted her to stay with us and blame me for separating the mother and child. The maid

has in turn treated me with distaste ever since, she believes she is worth so much more than me because she has given my husband a son when I couldn't.

It is terrible living here Lizzie I have no room to mourn of the lost of my son, my daughter on the other hand is becoming more and more distant with me, you will think I have been converted into an insane woman but I believe the maid is trying to take my daughter away from me for I, in her eyes, have taken away her son...

I have no one to talk to, no one that can truly understand. I believe my own daughter has the devil inside of her, I know it is not a very motherly thing to say but the maid has changed her, she still looks like me in every way but she is not my beautiful princess anymore Lizzie, she is a dark creature with evil in her eyes. I have been having bad dreams of late Lizzie, dreams that my own daughter in trying to kill me and both the maid and my husband sit and watch laughing. Something is going to happen here Lizzie, I foresee my own death; please take me away from here Lizzie please!

I would not ask you this if I did not believe it so.

From your darling older sister Lotty x

Tears fell out of my eyes when I finished reading that letter, how very sad and lonely Charlotte must have felt in the last days of her life, maybe death was the only way for her to feel at peace. I put the letter on the pile with the other documents and looked again within the black box. I found a photograph of what must have been the said daughter within the letter, her mother was right she did look like her in every way but there was something more shocking for me to find as I recognize the daughter... for she has grown up now and has become my maid!

1888

It did not take that long to find the enigmatic Billing Club, I suppose it was quite an insignificant building for the area that it sat in, but for me it stood out like a saw thumb. The front door is made of a dark red wood that shined in the morning sun with two darker shaded wooden knobs that was positioned in the centre of each one. The door was covered by an ornate and most expensive looking porch and rested on a set of cream coloured marbled stairs that was the home to one stern looking guard.

This guard had already spotted me looking at the building he protected and instantly changed his standing position from his footing being placed together and his hands lying in front, to his feet being apart and his hands behind his back. He was not, under any circumstances going to allow me to walk passed him and into the building he worked for, that I could tell immediately, this is going to be a waiting game I thought to myself so I would need to find a place to sit. My eyes wondered around and directly became shocked by the sight I saw for the location for the Billing Club sat right opposite the Willow and Owl theatre, could this Sir Charles really be that evil to place himself a few feet away from his beloved at all times?

I moved through the busy crowd of people that filled this demanding street, over towards the theatre, it seemed a quiet and peaceful place at this time of the day, I found it hard to imagine the evil that lies within this tranquil setting, I wondered if the ghost of Ellen, the singing nightingale still haunted the stage singing her little heart out when a voice from in front broke into my thoughts.

'A penny for them,' said a man that was sitting in front of the theatre on a wooden bench eating a green apple that had seen better days. The juice of the apple ran on to his shirt but he didn't seem to mind as he focus was mainly on me, in truth I don't remember him sitting there as I crossed the road but I seemed to have stopped in front of him to look up at the theatre .

'Oh I am sorry I didn't see you there,' I said as I moved to one side.

'That alright love, not many people see me. I am just a part of the scenery.'

'I feel like that some days,' I said as I sat down on the wooden bench beside this mundane man.

'Surely not you, you being special and all,' he said still looking towards the direction I was standing in.

'What do you mean by that?'

'Well you are Mary Kelly aren't you?'

'Yes I am but I don't understand,' I said frowning at this quite strange man, for he reminded me of someone I knew but could not put my finger on whom.

‘Well I heard you were the special one.’

‘From whom may I ask?’

‘Does it matter?’ he said as he finished his apple and threw it into the street with some disgust by the passersby. He eyes were still focused in the direction in front of him, but for the first time I realised this young man was never looking at me when I was standing there for he was staring at the building behind, the imperative Billing Club.

‘Do you know me?’ I asked quietly.

‘I have heard of you.’ was his unclear reply.

‘What interests you about that building?’

‘I would imagine the same thing as you.’

‘Do you work for the government?’ I asked him to which he laughed.

‘What makes you say such a thing?’

‘Well you have the habit of not quite answering my questions so I just thought you sounded like someone official.’

‘What you mean to say is that I am not giving you the answers you want to hear.’

‘Something like that I guess.’

‘Well did you ever think that you are not asking the right questions, to get the answers you seek?’

'You like to be mysterious don't you?'

'I would hardly use the word mysterious to describe little old me.'

'Who are you?' I asked.

'And there it is.'

'There what is?'

'The correct question, my name is Jimmy Turner.'

'I remember hearing your name once, but I cannot remember where or when.'

'I am very surprised to hear that.'

'Oh?'

'She does not speak of me that often I know, but I guess you and her have become close, almost sisters I hear.'

'You are Maria's brother.'

'Yes amongst other things, I could say I am Maria's brother in name as such.'

'She does not speak of her family much I am sorry.'

'Nothing for you to feel sorry about missy, Maria has always been a funny lot when it comes to her family.'

'It is from her, you learned about me.'

'I don't get to see her that often, but I heard that you had taken her under your wing so to speak after you met the strange woman that used to live downstairs from us.'

'Yes, Maria seemed so lonely.'

'She is a lost soul indeed but I am glad she found someone to put her trust in, tell me is she well?'

How do I answer that question? In truth I had no idea how well Maria was at this precise moment, I hope to God that there isn't other death waiting for me when I got home but in my weakest judgment I have a feeling that might well be the case. How do I tell her own brother that she was pregnant for being a common whore like me? 'I would like it if she wasn't like me' I answered.

'So would I, not trying to say bad of you my love. I am sure you are a lovely girl but your line of work leaves a little to be desired.'

'Believe me, it is not the life I would have chosen for myself.'

'I believe you my dear,' he replied as he blindly patted me on my shoulder almost missing me entirely as his eyes were still firmly on the eminent Billing Club.

'Are you going to tell me, what is so singular about the Billing Club?' I asked.

'Are you?'

'I don't know what you mean.'

'Yes you do, I saw you across the road looking at it, you are here because of that building, or should I say who is in that building?'

'I heard a story that might have some dosh behind it,' I managed to say but feeling a little uncomfortable.

'I see, you didn't take me as the blackmail type.'

'I believe it would help Maria get on and out of Whitechapel.'

'Well isn't that rather interesting?' he said as he for the first time took his eyes from the building that was across the street to me and it was the first time I could really see the young man behind the secretive words. He was really quite sweet in looks, his bright blue eyes shone out from under his flat cap and his beard was well trimmed, this Jimmy looked after himself well. I wonder why Maria kept away from him. He seemed as if he could really look after her, but instead the role of looking after Maria has fallen to me and as led me here, ready to blackmail a gentleman who has more than likely killed before and for less, great move Mary!

'What is interesting?'

'You believe yourself to never leave Whitechapel.'

'What makes you say that?'

'You are willing to risk you life to blackmail for the money you will give to Maria not yourself, there is something I admire about that and not because she is my sister,' he said with my eyes shining at me. This Jimmy was becoming keen on me I can see.

'Well Jimmy you are not very gentlemanly are you?'

'Have I not been?'

'No, I have told you why the building means something to me but you have not said why the building means something to you.'

'What interests me is the person staring out of the window on the first floor, that my dear is Sir Charles,' he paused for me to look across the street and at the Billing Club one floor up. There I met the eyes of the devil. 'And I don't know about you, but I think there is something sinful behind that face.'

1898

I had been sitting there for a while, inside the butler's vacant room on his wooden floor almost caught in a gaze. Suprising it wasn't shock that I was feeling it wasn't astonishment either; it was more like the feeling of bewilderment and perplexity, for I felt as if my world was in chaos and disorder. Everything is not how it was anymore, somehow I knew from this day things would never be the same again for me; I was told once that everything happens for a reason, is this the reason behind my companion buying this house?

Surely he would not buy the same house as the one my maid lived in, there has got to be more reasoning involved, something about my friend himself. What I did not understand was that if my maid was the daughter to the lady and master of this house, why has she become the class in which she is now?

What is more compelling in the notion of if the lady of the house was right in her letter, that for some reason she did not send to her sister then did her daughter who is now my maid want to murder her own mother? She disappeared with the enraged maid of the house that night, never to return again.

But she did, she had returned as my maid with Charles when they had heard of the break in for I had called her Charlotte. It must have been a great shock to her to hear me call her my her mother's name, the mother she may have murdered, so it is no wonder that she left this place as fast as she came.

But had she been here before? I only ask myself because of the words of the butler running through my head,

'Do you believe in ghosts Sir?' he had asked me. *'I have not taken leave of my senses for it is true in what I say. I have seen a ghost.'*

'A ghost of who may I ask?' I had asked the butler almost without thinking about the conversation I was having. I regret that I did not pay sufficient attention to the kind, old man's words when he was alive, I feel as if I had missed so much information of great magnitude, how many

times have I done that? How many times have I not listened and not understood?

'Charlotte Sir, at least I thought it was her Sir,' he had answered. *'At the time I saw her I was so very sure it was her, she looked so beautiful Sir, but the master, your friend said I was mad and if I don't forget what I have seen he would ask me to leave.'*

Why did Charles behave in that manner towards his own butler? It seemed so unlike him but on the other hand I am slowly learning the truth about my friend and the more I learn the more I sadly do not like. Clearly the butler had seen my maid on a separate occasion here and had mistaken her for the past lady of the house and as I look again at her photograph I can understand why. But for Charles to dismiss the idea so lividly, makes me wonder why he wanted severely not to be connected with my maid here? For he must have known the butler was talking about the maid and not really about the vision of a ghost.

'It sounds as if you had seen this ghost recently is that not so?' I had asked him.

'Yes Sir, it was a few days ago, just before you arrived Sir,' the butler had answered.

So when I was thought of missing when I left the hospital, my maid was here with Charles, I feel I am getting nervous and a little uneasy about the situation between both my maid and my friend. There is something drawing them together, something dark and evil I can tell. It makes me wonder what power mutually they have and what they have done with it.

I turned back to the box to see a other photograph modelled in almost a repeat of the portrait downstairs of the master of the house, but there was something different, the business books had disappeared, the clock was still there in the background but the man was younger, for he was almost the same age as me in this photograph, but is wasn't the background or the age of the man that bothered me, it was the man's face.

For now the master's face was younger I could tell the answer to the connection between my maid and my friend, because although I was looking at the face of George the vile man of this house, the man that had made his wife's life a misery by flaunting his mistress in her face, a mistress that had given birth to his child I was also staggeringly looking at the face of his bastard son, a son I had come to know for he was my friend Charles.

My friend was the bastard son of the master of this house, that is why he had brought it and hanged the portrait of his father back up in the sitting room, he is proud to be his son and I can imagine the hatred he felt for the lady that in his eyes, took his mother away from him.

He had made friends with the lady's daughter because the daughter had become fond of his own mother and that friendship had stayed with them through thick and thin because there is a bond between them. A bond of loathing and revulsion against the lady of this house, a bond so strong maybe that is drove them to a sinister side of both their characters; it perhaps drove them to the worse of all vices, the criminal vice of the murdering of a family member.

What have I gotten myself into? Could my friend really have murdered his step-mother at such a young age? Normally I would have dismissed the whole silly idea, but now I am not so sure, for I am beginning to lose faith in my friend as I believe I do not know him at all and what is more shocking to me is that there has been so many people trying to warn me about him. I thought to myself as the words of the strange lady ran deep inside my brain for she did once say to me something that I had thought at the time was just designed for my maid, but now I believe she truly meant my maid and my friend when she said;

'Beware of the company you keep.'

Chapter Twenty

1888

I was left alone on the wooden bench outside the Willow and the Owl theatre for some time before I saw movement in the first floor window of the famous Billing Club, Sir Charles was leaving and when I was deciding when to make my move he surprised me for when he left the building he made his way over to me.

'You are new here, are you not?' he boomed.

'Yes,' I plainly answered.

'A woman of short words I see, well that suits me very well. I cannot stand a woman that talks a huge amount because they never have anything good to say,' he said as he stood in front of me. 'So are you going to tell me why you and that other fella was staring up at me or not?'

'What makes you think I was staring at you?'

'Well,' he started.

'In actual fact I was staring up at the building you had just come out off, I like these aristocratic buildings they give a certain atmosphere to the place don't you think? It will be a great place to start my career,' I said looking around; I thought to myself that lying is so very easy. 'That is why I was talking to that fella as you call him, he might be able to put me on the stage in here.'

'You sing?'

'Yes, you see it runs in the family. My cousin used to work here you see, do you know this theatre well Sir? You may have known her.' I said building up my muster to tell him the ghostly name of his loved one.

'What is the name?'

'Ellen Sir, Ellen Rose,' as I said the name I stood up to face him, I looked at him sternly in the face and I could see the colour drain from him in an instant. 'But surely you have Sir, for you are Sir Charles are you not?' I asked.

'You know of me?' he asked quietly.

'Oh yes Sir, I know all about you,' I said as I moved away from him to which he grabbed my arm, like I knew he would.

'What do you know?'

'I know many things Sir, many dark and sinister things.'

'What do you want for me?'

'Now Sir, do I really have to tell you that?' I asked cheekily.

'If it is money you want, you will have to show me what you know.'

'Come to my home, in Miller's Court, tomorrow night, the 9th, and I will tell you all I know.'

'How can I trust you?' he said maliciously.

'You can't Sir, but I think you will find what a more important question is, can you gamble on not trusting me?'

'You do not know who you are dealing with!'

'I think I do,' I said, hoping that I might have changed the future for this Sir Charles might even bump into Jack the Ripper, now that would be something shocking for all wouldn't it? I tugged away from his grasp and walked away. As I passed the clock shop again I suddenly stop and look in the window for a thought had passed my mind.

What if? What if? I repeated to myself, no one knows who Jack the Ripper is, I do not know who my killer will be, what if the strange woman is playing a game with me? What if she is completing my fate for me? What if the person I had just met is Jack the Ripper himself? I have just invited the devil inside my home, is that why I get killed there? Is it really because of my own undoing that I meet Jack the Ripper? If this is to be the case, Sir Charles had not only killed the singing nightingale but all my friends too. I wonder how many more he has killed that I do not know about? But whatever the answer to that question I am now ready for him, I will be ready to meet Jack the Ripper on the 9th November in the year of 1888, for I am Mary Kelly, his next victim.

1898

Everything was starting to fall in to place for me when a thought had occurred, making me stand up and walk downstairs and into the study and straight towards the medical books, I had seen before when I was in here. Charles's father used to be a doctor, so these books would have been easy access for a girl with the mischievous sprite on her mind and now they stand here with no purpose but for decoration unless their purpose has arisen suddenly, say maybe the poisoning of the mother of a treasured one, or maybe an addiction given to a friend.

There were many well used and dog-eared books, Charles must have spent a long time in here, but there one book I was looking for was about drugs, my drug in fact and sorrowfully I found it, I had hoped in a foolish way that I wouldn't find it. I just did not want to believe my own thoughts about Charles for he had been my only true companion for many years, so I wanted to prove myself wrong but the truth was always there and the truth is such a powerful thing. Once you know the truth, you can never go back to not knowing it, as looking down at this one medical book shows me.

It had been ringed; Charles had made a note of this drug. This book told me everything about the dominance the purple poppy has and its side effects. Side effects which included memory loss and seeing things that is not there, side effects I was feeling. Charles knew about this and he did not help, in actually fact he was the one that ill-advised me to take more. Charles had used this against me, for he had used me. I slammed the book shut with disgust and put it back on the shelves.

It was then as my eyes wondered with anger I noticed another medical book had been used often as the spine was breaking away. I took hold of it and flicked though the pages, there was another ringed piece of information, but this time it was about madness. How one person could be sane one minute and mad in the other, was Charles making me mad on purpose? Was Charles himself mad? As I threw the book on the table, a piece of newspaper that was between the pages fell out. I started to read it;

Last night, a most ghastly murder happened in the back stage of the Willow and Owl theatre, in the East End of London. The victim was the young and talented Ellen Rose, her family are greatly upset, and she was meant to be married to a young duke within a few months. For someone to get backstage, she must have knew them. She was found with her throat cut from ear to ear, and in most appalling way her body was cut to pieces with her heart missing.

I heard the footsteps of the servants returning home, I placed the newspaper clipping back my pocket and placed the book in the bookcase and left the room. I ran upstairs to the box and emptied my pocket into it. I placed everything back into the box, locked it and placed the floorboard back in its home and left the butler's room for the last time. I decided there and then that this information will not go unused but for the time being I will not let on what I now know of my foolish friend for my life may well be in danger if I do.

I found that my acting skills came into question a little sooner than I had hoped for the very next day Charles came home to his Blissful Hill.

'Charles!' I proclaimed with mock delight.

'Hello Thomas,' Charles said without looking at me. He was starring at something; I moved closer and looked over his shoulder to see him studying two kinds of different maps of Whitechapel. One I had seen many times in the hall of the Billing Club, it shown the varied homes all painted in different colour to demonstrate the discrepancy of wealth within the part of our city. I had often thought it was bad taste to have a copy of this map hanging in such a fine hall, as it felt to me as if we were boasting that we were better, to even have the map at all. The other map was of the sewer works of Whitechapel. It shown every drain covering and where every pipe ran to, it really was a piece of art and very detailed. It was then, that a curious thought popped into my head almost as a whimsical jest at first.

Jack the Ripper would have loved to have a map like that, to use it when on the run and to disappear into the murky depths of the East End sewer system, while everyone was running panicked and terrified over his head.

But then I recognized where I was, what I had found and whose hands that map was in and the little harmless jest turned into the most shocking horror for a jest cannot be a jest if it is true. I suddenly felt weak and giddy, I was sure the colour had drained from my face and instinctually I grabbed a back of a chair to hold me up.

Could it be true? Could I have spent the last how many years, with Jack the Ripper? Could I have called Jack the Ripper my friend? But when I look back at all the things I now believe Charles to have done, is killings four prostitutes in the poorest of streets really so far of an idea?

I saw firsthand the fright this murderer had caused to many lonely and destitute people, the things he did! The evil he had done! Jack the Ripper was the devil, but Jack the Ripper is my friend. I am in the same room as the devil, the madman for I am in the same room as Jack the Ripper.

I felt queasy and my anxiety had reached new heights for my breathing had become faster, with all the bloodied corpses I had seen of late and the ones I had read about all running around in my head, fighting against each other to place themselves in the foremost of my mind believing their one to be the most gruesome, I had a sensation of coolness running over my whole body for although I knew this situation was new to me, something felt similar, *almost identical to an situation I have experienced before.*

1888

As I walked back towards my part of London town and towards my own class of people, I felt changed. This trip into the aristocratic and genteel boundaries of the Square Mile was meant to have been a way of getting money for Maria, yes maybe it was a dishonest way of doing it but how else is a girl like me going to come into some gold at this late moment in the game? But this trip has been so much more for it has transformed me into a stronger woman, before I was altering my mind between staying to face my death or leaving on the first cart out of here but now I have made my decision and cannot adjust it for if I have just met the taker of my life, he now knows where I live. Most people would be terrified at this prospect, but you see I now have a reason for dying, when I die Maria will have money and live a better life than I could have wished for and that is all that I am thinking about right now.

I came closer to my home with a bounce in my step, behaving childishly by dodging all the cracks in the pavement. When in the distance I spot a similar sight I have seen many times before, a common street walker standing on the corner of where Dorset Street ends and my Miller's Court start. The morning was turning into late afternoon and there was a certain dense mist hanging around, clinging to the walls of every home so I was finding it hard to see exactly who it was standing there, I slowly moved closer and I don't know whether it was breathing in the misty smoke of the London air or it was my mind playing tricks on me but the way this woman was standing, the way she was holding herself it was as if I was seeing my friend Lizzie Stride and my mind wondered back to the past...

'Hello my dearest Mary? You are looking rather rosy on this fine afternoon,' Liz said in her best mock posh voice as we met at the Embankment opposite the Houses of

Parliament, she was wearing her best hat and dress and looked overall quite sweet.

'Why, so do you young Elizabeth. If my eyes are loyal to me, do I spot a new necklace?' I replied in my finest imitation of how ladies speak in the West End.

'Why I do believe it is! How absolutely delightful of you to notice! It is made from the finest glass one could get at the exceptional little cart in Petticoat Lane, because you do know that is the only place to do for first-rate jewellery!'

'Quite so Elizabeth! It is simply to die for!' I replied as we burst out laughing causing all the other ladies turn from the Thames on to us, who straight away gave us a look of distaste and loathing which if truth will be told made us laugh even more.

We had decided to meet at the Thames as this was the only place to be today for the Queen of all people was travelling along the river on the Prince Eddy. This was the first time old Vicky would have been seen out since the death of her husband Albert in 1861 and it would also be the first I have got to see her at all. I was young and very excited for I knew this would be a moment I would remember for years to come.

'I don't know why we are here,' Lizzie whispered to me.

'It's our chance to see our Queen.'

'Yeah so?'

'What do you mean, 'yeah so'?' I whispered.

'What has she done for us? Apart from sulking around her posh houses dressed in black.'

'She is mourning the death of her husband; I know if I lost my Joseph I would be terribly upset.'

'For this long?'

'How long should you mourn for a loved one then?'

'Well, I believe you just get back on with your life. It's unhealthy to think in the past.'

'Oh look here she comes!' I proclaimed, dismissing what Lizzie just said.

'Oh righty oh then,' she said solemnly.

The boat was very grand, with dark varnish woods and gold plated rims and statues; the base was the colour of pearly white with the Royal Coat of Arms placed in gold and reds on the back. I could see many people walking about on deck, the Queen's son was there, I couldn't make out his face but he is always famous for wearing flamboyant fashions and there is one large man in a red tunic with blue slash, his gold buttons were shining ever so brightly. His hat reminded me a ship's captain hat with colourful feathers poking out of the middle, he was standing behind a gold plated chair with purple padding talking to a woman in a green dress and her hair was pinned up.

But the most important person was the lady sitting in the gold plated chair, for she was the Queen. I could not see the expression on her face as I was so far away but she held herself straight, her greying hair was tied underneath a small black hat with white lace. Her dress was simple, black and not over the top, a great difference between her and her son, with one white glove she started to wave at us. Which prompted all the children to start to scream and some of the adults to wave flags, everyone was smiling and being happy, I even caught Lizzie smiling and waving back to the Queen.

'Mary?' Lizzie asked as we left the Embankment.

'Yes.'

'If I was to tell you something, will you promise not to tell anyone else?'

'Of course.'

'I am in love.'

'Really? With whom?'

'He is quite high up in government, in foreign affairs.'

'Very nice.'

'You do not think of me as, what you English call, silly?'

'It is never silly to be in love,' I said as I hooked my arm around hers.

'When everything calms down overseas, he said he would take me away from here as long as I stop walking the streets.'

'Sounds reasonable, have you stopped?'

'I try; I only go out when I am hungry.'

'He can't blame you for that.'

'That's what I thought,' she said as she hugged tighter around me...

In my mind my thoughts brought me slowly back to my time, is that why you went out on the night of the 30th because you were hungry? My dear, dear friend, how I miss you so, how I miss all of you now. I had almost reached the woman on the corner when I realized who she really was for she was the strange woman I had met on the night my Lizzie had died.

'Nursing a bad head are we?' I asked to which she jumped out of her skin.

'Oh Mary, I did not see you there. I was just getting some fresh air.'

'Are you still playing that game with me?' I asked with my hand on my hips.

'What game? Don't we all play a game in the end?'

'None of this mumble jumbles now, I know who you are.'

'I am everyone and yet I am no one.'

'You are a caring mother,' I finally said. 'Who is worried for her own daughter.'

'I don't know what you mean.'

'I saw it on the first night; I saw both of you in the same room. There was a moment when you both looked at me, I knew there was something. I saw it again in Newgate, when I was claiming to be your daughter, before you turned around to see who it was you called me by another name. The name of your daughter and now you want me to blackmail a rich man so I can give your daughter some money, do you think I am that silly?'

'She will not see me,' the strange woman finally submitted, 'I saw the nurse leave so I tapped on the door, she is still so angry with me.'

'Are you going to tell me what you have done that is so bad?'

'No.'

'I thought not, but you would like me to see how she is?'

'Yes.'

'Lucky for you I was going home anyway,' I said as I walked passed her.

'Can you tell her something?' the strange woman asked, so I turned back to face her.

'What is that?'

'That anything I have done, no matter how bad and cruel it may seem to her, I have done because I love her.'

That statement was the truest thing the strange woman had come out with, so in turn made it sound very powerful to me. I looked at the strange woman for a moment and I saw her true nature, yes she still looked strange and quite monstrous but she was a mother, a mother to my dear friend. Everyone makes mistakes, everyone does something wrong in their lifetime but she has always loved her daughter, although this moment was important to both of us my hatred for this woman for being lied to still had me replying in three simple words which were; 'I will do.'

Chapter Twenty One

1898

I pulled myself together and pushed the horrific thoughts of Charles being the most notorious murderer of our time to the back of mind, took a few breaths because if I am going to get out of this place and back to the safety of London I am going to have to play along with this horrendous circumstances I have found myself in.

'What's wrong, Charles?' I asked him to which he seemed to answer in a dream.

'That bloody girl!'

'What girl, Charles?' I asked and with that he seemed to notice I was there for the first time and said

'Ah Thomas! There you are!' He pushed the map in his drawer. 'How are you feeling? Any better?'

'Much better, thank you Charles, how are you? You seem distressed.' I said in a mock caring tone.

'Oh that, that's nothing. I was just working on the case.'

'The case you say? Oh the 'missing bodies' case, yes I almost forgot all about that,' I said, as Charles sat down in his chair, crossed his legs and pressed his fingers together in an almost praying action.

'It's funny what one person can *forget,*' he said not to me but to the drawer he had put the Whitechapel map in. 'and yet, other person will remember.'

'What Charles?' I asked. He shook his head and looked at me. 'Can I help with the case?'

'No, I want you here,' he said, in a rather malicious way, he eyes went dark and his face looked quite mad. He seemed to change, physically as well as mentally in a matter of seconds.

'Charles you can't force me to stay, I thank you for you care but I feel much better now and I would like to return home please. I am dearly missing it.'

He face, warmed as he said 'Of course you do, my dear boy! Of course you may go home whenever you like, I'm glad you are feeling better. Maybe we could meet at the club? We could discuss a little more about the missing bodies.'

'Has there been any more?' I asked as I sat down on one of his armchairs.

'Haven't you been reading the papers?' Charles asked. Yes Charles I have been reading a very interesting newspaper clipping, I thought but said;

'No, I have been spending my time walking and painting.'

'No writing?'

'Well in truth, I have been thinking about another book and that's why I wanted to go back home for research,' I said. Here we go Charles, I am letting you know I am starting to realise who you are, I thought.

'Research you say my dear boy?'

'Yes, I have this idea, about Jack the Ripper.'

'The Ripper? Why do you want to bring that up? It was a few years ago, it's old hat!'

'Yes, but it's still fresh in people minds isn't it? And he's still alive,' I said, isn't he Charles I asked in my head.

'What?'

'Well, he was never caught. So there is a high probability that he still lives, what has happened to him?'

'And that's your book idea is it? A fictional story about a man that kills and then what exactly? He just goes back to normal life? It doesn't have the same ring to it as the missing bodies in London, does it?' He said. Are there really any missing bodies, Charles? Is it what your mind has made up? No one else is talking about missing bodies? There is no police case. Is it your guilty mind for what you did to Ellen? You think Ellen is sending you messages, are you truly going mad? All these questions were running around head as I sat there, opposite the person I thought was my friend with a blank expression on my face.

'It was just a thought,' I said

'Well it is a bad one my dear boy,' he said, as he almost waved the idea away. Well you would think that Charles wouldn't you? I wonder, you managed to kill your own step mother at an early age, you probably killed Ellen, maybe even Ellen's mother by all accounts but how many more? Something was telling me the thought of my friend as Jack the Ripper didn't quite cover how far he has truly gone. I stood up and turned to leave the room but stopped and with my back towards him he boomed 'what is wrong my dear boy?'

'Nothing Charles, I just suddenly thought.'

'You have been thinking a lot lately, I am glad to hear it. It is almost like I am getting the old Thomas back, which I think is highly Capital! But I digress, you thought what Thomas?' he asked to which I turned to face him.

'I see you have new gloves,' I plainly said.

'My gloves you say? You are interested in my gloves? You have got to get more!' he laughed.

'Yes, you are quite right Charles. But you see it has reminded me of something, something the butler had said, that your gloves had got ripped and that they needed mending.'

'Yes well, in the end I wanted new ones instead, can't go around with mended gloves can we? It is a gentleman's disgrace after all.'

'Do you remember where you had ripped them now?'

'No I have quite forgotten.'

'Yes well it was some time ago wasn't it?'

'Yes Thomas, I believe it was,' Charles replied to me with a questionable look on his face. I turned once again and left the room. I stopped outside and thought to myself, you may have forgotten Charles but I do remember, I remember now...

The white material I had found and kept with me ever since was from your glove, the white material I had used to stop the kettle from boiling in the theatre. The white material that was at the scene of the murder of Jimmy Turner, for you was his murderer wasn't you?

Jimmy looked up at you when we had entered the theatre for you was sitting in your chair in the Billing Club, seeing your face again trigger off something in both your minds for his face was horrific at the sight of seeing yours, that is how you knew where I was for you had seen me enter the theatre not because of the reason you had said?

'But tell me, how did you know I had been taking to a police station?' I had asked you, Charles.

'I asked the delivery boy.' was his reply.

'The delivery boy you say? Oh yes, I had quite forgotten about the delivery boy,' I had absent-mindedly replied.

'I haven't,' he had mumbled at me. 'He hadn't' Charles had replied, I wonder what he had meant by saying that. No wait, it cannot be, my mind is playing tricks on me, and he could never do that, what dark thoughts I have! But after everything I have learned is it so impossible to contemplate? He was just a boy Charles, a young boy like you was once. My mind went back to the night I was sitting in William Jenkins house and once again I was sitting in that chair, drinking his poorly made tea.

'You mentioned you saw a man at the window when you last saw her, could you describe him?' I had asked the delivery boy, Will.

'But it is funny, we are talking about him as I am sure I have seen him again recently, well that is what I thought but I could have been mistaken.'

'When was that?' I had asked.

'Well it was the same day I saw you, Tom. Funny how things fit together isn't it Tom?' You are quite right Will, Charles had seen you seeing him at the scene of Jimmy's death, and you had to be silenced. Poor, poor Will you weren't to know, you didn't understand what danger you were in...

1888

I entered 13 Miller's Court, to see that the room had been cleared and cleaned as the bucket had been emptied and the only other set of bed sheets had been placed on the bed leaving the soiled one in the corner by the fireplace.

Maria was sitting upright, and I could see that she had been washed; her eyes were once again bright and wide.

'You look better,' I said as I placed myself on the wooden milking stool that I took from the back of John McCarty's Chandler shop when his wife wasn't looking.

'Is she still out there?' was her reply.

'I don't know to be honest with you.' I said looking at the floor.

'She will not go away,' she replied as she threw her arms in the air.

'A motherly instinct to protect her child come what may, I suppose,' I said still looking at the floor, that statement was met by silence as I knew it would. I glance up at Maria to see the expression of shock mixed with guilt. 'Look I understand you do not want to talk about and it is only because I care for you that I will let this whole thing about you being her daughter, slip.'

'I am sorry for not telling you,' she whispered.

'It is alright.'

'Did she tell you?'

'In her own way, I guess she did.'

'I am sorry I wasn't the one.'

'It was a sister's promise wasn't it? How are you feeling?'

'I'm a bit weak to be honest with you.'

'Fancy some tea, now?' I asked as I stood up and grabbed the kettle.

'It would be nice.'

'Oh there was something she wanted me to tell you.'

'I don't want to hear it.'

'It was quite heart warming.'

'If you truly knew her, I bet you wouldn't think so.'

'If you say so,' I said as the kettle boiled.

After we had our tea, I felt a little better and by the look of Maria, she was feeling better too. It was unusual sensation sitting in the one room that had been my home for many years, knowing that today was going to be the last day I would enjoy being around my own stuff, I felt as if I needed to say goodbye to everything even though the things were not living. It was when I was half way through doing that Maria suddenly turned to me and asked 'Why have you not asked what happened when you left me?'

'Because I do not want to know, all I know is that you are alright and that's all I care about.'

'What would have I done without you Mary?' she started but there was something in her eyes when she said this, it almost looked as if she was sad which prompted to ask

‘What is wrong Maria?’

‘What is wrong you ask! How can you be like this! Don’t you think I know what today is? What today means to you?’ she shouted as she cried in the pillow.

‘What is wrong?’ I repeated. She seemed to behaving as strange as she did, down by the Thames.

‘Don’t ask Mary, please don’t ask!’ she said through the pillow.

‘Okay, okay,’ I said as I moved over to the bed and I started to rub her shoulder ‘Please calm down Maria, you still are very ill and so not need this stress, for me Maria please’ she wiped her nose on the edge on the pillow and said,

‘I will stop, I am sorry.’

‘It’s alright, truly it is. See what I got you,’ I said trying to change the subject and to cheer her up, so I showed her the clockwork on a gold chain.

‘Where did you get that?’ she said as she held it in her hands.

‘I got it from a very nice and undervalued guy.’

‘Who was it?’

‘Oh I don’t know, I can’t remember his name. Something like, Thomas Dunn. Although I am sure I have heard of that name before *somewhere.’*

1898

That same night I left for home, Charles did not see me off. There was something about him, something was going on, and something was changing him. I knew I had to get away from him and his servants to think about everything that had happened and the coach ride give me that time, so armed with the black box I left Blissful Hill, for the last time.

I got home and the maid was waiting for me, just as I knew she would. She took my bags, just as I knew she would. But I made sure I had hold of the black box and I was not about to let it out of my sight, while she was around. After she had put away my other bags I call her to enter my drawing room. It was time to let the cat out of the bag, so to speak.

'Yes sir?'

'Ah, there you are. What is your name?'

'Well its Sarah Sir, Sarah Biggs.'

'How long have you been working for me?'

'Years, Sir.'

'And yet, I didn't know that. I don't even know your name and when I ask you what your name is, you tell me without looking shocked that I am asked you this.'

'I don't understand.'

'That's the thing, Ms Biggs. I didn't understand any of this, do you know I don't remember buying this house. Well of course you knew that, because I have never brought this house have I? And you don't work for me.'

'I think you need to see the doctor.'

'Oh the doctor, yes that's another thing. How comes I don't remember ever seeing this doctor? Yes I saw the medicine that you kindly gave me every time I had a famous fever, but I saw no doctor, strange isn't it? I think that's strange. What does my doctor look like? Is he similar to someone we both know, very well by chance?'

'Well, I don't know what you are getting at!'

'Come, come Ms Biggs, there is no need to get angry with me. I asked simple questions, what does my doctor look like? Because, strangely I don't remember him, I don't remember him at all. Instead of answering me, you get angry. Why?' she was about to speak again when I said 'Don't answer that question. I'm sorry, I'm getting ahead of myself; you know a friend once told me to ask the right questions. But I think I need to ask the right questions to the right person,' I said as I walked past her.

'Where are you going Sir?' She asked.

I stopped and turned back to her. 'Can I ask you a question that only you can answer, was it you that kept filling up my flask with the uncontrollable drug?' I asked but she said nothing. 'Well maybe you can answer me this, was it you that dragged me into the den that night, making sure I would have more because you could see I had changed my mind?' I asked louder but again she said nothing.

'Not talking now are we? Well maybe you can tell me exactly what did you have in your hands that day to make my bed sheets red with 'blood'?' I asked her heatedly but she said nothing. 'I see' I answered myself as I knew she would have never answered those questions 'One last question, how far have you gone in the past for a *family member?'* Again that question was faced with no answer 'well you can fill in your report and hand it to the person that pays you,' I said as I walked out the door and headed eastwards.

I had one important stop to make before I was in Whitechapel again and feeling like I was home, with no box in my hands as it was in a safe place now.

I walked in the Ten Bells and there she was, like I knew she would be. I nodded to her, she walked over to me.

'You seem to know me,' I said.

'Why wouldn't I?'

'I need to know things, I need to understand.'

'Ah, you are ready to know the truth, I can see it now, and I can see it in your eyes.'

'Is there any where we can talk?'

‘I have people after me, we need to speak fast.’

‘Why are people after you?’

‘For what I know, it’s risky but I know a place we can talk that will make it easy for me to explain.’

We walked out the pub and down a few streets, with the girl constantly looking around her. We arrived in Dorset Street, I turned down an alleyway and headed right to the end of the tunnel, to the old wooden door, I looked around the corner to see the window was boarded up. I looked back to see the girl walking slowly up the tunnel.

‘Don’t you find it odd?’ She asked.

‘What is odd?’

‘What have you just done? Think about it, you were following me until we reached Dorset Street, then YOU turned down here, YOU looked around to that window because YOU knew, there would be a window and now YOU are standing in front of number 13 waiting for me because YOU knew this is where I was going. YOU know this place, YOU know 13 Miller’s Court.’

‘Miller’s Court, why do I know that name?’

‘When I first saw you, I thought it was you and that I was going mad. I mean it can’t be you, look at you. You are everything but you, but watching you and what you have just done I understand I am not as mad as I thought,’ she said as she walked nearer to me. ‘Tell me do you believe it past lives?’

‘Past lives? Yes I do. I know with my background I am not meant to, but I write about them.’

‘Your background you say?’

‘Yes, I mean, I don’t know, I don’t know anymore. I don’t know anything about my background I don’t know why I just said that. I can’t remember anything that I did before the murders.’

‘The murders you speak of are they the famous murders? Do you remember Jack the Ripper?’ She asked quickly.

‘I remember the murders, I was in Whitechapel at the time, and I knew those women.’

‘Yes, you did.’

‘Poor Mary, Poor Annie, Liz and Kate.’

‘Yes, yes and?’

‘And? What exactly do you mean?’

‘Is that it?’ She asked. I nodded. ‘Most people, when they mention the murders, they mention five women, but you mention four, tell me do you have dreams?’

‘Dreams, yes I do for I have already mentioned that I have to you.’

‘What are you dreams?’

‘There is this woman screaming at me to save her, she is covered in blood. I feel like I’m looking at her threw a window. I can’t get to her, there’s blood everywhere.’

‘Oh my dear god!’ she proclaimed as the colour drained from her face.

‘I know I sound mad,’ I said.

‘It’s not that, please say you understand me when I say this, you are her! You are Mary Kelly! Jack the Ripper killed you! You have come back, Mary please believe me. Do you remember me Mary? Do you remember Maria? You are standing outside your own door, for God’s sake!’

I can’t believe what I was hearing, I am no woman. I do not know this Mary Kelly. Jack the Ripper killed four women, not five. If it was five I would have known I was here, researching my book, I would have known!

‘No, I don’t believe you. You are mad! I am no woman! I thought I would understand more by speaking to you but I don’t! Leave me alone!’ I shouted as I run past her.

‘Think back Mary, you know who Jack the Ripper is! You are the last one to see him! Think back! You need to let her spirit go!’ She shouted back.

I ran as fast as I could, until my legs went wobbly. I leant against a cart, to catch my breath. *Think back Mary, you know who Jack the Ripper is! You are the last one to see him! Think back! You need to let her spirit go...*

This is madness. How can I be this Mary Kelly? I am a man, look at me. But why do I not remember her as a victim of Jack the Ripper? Why do I not remember my life before Jack the Ripper? I do feel at home here, I did know where she was taking me, even though I, myself haven't been to Miller's Court. And yes, I did know there would be a window, I looked for it because strangely I thought that, that would be a way of opening the door for me. Why did I go straight to that door? What am I saying? If I am saying, if I am trying to justify myself being Mary Kelly, I am saying I am dead, I have died. I started crying as I slid down the wall.

But dead bodies do tell tales...

And maybe, just maybe this is the tale for this *dead* body to tell. But one question remains floating around in this dense fog that is my brain, if I have died, why have I come back?

I know who Jack the Ripper is! It all makes sense! My dreams are of my death, I am the woman in the lake of blood, I am the only one that knows, and I am the only one that knows her! So I am the only one that knows my killer! I was calling out to myself to help. But I was meant to forget, I was meant to forget who killed me and who was making me forget?

I ran back to Miller's Court. 'I understand,' I shouted. 'At long last I finally understand!' I ran to the door, there was no one there. 'I understand,' I shouted again but there wasn't a sound. I looked around the corner to see that the boards up at *my* window were now bloodstained. I looked to the floor, she was dead.

My friend Maria was lying in a pool of her own blood, her dress was strained and her throat cut and the blood was pouring out and dripping on the cobbled stones. She had a life to lead, a life that was cruelly taken away from her, she looked such a sorry state, I instantly felt pain seeing her in this way, a pain a mother would have or maybe a *sister.*

I then noticed that in the half closed palm of her left hand something small and shining was inside. I bent down and took the item at first I was a little confused how a street walker would have such a thing as a gold chain with a time piece at the end of it and although it was the first time I had seen this item, I felt as if I have *known it all my life.* I placed it into my pocket and said a few prayers over her lifeless body. He had got her too. I felt sick, and then things went black...

Chapter Twenty Two

1888

Knock, knock. 'Come in dear,' the door opens.

'I don't understand why you want to meet here, Mary.'

'Because love, I am leaving here, I am going aboard but I need some money first,' she lied.

'And you think I will give you money?'

'Yes, you are.'

He laughs, 'Why would I do a thing like that, you are just a common whore?'

'I am a common whore that knows.'

'Knows what?'

'I know you killed Ellen, all those years ago. All because she wouldn't go with you, because you knew where she had come from. You knew she was a whore but the other man didn't. She wanted to break away from her past life.'

'Her past life you say? I could have taken her away from her past life! I could have taken her away for people like you!'

'But you would have known. Deep down inside, you would always have known. She wanted a fresh start but you killed her and took her heart.'

'It was mine to have! You have waiting a long time to black mail me!'

'I thought that would be that, but then you killed again.'

'What?'

'Don't be stupid, I know it was you in Buck's Row. You are mad, but there are a lot of people who are, so I want money to go back to Paris.'

He turns his back to her and laughs. 'You are playing a dangerous game Mary.'

'Everything is a danger around here.'

'That includes me!' He shouted as he ran at her with his knife in his hand.

'Help me, Help me!' She instinctually shouts. But no one does, because no one is meant to. Her throat is cut and everything slows down, her glance draws itself towards the window and she what sees is a ghostly figure starring at her through her broken gap in the window and she knew then that she was always the maiden, like the strange woman had told her for the spirit that she saw outside her window was of herself looking through her looking glass.

Her body falls to the floor and the last thing she sees is the book she had taken from the strange woman's lair, the book the strange woman needed to convince herself to tell Mary her fate, laying underneath her bed. Someone had been reading it for it was open, near the end of the book.

The sight she saw confused her, but only for a short while for there was a photograph of Maria Harvey lying on her bed, she was cut into so many pieces that she could not recognize her, if it wasn't for her being able to just read the two words of 'Maria Harvey' written underneath it.

But as she watched, the photograph changed in front of her eyes and so did the name, for now she saw herself cut to pieces on her own bed and her name was underneath the photograph and suddenly everything she had been through these last few months had made sense.

For she had been tricked. She had, had a game played on her, she was never meant to have died tonight, it was never her fate for it was Maria's. The strange woman had the power to change the past, so she did her best to change it by using her. She put Mary in the place of her daughter, she had changed history.

Everything she told her was a lie, to get her to play the game. She was never this maiden, there was nothing special about her, and she was just there to be used.

The dream she had at the strange woman's lair was just a hallucination brought on by the strange smoke the strange woman had burned for Mary had breathed in and she didn't because she made sure she left the room. Mary was never going to die at the hands of Billy Bo, that was the strange woman's way of keeping her here, making her not run away from Jack the Ripper.

Her own dream she had in the pub, was the opposite of the dream she had in the strange woman's lair, for her own mind was trying to tell me that she had been placed in Maria's circumstances but she didn't listen to herself.

Then at last the strange woman played her last card, she made Mary sort out Jack the Ripper herself, she made her, her own victim under the pretence of blackmail and foolishly Mary did it. But what makes her the most sadness of all is that Maria had known, Maria had always known.

She even played along for a bit, but seeing the Thames for herself, the place the strange woman had placed in Mary's head, the fabricated meeting for Mary and Billy Bo, that Maria had started to doubt everything they had planned, Maria had become fond of her so in turn hatred everything that had been done to her. She could not face the person, who was doing this to her, but she could not explain to her why, but she understands now Maria, for she understands all.

She thinks the strange woman summed it up well, when she told her, 'that anything I have done, no matter how bad and cruel it may seem to her, I have done because I love her'.

After all what would anyone do if they had the power to change history? Would they change it to save a loved one?

1898

I awoke, to see Charles starring madly at me, I looked around I was back in my home, no I am wrong, my 'friend' has held the deeds to my home for years so I am actually in Charles's home, lying in his bed.

'Why were you there Thomas?' he boomed.

'Did you name me?' I asked.

'What?'

'Did you name me Thomas? Was it you that had given me my life here, because it was you that took it away, there?'

'That's what you meant by shouting 'I understand' then.'

'How can this be?'

'I don't know, I didn't believe it until I saw you, I could see right through you, I could see her eyes in you. I needed to keep you in my sight, I needed to know if you remembered, but you didn't. I even tried pushing you to remember, but you still didn't. I felt safe and I guess I started playing games with you, for I have always liked a good game. I even took you into Whitechapel, made up some story about missing bodies, you still didn't remember. I was feeling quite great about myself, but then Robert

Mann remembered you. He saw in you, what I did and remembered your body. He had to go.'

'You killed him?'

'Yes I killed him, are you really that stupid? Did you really not know? My god! I must admit I thought it would have been strange to kill him, but he was so simple, he would have killed himself if I had told him too,' he laughs.

He looked surprised that I wasn't laughing along with him, so he carried on talking. 'It is what I call thinking on my feet, so I killed him and took you there to see it, to see my handy work. I was even trying to remind you of who I am, I left the same knife I killed you with, in his back, but still you didn't remember. I knew then that the medicine was working, you were forgetting yourself. And every time I saw you take a drink from your flask or followed you to a den I knew you were forgetting a little more. But then that girl appeared.' The last sentence he said with a more angry tone.

'That girl knew me.'

'Yes, she was your friend Maria Harvey. She saw the Mary in you, she took you to hospital and gave your name as Thomas Kelly, which was a hint towards me, she was taunting me. She was letting me know, that she knew who you really were, so in turn what you would really say. I had to get to her! But sneaky as she was, she run aground. I had to get you away from her, so she didn't make you remember.'

'So hence why I went to Blissful Hill.'

'That's it, you are beginning to understand. With you at Blissful Hill, I could search for her undetected. But I still couldn't get to her. Then you wanted to go home, at first I thought that was a bad idea but then it might work in my favour as she will come to you, which she did. I wasn't able to get to her straight away, but I watched you run out of Miller's Court shouting at her to leave you alone. I thought you didn't believe her and that if I killed her, that would be the end of it, but just as I left I heard you shout, you understand. I ran back and hit you over the head.'

'And that's why I am here, once again.'

'It's funny, I never thought I would become attached to you, in the way that I have, but I'm afraid our friendship must come to an end,' he laughed 'I have to kill you all over again! If you think about it, it's really quite hilarious,' he said as he brought out his knife.

'Maid!' I instinctually shouted.

'Don't be silly now, she works for me,' he sat as he moved closer to the bed.

'Oh yes, she is your half sister isn't she? Tell me if I have guessed right Charles, but did you kill your stepmother?'

'Charlotte? Of course we did! She took me away from my own father, she had to go, it was quite simple of me what with all the poisons my father left lying around. It was the others that I had to be a little more creative.'

‘Your butler you mean? Jimmy Turner? Will Jenkins? Ellen’s mother as well? And of course there wasEllen Rose? Did they all have to go? Did your Ellen have to go?’

‘Yes, they all got in my way, and Ellen was going to leave me. I couldn’t let her go to someone else!’

‘Foresight! Inspector Foresight!’ I suddenly shouted.

‘What?’ Charles asked as he stopped short in his movements. With that the bedroom door burst open. Policemen came flooding in, one of which had got hold of Charles and struggled with him. A knife dropped for his hand and P.C Abberline picked it up.

‘Well now, my father has been looking for you,’ he said to the knife while he winked at me.

‘Now, now Sir Charles, give up, we have you at long last, we bloody well have you,’ said Inspector Foresight right in the face of Charles.

‘Let me go!’ Charles shouted.

‘Not until you hang,’ said the Inspector as he walked over to me, lying in the bed, and shook my hand. ‘Hello Mr Dunn, well where is then? Is it under the bed today?’ he asked moving my pillows around, pretending to search for something.

‘Where is what Inspector?’ I asked a little puzzled.

'The dead body, when I always meet you there's always a dead body. It almost doesn't feel right without one!' he laughed. If only he knew that he was glancing at one right now, I thought to myself.

'Well I am glad for my own sake that you didn't find one in this room!' I said as I joined in with the laughter.

'And as you can see I got your message and your little black box of evidence. Yes, you were right if would be worth my while to come here, we heard all we needed. Thanks to you, Jack the Ripper will hang!'

'I don't understand!' shouted Charles, who I had forgotten for a moment was still in the room.

'Let me enlighten you then,' I said as I sat up in the bed, noticing I was still dressed. 'I knew who you were when I left Blissful Hill; I knew what you did to Ellen and the rest. So I asked your servants if I was to protect them, would they give me statements I could give to the police and any proof. Your trust in your man servant was wrong Charles, he wasn't working for you because he wanted to, he was frightened off you, and they all were. Your butler was a very clever man and kept the history of your family. So armed with this information I went to the police station before I went to Whitechapel and told Inspector Foresight here, if he wants the ripper to meet me here. I just didn't think about the girl, I didn't think you would be after her! If only I thought.' I said sadly.

‘Mr Dunn, you alone have saved the world from a monster, do not feel down’ P.C Abberline said to me.

‘You don’t believe a word he says do you Inspector? He thinks he is Mary Kelly in a past life! He is quite mad!’ Charles proclaimed.

‘Not as mad as you! Anyway we know Mr Dunn was playing along with you! Past life indeed! Take him away!’ The Inspector said.

‘Tell them! Tell them who you are!’ shouted Charles at me while he was being dragged from the room.

‘I don’t know what you mean, Charles. I am Thomas Dunn,’ I said. As Charles disappeared from view, Inspector Foresight gave me some papers.

‘There are the deeds to your house, like you said Mr Dunn.’

‘Thank you Inspector.’

‘So what are you going to do now, Mr Dunn?’ He asked me.

‘Well I think it’s about time I write another story, don’t you think Inspector?’ I replied.

‘But can you remember what has happened?’ he asked with his eyebrows raised, to which I placed my hand in my pocket and brought the time piece on the gold chain out and placed it in my palm and as I ran my finger over it, I answered to the clock rather to the Inspector,

'Yes, for I *now* remember all.'

'But what if, like you had said once, what if people won't believe it?' he asked.

'Then I will repeat the words of a very clever and wise policeman when I say, what does it matter? For if it becomes a classic it will have its own history,' I answered as I winked at the Inspector.

'And as we all know, we can't change history,' he said as he raised his hat to me and left the room, leaving me alone for what felt like the first time in a very long time.

'But of course if we chose to Inspector, if we had the power to, I am sure we could all change history,' I said to myself out loud as I looked out of the bedroom window to the side of me and in the brightness of this wonderful morning I saw a grey mist floating up to the heavens 'Goodbye Mary, I have finally let my spirit go,' I whispered, as my eyes glanced towards my unused pen and paper. I will get to work once more...

The End.

Or is it?

COMING SOON:

THE STRANGE CASE OF CAROLINE MAXWELL – A SHERLOCK HOLMES NOVEL

It is the start of a new Edwardian century and Amelia Christie is struggling to prove herself as a great *female* journalist for The Times Newspaper in London. To prove herself to her editor leads her to ask help from the celebrated detective, Mr Sherlock Holmes.

Sherlock Holmes has always known that, the now famous names of the women who died at the hands of Jack the Ripper was wrong on one count, as Sherlock never wants to leave a case open, even after sixteen years, he decides he needs someone else's help. Someone that is quite different from himself and *womanly* to crack the case. He decides to put his trust in a female journalist who against the odds managed to get the one and only interview Sherlock has ever given, Amelia. She, at first feels uncomfortable to be another journalist who writes about Jack the Ripper. But in his distinctive and unique way, Mr Holmes persuades Amelia that not everything is known about the case.

He starts the case for Amelia by leaving clues as to what ex-policeman to talk to and departing from Baker Street Amelia takes on the role as Dr Watson's story telling narrative and the reader followers her to Scotland Yard, The Times News Agency, Hampshire, London's East End and to the railway village of Ashford in Kent. While on her quest Amelia learns about the real criminal crimes of The Cleveland Street Scandal, The Poisoner George Chapman, and The murderer Henry Wainwright.

What is so strange about the real person who was involved in the Jack the Ripper case, Caroline Maxwell? Who does not want Amelia to find out the truth? And more importantly where is Sherlock Holmes when we need him?

COMING SOON:

THE TAILS OF BINKY THE TABBY CAT SERIES: THE HISTORICAL TAILS OF BINKY.

Binky the Tabby Cat transforms herself into famous but cat like versions of historical characters in this continuation of the funny series. Binkton Churchill, a Roman Catiator, Henry the eighth and his Six Fishes and Leonardo Da Kitty all get a mention and many more.

VICTORIAN LIVES BEHIND VICTORIAN CRIMES SERIES – VOL:4

'WE ARE ALL MAD HERE'

This e-book is where people who got sent to an asylum in the Victorian era, talk to the reader about their lives as if they were in the same room as each other.

Author Information

Amanda Harvey Purse is a twenty eight year old, Ripperologist and Sherlock Holmes enthusiast who has spent the last twenty years researching Victorian and Edwardian Crime. She has worked for the City of London Police Museum, where she has given tours, researchers, has written the guide book and given lectures about Jack the Ripper. At the moment she is designing a 'Jack the Ripper Day' for schools and the public at the museum.

She wrote **Jack the Ripper's Many Faces**, a set of four short linking stories sending the reader on a quest to find out who wore Jack the Ripper's face, as an entertaining introduction to the Jack the

Ripper crimes for the reader, mixing a little fact with fiction.

She also wrote a series of e-books called **Victorian Lives behind Victorian Crimes**, where the reader listens to Victorian people who were involved in Victorian crimes as if they were sitting down in front of them, as a new way of explaining about the crimes that has never been done before, hoping to catch a new generation of interested public.

For fun, Amanda Harvey Purse has also written a series of e-books about her cat, Binky. The first called **The Detective Tails of Binklock Holmes, Purrirot and Miss Meowples**, where Binky the tabby cat changes into costumes of her favourite detective heroes, Sherlock Holmes, Poirot or Miss Marple and the reader follows her into similar but cat-like versions of the famous stories, such as The Speckled Collar, Murder on the Feline Express and Pocket Full of Cat Nip. She wrote this after imagining all the things her cat Binky could do and say when she thinks she is not being seen by human eyes.

Amanda lives in Kent with her husband Benjamin (who is also writing a novel about Zombies) and with her mischievous cat Binky.

Lightning Source UK Ltd.
Milton Keynes UK
UKOW03f0207080414

229572UK00003B/58/P

9 781782 998754